Prettybelle

Also by Jean Arnold
FAUSTO'S KEYHOLE

Prettybelle

A Lively Tale
of Rape and Resurrection

JEAN ARNOLD

The Dial Press, Inc.
New York 1970

For my son Andre

Library of Congress Catalog Card Number: 74-92735

Printed in the United States of America

Design by Thomas Clemens

First Printing, 1970

CONTENTS

. . . Yes, we have lost track of the light, the mornings, the holy innocence of those who forgive themselves.

—CAMUS
The Fall

In my hometown nobody will speak to me, nobody, not one soul, black or white, much less my own daughter. Not really speak. All on account of that wretched Rape of mine. Only my doctor, and HE sent me over here to Pummicami Mental Sanitarium and said I was suffering from nerves. Well, he did that to be rid of me, and also because I vowed I'd seen my husband Sheriff Sweet, which naturally enough he didn't believe, since my husband Sheriff Sweet is dead. But let me tell you, I did see my husband, and never mind, I know what I know. I guess I know my own husband when I see him.

Well, he sent me over all the same, and here I sit in Pummicami biting my lips, and one morning my doctor comes up to me and says, "Miz Sweet, aren't you interested in anything?" And I said, "Why Doctor, whatever can you mean? I am interested in everything and everybody, always have been, just give me a chance," and he said, "I mean, Miz Sweet, anything in the work line, arts and crafts, needlework, knitting, like that." "Well," I said, "I'll tell you a secret that I've never told a soul before. I always wanted to be a writer! I always thought I could be a good writer if ever I tried, and that was my secret ambition. I got an A in English, it was my best subject, and I could rhyme too, believe it or not, I could! But then, I got married——" Well, he never let me finish. He said, "That's FINE. We just happen to need a writer for the Sanitarium newspaper. You can start right in." And I said, "Dr. Dimmer, that is simply thrilling, and does it mean when I get out of here, I can work on a real newspaper?" And he said, "Well, Miz Sweet, I wouldn't go THAT far!" And I said, "I bet you wouldn't," and we did laugh. I said, "Now what can I write for your newspaper, let me think. I know what! I have it! I will write my own story on the installment plan."

Well, he scratched his head and looked doubtful, and said, "Why don't we start with a poem or two?" and I said, "Oh Dr. Dimmer, come on, please let me do it! It's a lively story, it really is!" "Well," he said. "We-ell . . ." "I'll stick some verses IN it," I said. "Oh please, come on." "Well, you write it," he said, "and then we'll see."

So without further ado I started writing, and here it is— the Truth, the Whole Truth, and Nothing But, so far as in me lies, and as Granpa Beesly put it (not wishing to say GOD except in church), *So Help Me Deity*. I call it *The Rape of the Sweet Women*. That's a tricky catchy title, I think, don't you? So take a deep breath, now, and we're on our way.

Farewell, Sheriff Sweet

The funeral of my husband, Sheriff Leroy Sweet of Cach-attow County, was on a real hot breathless day, and Fourth of July. My, it was HOT. The sun just baked and broiled. But Leroy had the darlingest place, near the wall with ivy and honeysuckle vines, and magnolia and hummingbirds and butterflies, and mockingbirds just singing their hearts out under stickly prickly little blue and pink and yellow flowers. The red clay was covered by a nice green artificial-grass carpet, but you could smell it anyway, alas. I person-ally just HATE the smell of red clay, don't you, it is abso-lutely the smell of evil to me. Well, thank heaven the flower smell was even stronger, so strong you could almost lay back and float in it, the honeysuckle smell, and the fu-neral-flower smell, both of them proclaiming *Life is sweet, Life is short but sweet!* until you would almost believe it, except for that old cold red clay smell come sneaky-finger-ing its way into all that bliss, like the serpent in old Eden, saying, *No it ain't, oh no it ain't! Short it may be, but sweet——? Don't fool yourself!*

Down our way we don't celebrate Fourth of July much. Or am I mixed up? Lordy yes, that's Lincoln's birthday we don't celebrate—— Well, let it go. Anyway, it sure was HOT. The sun just fried and cooked. Let me tell you, the pallbearers were PERSPIRING. (Or as they say down here PREspiring, and Lord I even catch myself saying it now and again.)

Yes, the pallbearers were perspiring fit to melt and float away. Leroy was a heavy man. I mean, over two hundred, that's heavy. I weigh only one-ought-nine myself. Folks used to say he'd make two of me, and they were right. But even if I weighed TWO-ought-nine I doubt that I'd have crossed Leroy. Nobody crossed Leroy, except our daughter Saralizabeth, and Leroy he just pampered her so, she didn't even *have* to cross him. As for me, don't think I simply cringed and knuckled under. Oh my no! I had my ways and means. But if you can imagine a smallish pussycat joined in wedlock to a giant hound with his jaws wide open, why that was me and Leroy. Considerable spitting-and-clawing on my part, and some perplexity on his, but a clear agreement by both sides as to where the power lay. Well, the pallbearers passed by carrying that great coffin which must have weighed 500 pounds easy all alone, and then you add 240 pounds for Leroy, and that's a heavy weight on a hot day. As they passed by I could smell them, the ones on my side, yes, I could smell each one. Gawky old Jim Peabody who was now Acting Sheriff, well, he had a sort of frank and honest sweaty smell, but with an after-taste, so to speak, on the rancid side. And Cousin Clayton Tew, he smelled like a distant skunk on whom someone had hopefully poured Mennen's After Shave Lotion, and Deputy Hargrove smelled of cleaning fluid, strong. The sweatiest of all was old Bubba Tew, for he had just perspired right through his seersucker jacket in great dark circles, and the perspiration smelled of gin. It DID, I smelled it. Actually it smelled right good. That sounds funny, but it did.

I just couldn't get my mind off how Leroy was dead inside there and on his way back to the earth from which he sprang. Hard to believe. Oh he was a good-looking man in his day, before he put on weight. And Lordy didn't he give me a time. I caught myself quietly sniffing to see could I smell Leroy—which is a shameful thing to say—and naturally I couldn't through the metal coffin, nobody could, but a woman's mind knows not sweet reason. (Granpa Beesly.) I had the craziest feeling Leroy wasn't truly dead at all but only playing possum in order to catch me doing something I oughtn't, and he was going to explode right out of that coffin and give me merry Ned! I mean, who could believe Leroy was dead? He just wasn't that kind of a man.

Maybe that's why I didn't shed a tear, not one. I just could not take it in. I stood there in that raging sunshine, looking out at the sweet lovely cemetery through my heavy black veil, listening to the birds and smelling all the smells, and it seemed unreal just like a dream. Nothing like a veil to remove you, a good heavy black veil. I would have been as snug and private as you please behind that veil, if I hadn't had that constant worry about Mother Sweet— that's Leroy's mother, and believe me she is capable of doing *anything* to attract attention. Sometimes she's as sharp, and other times she is like a two-year-old child. I expected any minute she'd do something awful at Leroy's own funeral, like say in a loud voice she had to go to the bathroom, or was hungry, or the judge was a great big fathead. But she behaved like a lamb, a perfect lamb, just stood there with her little gray eyes twinkling and glittering, and only mumbled to herself now and then, and chomped her false teeth together, and slapped Saralizabeth on the hand a time or two, for no reason that I could see, some old something she was remembering, no doubt.

Well, Judge Collie Meggs, dressed all in white raw silk, in the old style, gave the most eloquent and moving speech you can imagine, about Leroy, how he fought all his life to preserve our Southern Way of Life. Yes, that same old weary stuff, and you'd think we'd be immune to it by now! But no. I swear it brought tears to everybody's eyes, like so many Pavlov's dogs. Yes! I even got moist myself, and can you believe it, I saw even *Lily* sniffle and blubber a little bit—that's Lily Black, our Nigra cook's been with us since we got married twenty years ago. Think of it, twenty long years. And Judge Collie Meggs he was so overcome himself he had to stop now and then to blow his nose. His voice would crack and falter, he'd gulp a few times, and then he'd blow his nose, which sounded like a trumpeting elephant, and made Saralizabeth FURIOUS! "Mother, if he does that once more I'm going to walk out!" she whispered. "I just cannot and will not stand it." Saralizabeth has a very fine sense of right and wrong.

Judge Collie said how Leroy gave his very life for us, and pointed to us three—Saralizabeth, Mother Sweet, and me—and said how we were Southern Womanhood and Leroy died for our Purity. I mean, it sounds plain silly when you write it down. But when he said it, it like to give everybody chills and fever, like hail in a summer storm. Of course he surely overdid it, to my mind, but old Judge Collie being of the old school and loving to swoon at his own oratory, he truly believed every word and just put his stomach in it. How Leroy had not Died in Vain! How the spirit of the Southland would, like the phoenix, Rise from the Flames, and a whole lot more along the same familiar line.

Then, somewhat to my surprise, the preacher said we would sing a hymn or two (which to my knowledge is not customary in the cemetery), and we sang "Nearer My God to Thee" and wouldn't you know—despite what I had told them beforehand—"The Old Rugged Cross." I was mad as a wet hen! I had particularly said which hymns to play in church, but I never thought about the cemetery. Well, that was Mr. Wimbly's doing, I knew full well, and it made me even madder than any wet hen because he was simply CLAIMING Leroy for the Klan, that being their pet song, whereas Leroy dropped out of the Klan ten years ago, he told me so himself, and only went to meetings now and then to check up and amuse himself. I am just DEAD SET against the Klan, and I don't care who knows it and what anybody thinks. And I looked around, and sure enough there he was, that horrible Mr. Wimbly, standing right next to the preacher, his mean soft face looking all pious and sorrowful, and just aching for a cross to burn I have no doubt, he being some Lord High Muckymuck of the Klan. I told him beforehand, I said, "Mr. Wimbly, we will NOT sing 'The Old Rugged Cross' I don't care what you say," and he said, "Why Miz Sweet, the White Knights don't have a monopoly on that good old hymn. I think you carry spite in your heart against us," he said, "and that would cause me MORE GRIEF, ma'am, than I can tell, since our late sheriff and dear friend, the finest bravest man our county has known in many a long year, was our very mainstay and bulwark, ever present help in danger," and so on. "Well," I said to him, "the truth is, Mr. Wimbly, I cannot keep you out of the church, but the burial is private." Where I got the courage I will never know! But I said it, and Mr. Wimbly looked astonished and aggrieved, and then he kind of looked at me speculatively with a tender little secret smile, and I swear it flitted across my mind, it DID, that all my moderate views on the Nigra question might just plop me into trouble—now Leroy was gone. Yes, it flitted across my mind, a kind of premonition, a rat running over my grave, but I squared my shoulders and I didn't care.

I absolutely hate Mr. Wimbly, and I always will. I hate him on general principles, and I would hate him just as much even if I HADN'T had those repulsive personal experiences with him, like that time just three years ago when he actually put his one hand inside my blouse and his other up my skirt—yes, he did, in the church vestibule—and he held me like a vise! and PINCHED! And he said if I told Leroy he'd laugh, and nobody would believe me because I was so rattle-brained. Well, that alone would be cause enough to hate him, but I hate him as I said on general principles, in the abstract as well as the concrete, and truth to tell I simply hate his FACE, that soft mean good-looking face of his, well, not unlike Leroy's face (after he put on weight), only Leroy was a bigger man, and nobody could say Leroy was a hypocrite. Leroy never went around spouting the Bible to cover up his filthy thoughts like Mr. Wimbly, who is some kind of absolute SADIST in my opinion. I mean, that time three years ago in the vestibule, he gave me this mean hard squeeze or pinch, and I swear he had more will to hurt me than to feel me, and I took my fingernails to him, and I went for his face, and drew blood on his cheek and proud of it, and he turned me loose all right, but then he SLAPPED me good, I mean as if I were somebody he had the RIGHT to slap! like a dog! or some poor helpless Nigra! and he said he wouldn't forget it, no sir. And then he added something so repulsive I won't even mention it, about what he said would surely happen one day between him and me, and I said, "Oh is that so, Mr. Wimbly, and would you care to place a wager on that like one million dollars," and he said yes he'd take that bet. Well, after *that*, you may be sure I did the best I could to poison Leroy's mind against that man, but I doubt it was much use, for Leroy rarely listened much to my opinions. Not since the early days, you know, when he came courting.

Well, we sang "The Old Rugged Cross," and that was Bad News enough, for one funeral, you might think, but no. For right smack in the middle of it, BAM! BAM! BAM!

Now I want you to see the picture. There is a crowd, a good big crowd round the grave, standing all amongst the tombstones. The lieutenant governor is there, everybody is there! Saying good-bye to Leroy, paying their respects, when all of a sudden BAM! Somebody threw an old-fashioned string of firecrackers right over the wall! Yes! They landed over to the left, about twenty feet from the crowd, on the grave of old Mrs. Gulpin. Bam-bam-bamety BAM! And not one soul had the nerve to run over and step on them! It wouldn't be dignified. No, we just pretended it hadn't happened. And then, when old Reverend Muncher was pronouncing the benediction, BAM! you won't believe it, but it happened again! Yes! This time they landed to the right of us, and I swear I heard, from over the wall, the sound of running feet. As I glanced round, I saw Lily our maid clench her hands together and roll her eyes, nervous as could be. The rest of us just froze, sweet and pious, tableau, and pretended nothing had happened, everything was lovely. No noise, nothing! Reverend Muncher didn't miss a beat and Mr. Wimbly, why he was just the sweetest and most pious of anybody. Now I find that amazing! A whole crowd of people just pretend a thing right out of existence! I declare. But underneath, I suppose, all our minds were working the same. It must have been some naughty child, was what we thought. Some bad boy. And then behind that, lay that other thought, enough to make Mr. Wimbly dampen his breeches with sheer joy, and that other thought was: Nigras.

Lily, squirming and looking around uneasy, made me wonder. Yes it did. But oh, I never dreamed what turned out to be true! Well, the instant Reverend Muncher finished his benediction and everybody began a kind of mournful conversation, Lily just quietly faded away. By the time she reached the cemetery gate, she was really *running*, that big round bottom of hers just working and churning away. Mr. Wimbly also faded away, and the new sheriff, and one or two others, and they all had light in their eye.

But truth to tell, Reader, I still didn't make much OF it; you see, our house was just a block away, and I calculated Lily was hurrying on ahead to get ready for the funeral party. That is what I figured insofar as I figured anything at all, for only one small morsel of my brain was out scouting for Reality, and all the rest of me was just so light-headed with heat and strain and unbelief and shock, I vow Leroy himself could have risen white-faced from the grave and I'd have said no more than *howdo, Leroy, chicken and greens for dinner.*

You see, Leroy dying, it happened so fast, no warning. Why, I was all set for Leroy to last forever. Well, twenty more years, easy. I told myself, "Prettybelle"—that's my nickname, always has been since I was tiny, I hardly even recognize my real name which happens to be Annabelle—I told myself, "Prettybelle, Leroy is going to last another twenty years, and the question is, are YOU going to last that long," and I decided I was not, and therefore I determined to make out a Will. Because I had money of my own. Yes. And I do have to say for Leroy he never touched that money, which I got from my mama and from Aunt Millie Lou Ruffle. He respected it and never touched it—not after he got to be sheriff anyway. I guess a sheriff makes money enough. So they say! I'm sure I don't know for certain. And Leroy has simple tastes, just give him guns and dogs enough, a couple of cars, and a pickup truck, and Leroy is content. I mean, WAS content. Anyway, some of Mama's money was still sitting in the bank, and most of Aunt Millie Lou Ruffle's money, and I swear, I'm that mean that I didn't want Leroy to get it. So I made out a Will, favoring a certain few folks and one Secret Charity which nobody will learn about until I'm dead, because I have been stoned and reviled enough already. When I am gone, let them dig me up and spit on me some more, I won't even care. Of course back then, I hadn't yet been reviled by anybody, but I nevertheless stood in some dread of it, I admit. So I made my Will, and I honestly figured I would be gone before very long, what with nerves and shingles and my slipped disk, and I kept thinking how funny it was going to be for Leroy when they read my Will and discovered WHO GOT THE MONEY! I thought about it night and day and I just chuckled and chuckled, and laughed out loud—well, I guess I can tell you it's a certain National Organization and the initials begin with N and end with P—I can tell you that much because, Lord, you'll never guess, never in this world! Well, I just snickered and snickered, mean as a snake, and I got stronger and healthier every day that passed! Until one afternoon the telephone rang, and Leroy was dead, not me! Dropped dead at his desk, would you believe it? Cigar in one hand and a Dr. Pepper in the other, went right down splat face first on a pile of tax bills. Never knew what hit him. Doesn't seem like Leroy would be content with a death like that. Man like Leroy, right in the middle of a Nigra voting drive? Seems like he just wouldn't put up with it. I tell you, I felt uneasy. It just did not seem reasonable to me that Leroy was truly dead.

Well, I went to visit him in the funeral home. And feeling the way I did, my heart was beating fit to break out of its box. The organ was playing and the light was all dim and rosy, and there stood the coffin at the far end of the room surrounded by a million flowers. I crept over that carpet up to that coffin in sheerest terror, and I looked inside like peering over the edge of a precipice. And it was Leroy, apparently, looking neat and clean and peach-complected, and not sweating the least bit, wearing his blue suit, and lost his fat somewheres along the line (now there's a mystery). Well, I reached my hand out to touch his hand, and *crack!* Do you know what he did? He gave me a shock! That's right, an electric shock! Well, I want to tell you, I let out a screech, I really did, and fell down on my knees.

"Oh Lord, Miz Sweet, whatever is the matter?" They all came running.

"He gave me a SHOCK!" I hollered, scared out of my wits.

"Poor child, fetch some water!" they all said.

"I mean, an electrical shock," I said.

And they were all embarrassed and explained how walking over all that carpet scuffing my feet and everything, how it really *was* an electrical shock, and perfectly normal and nothing to worry about. So I got up off my knees, but I wasn't about to touch him again, I can tell you. Anyways, I had felt enough to know that he was cold and hard for sure. After those folks had retreated (padding off discreetly with lowered pious eyelids in their fashion), I looked at Leroy gingerly, and I whispered, "Leroy?" And then I said, "Leroy, is that you?" For to tell the truth, it seemed more like some statue of Leroy than it did Leroy himself. Deputy Peabody (now *Sheriff* Peabody, God save the Mark!) told me that the stroke or heart attack, whichever, gave Leroy two big black eyes, well I couldn't spot them, so I padded over to the funeral-home lady and asked her, and she said they covered everything up with Touch and Glow Liquid Rose Foundation Cream. Imagine Leroy wearing Liquid Rose Foundation Cream! Lord, I vow I almost giggled. Don't think I'm flippant in the face of death, far from it, hysterical I reckon would be closer to the mark. And back I padded to the coffin and looked in once more, mighty careful not to touch. Well, whatever it was, Rose Foundation cream or whatnot, he surely looked a waxworks man. So I whispered, "Leroy?" and he didn't answer, naturally enough, and I said, "Wake up, Leroy," and he still didn't say a word, and I said, "Dobie's had her pups, Leroy" (which wasn't true, she was still expecting; but I thought if anything in this world can arouse Leroy it will surely be a black-and-tan) and he lay still as the grave. So I said to myself, that's Leroy and he's surely dead. And I went away, but do you know I was not convinced deep down that Leroy had gone forever, even though on TOP I knew perfectly well, I'm not a fool, that he was dead as he could be, and would never, for example, find out the contents of my own last Will and Testament. Unless . . . unless he read it from Beyond the Grave—and THAT thought gave me the chills, because to my way of thinking Leroy would be capable of it. I tell you, I could not shake off this uneasiness. If the dead know all, if everything is Revealed Unto Them, well, Leroy would learn about my Will and he would surely not let it pass in silence. But Reader, I do not believe in indulging myself in morbid thoughts, so I said brightly, "Prettybelle, you're about to find out if the dead return, and won't that be INTERESTING to know!"

But listen to me, running on about Leroy, when my story isn't mainly about him at all. I don't know why I do that. Let's get moving, forward march! Where'd I leave off? Yes, I'm at the cemetery and I'm in a daze. Saralizabeth is sulking. Mother Sweet is pawing the ground to get back to the TV set. And Lily is running off as fast as she can go in her tight-fitting Sunday dress (maroon color), her Sunday shoes, which pinch, and her Sunday hat, which bounces, and she is disappearing through the cemetery gate. Oh she is a good woman, that Lily, been with us twenty years, honest as the day is long, couldn't do without her, I can tell you, and her spoonbread is the best you ever tasted, not stiff, like some people think it ought to be, but crusty on the outside and soft as custard yet springy within. And pecan pie! And caramel cake—why Leroy'd eat the whole thing alone give him a chance. And I'd be fat as a hog if it weren't for Nervous Distress. Anyway, there she goes, there goes Lily, her big old comfortable behind is bobbling in her maroon silk dress, and she's all anxious and upset.

And as I come to the end of this Installment, Reader, the questions I hope you will ask yourself are, well, WHO threw the firecrackers? WHERE was Lily running? WHAT will happen next?

END FIRST INSTALLMENT *

---

* Dr. Dimmer, I just couldn't find a place to put verses in here but I haven't forgotten, don't think I have, I've got it right here in mind, and by heaven I will surely get some in my next. Also, I would like to add, I am an excellent Speller, and if I have misspelled that word NEGRO it is by design, not ignorance! Yes. For I would simply CHOKE if I had to spell it NEGRO and think NEE-GROE, for to my mind, Nigra is warm and friendly, whereas NEGRO is simply awash and a-crawl with prejudice and hatred. (As a matter of fact, in my opinion, a very great DEAL of our orthography could stand a change. Yes it could. Oh Dr. Dimmer, don't worry, I'm not about to undertake it! But I do point out to you, as an example, how much *thicker* and *throatier* is CHOAK than simple CHOKE. Now come on, admit it!)

Watermelon Boy, or, The Dumb Chicken, The Nervous Rabbit and The Fussy Mule

Well, where *was* Lily running to?

I can tell you. She was running right back to the Sweet Residence, just like I thought she was. Only, it wasn't the work that sent her flying. No sir. She was running to find her son Billy, age nineteen, who was hired to help out with the funeral guests. For Lily had suspicions. Oh, she knew her son!

Now Lily is a strong woman but she is a heavy woman, and her shoes pinched and her hat kept falling over her eye, and when she got to the house, she was puffing and panting, and scared, and MAD. She cut around back and she busted in that kitchen—and he wasn't there. She came surging into the dining room like a Black Tornado Cloud —and there, polishing the glasses, wearing a starched white jacket with a smile to match, all sweetness and light, innocent as new-mown hay, is Billy. Now Billy is a real nice-looking Nigra boy, not very tall, a shade lighter than his mama, and he's got this big white smile like all the Watermelon Boys you used to see in the picture books (no more!) rolled into one, just a happy-go-lucky smile and great big mischievous merry brown eyes with lashes like a

16

silken fringe—but let me tell you, he was no Watermelon Boy at heart, no sir, he was NOT. And on the tip of his chin, if you looked hard, you could see these few scraggly young whiskers, no more than a shadow now, but ambitious, mighty ambitious.

Lily takes one look at him, and her eyes just snap, crackle and pop.

"Billy Black," she says, very ominous, "Bill-ee BLACK!" (Now Reader, should it cross your mind to ask me, "Prettybelle Sweet, how can you KNOW what happened when you weren't even there?" I will answer you that, truth to tell, I did NOT know it, not at that time, I did not, but I know it now, and have reconstructed it, like any author has the right to do, from keen and intimate knowledge of the parties involved, and if it wasn't JUST like I'm saying, well, it was mighty blame CLOSE, and if you have any complaints, why send the box top and get your money back, but you're making a big mistake.)

So Lily stands glowering, and Billy is polishing glasses and he looks up at her innocent as dawn in the country, and says "Huh?"

"Don't you huh ME," says Lily, and let me tell you she was MAD. Any mother will agree there is nothing like fear and terror for your Young Ones to make you want to fetch them a good clout.

"I mean, MA'AM?" says Billy, correcting himself, real polite, but with this little mocking sparkle in his eye. Oh, he was full of the old nicholas that boy. He'd been giving her trouble all his life. Him and his brother, they both gave her grief and woe.

"You come here to me," orders Lily. "I like to tan your hide." So Billy sidles up to her with his head on one side, cautious like, afraid he'll get his face smacked I reckon.

And Lily gathers herself up and she says, "That was you, now wadn it. It was, that was you, you done it sure as sunrise."

"Done what?" says Billy, all perplexed.

"Done what," says Lily, indignant. "You knows what. Set off them firecrackers in the graveyard, that's what. Don't you fib to me. I'm your mammy and I read you."

Billy studies for a while, and says, "Well, I spose—it MIGHT have been me. It just MIGHT."

Well, when he owns up to it like that, Lily just falls apart like a busted balloon. She lets all the air out, and shakes her head. "I knowed it. I knowed it was you. Oh, I pray the Lord to take my life away." Then she turns on him and just lambastes him. "Ain't I taught you nothin? You act like you still a little biddy boy. Ain't you learned nothin? You act like some white boy might act, some bad little biddy white boy. You think you white? Let me tell you, boy, you ain't white, and you ain't little biddy. Oh, I like to tan your hide."

"Why Mammy, it's gone tan already," says Billy Black, fresh as he can be.

"Smart!" says Lily, just hissing it out. "You goin to smart yosef right into the river. You got half the state police force looking for you right now, O Lord, O Lord Almighty, take my life away."

"Now Mammy, don't you fret," says Billy. "Didn't anybody see me, and if they had, I was wearing a DISguise." And he pulled out this false moustache, just like a child I vow. But don't be fooled—he was no child, oh no! "Besides," he says, "they can't tell one nigger from another, ain't you heard?"

"You think it's some kind of game?" says Lily. "It ain't no game."

"Ain't no game?" asks Billy. "Why Mammy, I thought it was a game." And when she turned away from him, ready to cry and weep, he says very soft, "Listen, Mammy, somebody got to stir y'all up down here, got to wake you up. You SLEEPIN."

"Is that what you come home for?" says Lily very bitter. "Throw firecrackers? Well jus go on back, go on back up North." (Did I neglect to say Billy was going to school up North in Chicago? Well, he was. But he came home for the summertime. And more about that, later.) "I mean it," says Lily. "Go on back. That's where you belong. You don't belong down here no mo. You jus trying yosef. You bound and determined to land yosef in jail or the river. Billy, I'll give you the money. Just carry yosef down to that Greyhound bus and climb on board."

And she starts digging into her pocketbook.

Billy looks at her and smiles real gentle, and says, "Don't you fret, ole Mammy. I'll be all right." And he started explaining how today was a special day, a great day, and how he just couldn't help himself, he had to celebrate. But did he mean Fourth of July? Reader, he did not. He meant Sheriff Sweet's funeral day. Leroy Sweet, my own husband. Yes! Well, he said by rights there ought to be dancing and singing in the streets, and since there wasn't, he figured SOMEBODY had to say hurray, hurray, the son of a b**** is dead! So he took it upon himself, he said, on behalf of the black folk of Cachattow County, to let the white folks know how pleased and happy he was.

Now I ask you! If that don't prove he was no simpleminded watermelon boy! And furthermore, Reader, he had this new Yankee accent he could just turn on and off like a water faucet!

Well, Lily, she's frowning and studying while taking off

her hat (the pansy one I gave her after Saralizabeth sat on it), and she's trying to figure out how to reach through to him. And at last she says,

"Billy Black, I speck you heard that story about the Dumb Chicken."

"What story's that?" says Billy.

"Well, this here Dumb Chicken," says Lily, "all his life he's been MOlested by one single old mean red fox. And that chicken kep on sayin, *O boy if only that old mean red fox would die!* Well, one day it happen, and that big fox just collapse and die. And what does that Dumb Chicken do? Well, he's so excited, he start in runnin. Runnin and squawkin. And all the time hollerin, *Hooray, hooray, the fox is dead!* Well, he runnin, squawkin and flappin his wings so hard, he run right out the chicken yard into the field. And you know what happen? All of a sudden, he come to himself, and he shift his feet and scratch his head, and he say, *My, my, it sure got might SHADY around here!* Well, you know howcome it got shady? He's standin right INSIDE THE JAWS OF DAT BIG FOX'S SECOND COUSIN. THAT's howcome."

And with that, Lily just marched proudly into the pantry and changed her Sunday clothes. She left him to think it over. And when she came back out in her white uniform, carrying a bunch of flowers, Billy, he says,

"Mammy, I got to admit that sure was one dumb chicken."

"I mean to tell you," says Lily. She fixes the flowers in a blue vase. Oh, there were flowers everywhere. Foxglove and dogglove, bleeding heart and merry widow, every kind of flower you can name!

Well, Billy looks at her real sly out the corner of his eye.

"Puts me in mind of the Nervous Rabbit," he says. "You remember that story, bout the Nervous Rabbit?"

Lily just went *Huh!*

"Well," says Billy, "this here Nervous Rabbit was scared ALL the time. He was so scared the dogs might catch him that he just stayed down in his hole. Yes sir, he just stayed there. Course he had no food down there, but never mind! He stayed there nice and safe, *eatin dirt*, until he died of starvation. And when he died, Mammy, nobody knew about it, and nobody cared. That's the story of the Nervous Rabbit."

"Never mind no nervous rabbit," says Lily.

"Y'all are nervous rabbits down here, and that's the truth," says Billy. "You're dead, man."

Lily shakes her head and says, "Uh-uh. WE is alive. YOU is the one is goin to be dead. Dead and drownded in the river like your brother. Oh Lordy Lord," and she started in rocking herself and wailing.

Billy makes a big speech about how he doesn't CARE if he winds up in the river, and how the Nigras in Cachattow County got to wake up because it's the worst county in the whole South. And did she know that, how it was the worst? We got to get ourselves a black sheriff, he says. And he pretends like he's shooting a rifle in the air, and goes *pow! pow!* like a little boy, and then he shakes his head and says, "Got to wake up, Mammy, got to wake up!" And then, looking his mammy right in the eye, he reaches out, and he fingers and toys with our big blue shiny vase, which is full of foxglove, and he shoves it little by little to the edge of the table, and then just lightly knocks it off. "Times changing!" he says. Pushes it right off the table!

Well, luckily it didn't break. But there's a big dark lake

of water spreading on the rug. Lily just gasped and picked up the flowers and picked up the vase, and sopped up the water with her apron, and there on her hands and knees she turns her face up and she gives him a LOOK.

Oh I tell you, Reader, children black OR white are surely a cause of grief. Yes, yes. They grow up and it's like having some stranger in the house, some mean stranger, who defies you every way you turn. Don't I know it! I had a son myself. Well, we won't talk about THAT. Anyway, Lily has blood in her eye and she tells that boy he can go ahead back up North and never come back. He can go ahead back and shoot off his firecrackers, and his firebombs, and run in the streets and loot the stores and throw bricks through the windows and all like that. "But down here in Cachattow County," she says, with this great Natural Dignity she does have, "down here in Cachattow County, we don't do like that."

"Oh we don't?" says Billy, and he raises his hand to push over another vase.

"NO WE DON'T," says Lily. And she confronts him eye to eye and chin to chin, her hands on her big hips.

Well, after a bit, he relaxes and grins that white old mischievous grin, and I have to admit he IS a cute-looking Nigra boy, and he grabs her round the waist and dances her around, and says, "All right, Mammy, you win! For now."

She splutters and fusses while he's dancing her around, but you can tell she's fond of him all the same. And she was, oh my. Yes, that boy just meant everything to her. Sunday, Monday, Tuesday, Wednesday, everything.

"Now is you goin to hep me round here or not," she said, pretending to be cross. "Funeral guests comin any minute. They is plenty to be did."

Well, he pitches in, but it couldn't last, not with that

boy. Only two minutes later he's asking if she went to some address he gave her, and Lily asks the Lord for guidance and says what address, she ain't been to no address. And Billy keeps after it and says Well, you going pretty soon? And she says, when does she have time to go to some old address? and he says, at that address they're going to teach her *all she needs to know so she can register to vote!*

Now Reader, I remind you, this is the private residence of Sheriff Leroy Sweet. And what is going on inside it? A Nigra Voting Drive!

Well, Lily says, We ain't talking about register to vote! But he says yes we are, we're talking about it. And he starts singing and dancing and clowning around, saying see how good he is, nonviolent and everything, worrying about the VOTE just like white folks. And Lily says is he going to hep her like Miz Sweet done hired him to or is he NOT, cause if he keeps on like he is now she don't need that kind of hep.

And here, Reader, I will pause briefly and reluctantly to symbolize and sum up the emotions of Lily and Billy in the following verses, because alas I have faithfully promised Dr. Dimmer I would work them in, somewhere, somehow, which is surely far from easy. I mean, how can you put *verses* in a *story*? How can you do it gracefully? Well, you purely can't. At least I can't. (And why should verses be any more therapeutic than prose after all?) Well, here is my first sorry attempt, Dr. Dimmer, and I confess I am sullen about it, because as far as I'm concerned it truly violates the mood and spirit of my work. Anyway, poor Lily, that good woman, is begging her son to behave himself. She is frightened to death for him, and Reader, she has good ample reason for her fear. She has lost one son already and she senses trouble ahead for this one. She recognizes the signs, she knows he is slipping away from her, and she is desperately fighting to bring him back. And this is what she says:

Please promise yo Mammy
    Behave and be nice!
You actin so crazy
    You'll pay a big price.
Don't touch what you shouldn't—
    Remember yo race!
Don't do what I wouldn't—
    Boy, keep in yo place.
Please promise yo Mammy
    Be nice and behave—
For I'd grieve to be weepin
    Alongside yo grave.

(*I hears deep sorrow in the wind*
    It's comin near.
The voice of sorrow in the wind
    The voice of fear.)

And he replies:

Oh Mammy I promise
    I'll surely behave,
Despite all temptation,
    Won't do what I crave.
I'll just be a model
    Of poise and restraint,
Won't fool it, I'll cool it,
    I'll be what I ain't.
Don't worry, old Mammy,
    I swear I'll behave,

And I'll hold to my promise
    Right down to the grave.

(*I'll toe the narrow line for Mom*
    I will not cross!
I'll be a first-class Uncle Tom
    I'se comin, Boss!)

But she can't trust him:

I knows how you promise!
    You'll never behave.
You started to promise
    When you started to shave.
I pampered and spoiled you
    Till you was too old,
I petted and praised you
    That's why you so bold.
I ought to have whipped you
    To make you be good
I ought to have scared you
    While I still could.

(*I hears deep sorrow in the wind*
    It's comin near.
The voice of sorrow in the wind
    The voice of fear.)

Well that's the best I could do, because Lord I didn't want
to take all day at it. "Do your best in Time Allotted," said
Granpa Beesly. "No one can ask for more." Right, Dr.
Dimmer? Right! And now, back to Reality. The real Lily
and her real son, in the kitchen of the Sweet residence, 137
Liveoak Street.

So anyway, Reader, Billy did promise his mother he would behave and control himself, and that his friend (some Yankee Nigra who came down with him from Chicago and who is also hired to hep out, I mean help out) —his friend will also behave and control himself. And I have no doubt he truly meant it at the time. But as we shall see, he surely did not keep that promise, he did not. Well, Lily told him to do this and that, fetch the plates and slice the turkey, fill the ice bucket for ice tea, dish up the cookies—

"And one mo thing," she said.

Billy Black pricked up his ears, because he didn't like her tone of voice.

"When Miz Sweet comes in," says Lily firmly, shaking her finger at him, "when Miz Sweet comes in, you step right up to her, and open yo mouf and you say, 'Miss Belle, ma'am, I sure am sorry yo husband Sheriff Sweet is gone!'"

Well, Billy threw a fit. He said he'd do most anything but he would not do THAT. He said he couldn't do it, because he'd bust out laughing.

And Lily can't believe her ears, and says, "Laughin!"

"Well, more likely, choke," says Billy, and he gets mad and he gets sullen, and says he won't do it, and she can't make him, and she shouldn't have asked him.

Then Lily reminds him of certain little favors I had done for him, which she wasn't supposed ever to tell him about. But she had, she had told him, and I was right disappointed in Lily when I found that out. And now she reminded him how he was obliged to me—well, I might as well say it right out. I paid the money that sent him to school up North. I did. I paid his tuition money and his travel money, and I paid $25 a week for room and board. And if you were to ask me WHY I did it, I could not tell you why. It is a mystery even to myself. I thought, well, he's a bright boy, considering. And Lily's a good woman, and Education is the Answer to Everything, so Prettybelle, here we go!

Well, they argued back and forth. Lily said how good I'd been to him, like a second mama (imagine!), and he said a whole string of stuff against Leroy which there's no use going into. And he mentioned his brother Skeeter, and Lily bristles and says that was an accident. That Skeeter wound up in the river by *accident*, but Billy would wind up in the river *on purpose*. Then she coaxes, "Come on, be nice, I don't say you got to *mean* it, I just mean you got to *say* it."

And Billy says he won't.

Well, just at that moment they hear US coming in the front door. So she shoos him back, and they duck and skedaddle into the kitchen, and in we come—Saralizabeth and me and Mother Sweet, all tired out and sweaty, and we sit down in a row on the sofa.

So Lily, she puts a tray of little tea sandwiches in his hands, and she gives him a shove. "You get on, now," she says. "Take that tray and seek yo opportunity."

Well, Billy didn't move. He just stood and fretted himself. He started to go, and then he stopped. And he started, and he stopped, and he grinds his teeth.

"Howcome she gave me all that money anyways?" he says. "Now howcome she did that? I don't dig that."

"Somebody hand you a cup of cold water on a hot day, you don't ax 'em howcome," says Lily.

"Yeah?" says Billy. "And what if it's POISON WATER. You ever think of that?"

"Lissen here, boy," says Lily, real short. "You heard about the Fussy Mule."

"What fussy mule?"

"Figured grass was dirty, so he starved to death," says Lily.

And there we will leave them, Reader, for the moment, Billy Black still undecided, teeter-tottering, gripping the tray, looking at the door, and grinding his teeth.

Can Lily control Billy? How much trouble is that boy going to cause? What does the future hold? Well, it holds a LOT, I can promise you!

END SECOND INSTALLMENT

An Uninvited Guest

Yes, home we came, we three Sweet women, and down we sat on the sofa one two three, all in a row like the Three Monkeys, simply tired out and all exhausted. And we sat there looking straight ahead in our black dresses. And I took off my hat and I held it in my lap. And we just stared into space, numb and unbelieving. Me and Saralizabeth did, anyway, and as for Mother Sweet, well, I just wonder and doubt if she took it all in. But maybe she did, because after a time, in a little old faraway voice, Mother Sweet says,

"That was a lovely funeral, just lovely. Wasn't the church lovely." And she put her lips tight together and nodded her head in approval.

And I heard myself saying, in the same little old faraway voice:

"It was just lovely. All those flowers."

"The church and all," said Mother Sweet.

"Never knew Leroy had so many friends," I said. "Why they filled the church and had to stand outside, all down the block."

29

So we sat there awhile in this dreamy silence, waiting for
the funeral guests to arrive, and remembering the funeral.

The Funeral

My wasn't that a lovely funeral?
The services were simply beautiful!
The sunshine and the birds conspiring
To make the eulogy inspiring.
Leroy himself could not have made objection,
More folks were there than voted at Election.
Too bad it had to end so soon and all,
It was a lovely, lovely funeral.*

"Did you see? The lieutenant governor was there!" said
Saralizabeth, and she turned to me and said, very petulant,
"I hope somebody asked him to come by the house.
I mean, did *anybody* have *sense* enough to ask him to come
by the house?"

Well, I simply did not reply. I always handle Saralizabeth with great personal dignity on my part, it's the only
way. And truth to tell, I had no clear recollection of inviting
the lieutenant governor to our house, which was an over-
sight of fairly grave dimensions, I admit it. (However, I
was not going to admit it to Saralizabeth, and give her an
excuse to throw a fit.) So we sat in flowery silence, and we
stared in shimmery space. (Granpa Beesly.)

After a while, Mother Sweet brightened up.

"The Nigras were mighty sullen," she said. "Did you see
the Nigras? I saw them. They were mighty sullen. We

* But honestly, Dr. Dimmer, I'm not at all sure these verses
have a *place* here. Seems to me they're purely bastardizing the
form. Yes, that's how I feel.

passed along Commercial Street, I looked out the window, and there they were, just as sullen! Lined up, four and five deep, in the dust, staring at the hearse. Well," said Mother Sweet, "*you* may think they were paying last respects. *I* say they were *restless*."

Nobody answered her.

"Restless," she went on, in a funny little thin dreamy voice. "Like crows before a storm. Did you hear me? I said, a storm."

They do claim the Very Old can prophesy, and I reckon that is what Mother Sweet was doing, all right, only she spoiled it by adding in the very same breath, in an ordinary voice,

"This dress is too tight, I am gasping for breath." And then, fixing her eye on Saralizabeth and starting to grab, she said, "Missy, those are my pearls!"

Well, Saralizabeth just held on to them (the pearls), and said, "They are *not* your pearls, they are my pearls. If you lost your pearls, it's your own blame fault."

"Lost! Ha!" said Mother Sweet, sticking her face in Saralizabeth's face. Saralizabeth just curled her lip with disdain and flared her nostrils as if Mother Sweet had halitosis, and turned to me.

"Mothuh," she said, very broadly sarcastic, "did you *happen* to think to ask the lieutenant governor of our state to stop by the house?"

"Why, honey, I don't rightly know whether I did or not."

"Oh Lord!" cried Saralizabeth, allowing herself to go all to pieces. "*How* am I going to stand it? Lord, tell me! How am I going to stand it without Daddy? There's not a *sane* person left in the household, not one!" And she began to cry, but remembered to add, "Except me," before she was completely carried away, crying and sobbing, and holding her Kleenex under her lower lashes so her mascara wouldn't get all messy.

Mother Sweet and I paid her no mind, having our own thoughts.

My own thoughts ran gloomily along like this: "I truly cannot believe Leroy is dead. I keep hearing his footstep. Even his voice. I've been his wife since I was seventeen. Leroy's wife. Sheriff's wife. And *now*—what on earth am I?"

Well, I certainly thought I said all that inside my head, but I must have spoken out loud, for Mother Sweet responded very sharply to my question.

"Well," she said, "don't start thinking you're his widow!"

I looked at her blankly, and I said, "If I'm not his widow, what am I, I should like to know."

"I'm the widow around here," said Mother Sweet. "I won't *have* two widows. I won't put up with it. I've been a widow since before you were born. My daddy always said, 'This child, this child was *born* to be a widow.' And I *was*, and I *am*, and I *like* it." And, Reader, that was Mother Sweet running true to form. "I like all those dead men," she screeched, practically flapping her wings. "In that cemetery, all those dead men, I like it!"

At that Saralizabeth cried louder than ever, lifting up her voice unto the Lord. And whilst they were thus busy, I stepped over to the refreshment table.

"Mother!" said Saralizabeth sharply. "What are you doing?"

"Why nothing, honey."

"Mother!"

"Saralizabeth child," I said with dignity, "on the day of

your Daddy's funeral, I reckon I can surely have one drink to carry me along." And I poured myself a bourbon neat from the bottle I had concealed behind a stack of *Saturday Review* and *House and Garden* magazines. Yes I do subscribe to that wicked magazine the *Saturday Review* and when Leroy asked me what it was, I said, Leroy, it is just a dumb old magazine for schoolteachers, and that satisfied him, and lucky for me he never looked inside. He only mentioned it one other time and that was when he said, "Why do you keep getting that damn magazine, you never read it." And I answered, "Why I do indeed read it," and I do, too, though I must admit it seems like there's a new one every five minutes. As for *House and Garden*, well I subscribe to that one as well, but mostly for appearance sake on the coffee table, a kind of protective coloration, for truth to tell I have never been great on domestics. Roses and wallpaper and such don't strike the gong with me; small animals are my line, yes, I am great with your stray cats, your squirrels and rabbits, foxes, fawns, even little furry fieldmice. I empathize with them madly and could be a veritable St. Francis of the small mammal world given half a chance. Oh birds too, naturally. My sympathy by nature leaps out to the hunted. Those poor creatures that Leroy and his cohorts just love to go out shooting—yes, I'm very strong for them. Not that Leroy would hunt a cat on purpose, but do you know, those men, if they *spot* a cat, they'll shoot it down as soon as look at it, poor little soft furry creature! And they defend themselves by saying "Cats Destroy Game." To which I respond, Ha! It is *men* and their blame *guns* that destroy the game, not some poor feline critter who is merely trying to keep her body and soul together!

"If Daddy were alive, you wouldn't *dare*," said Saralizabeth, spitting it out real spiteful. But I ignored her, I turned
my back with dignity, and I drank that bourbon down.

In Virginia where I come from, we don't have such foolish backwoods notions about alcohol. Why, in Virginia,
having a refreshing drink is something gracious ladies and
fine gentlemen just always do. Being a teetotaler is considered downrighty tacky and common, unless of course
the person has a History of Weakness. But down here, oh
my, folks are that rigid and old-fashioned. Imagine a poli-
tician in Virginia running on a dry platform! Of course I
was raised Episcopalian, not Baptist or Methodist, and
that is a crucial difference, I may say. Leroy always claimed
that I was haughty and stuck-up just because I'm from
Virginia, but the truth was, he felt his family was a bit on
the *crude uneducated* side, compared with mine, and he
therefore resented it. He did. He resented it, and he didn't
forget it.

Well, I drank down that bourbon and I poured another,
and let me tell you, I felt better right away. After all, I had
been under a terrific strain.

"Well, here we go," said Saralizabeth. "Back to the sanitarium! Back to the old padded cell!"

"The Nigras were restless, I could tell," said Mother
Sweet in her prophesying voice, and then she added, "I
heard gunshots. I did."

"Well now, I heard that too," I said, in my vague way.
It's an old habit. Say something pleasant, make yourself
agreeable. Never mind if it makes good sense or not. I knew
perfectly well those noises were not gunshots.

But Saralizabeth, she's not troubled by any need to make
herself agreeable. Lord no.

"Gunshots!" she fairly screeched. "Those were *firecrack-*

ers! They were celebrating! They were happy! They were
happy that my—Daddy's dead!" And she began to
cry again, whimpering and whining. "Well, they got
good reason to celebrate," she said bitterly after a time.
"What with that old fool Beansbody as the new sheriff. Old
Jackass Beansbody!" His name, Reader, was Peabody, but
Saralizabeth just insisted on calling him Beansbody. "You
mark my words," she said, trying out her hand at the prophesying trade, "there's going to be trouble in this town
now Daddy's gone. Daddy, he kept them quiet. They worried him into an early grave, but he kept them quiet. Old
Jackass Beansbody, he can't keep anybody quiet. Oh
Glory!" And she tuned up again, wailing and hollering.
"Everything is awful!" she hollered. "Everything is just
putrid! And what about *me?* What about my coming-out
party? What about that! I suppose I can't *have* it now. I
suppose I have to wait until next year, and be the *oldest,*
crummiest, most repulsive debutante in the whole history
of the South!"

Now what can you answer? I tell you, you cannot answer.
She's a spoiled child. Leroy did the spoiling, not me, he just
doted on her, almost as much as he doted on his hounds, I
declare. She's eighteen years old, and Lord, she thinks she
is Scarlett O'Hara. Well, truth to tell, she *is* a pretty child,
though a bit on the beefy side to my taste. She has a figure like one of your sex-kitten movie-queen types, which I
personally do not think is quite ladylike or nice. Of course,
she can't help herself, poor thing, and I shouldn't criticize.
God made her that way—she surely didn't get it from me.
I've always been delicately formed, even now my bust
measures 34, and my waist is small too, it's 25 (though
once it was 23 I must admit). Lord only knows what Saralizabeth's bust is. I expect it's 38 or some such shocker, and

her waist is like mine, 24 or 5. And Saralizabeth has hips, and a *fanny*—I declare, like some immigrant Italian girl. I suppose she got that fanny from Leroy, I don't know where else, though when I first met Leroy, I will say, his hindquarters were as tight and small as any flamingo dancer. My he did look elegant in his britches then. But time told on him and he kept expanding. Well, she's got good long legs, a bit solid in the thigh maybe, and feet—well, feet that are size ten! Lord, in my day, a girl with size ten would have locked her bedroom door and died of shame. I swear, I think she's proud of those great things, those feet. She could squeeze into a smaller size if she had to, but will she do it? She will not. She says Jackie Kennedy has bigger feet than she does. Well I say, What's Jackie Kennedy to you? And I say, What do you think made Jackie Kennedy so shy of public life if not those feet? In my opinion, Saralizabeth is somewhat given to vulgarity. Believe me, I have tried to root it out of her. I have tried and tried, but it grew too rank and strong. Time and again I have heard her say, in front of *anybody,* "Lord, my *feet* hurt!" Now what lady would say that? I remember my old Aunt Millie Lou Ruffle telling me, she said, "Prettybelle, a lady's feet *never* hurt." And I said to her, "But Aunt Millie Lou Ruffle, supposing they do, supposing her feet really do hurt." And she said, "A lady's *one* foot may hurt, child, that's all right!" "But supposing she goes to the doctor?" "Well," said Aunt Millie Lou Ruffle, "what she says is perfectly easy, child, just use your head! A lady would tell the doctor, 'Oh, doctor, my right foot hurts me so bad!' And then she would say, 'And, doctor, my left foot hurts me mighty near as bad!' " Well, I tried to pass this on to Saralizabeth, but she was rude as she could be, and turned her back, and said I'd told that old story about a million times. Which was *not* so.

So I raised that glass of bourbon to my lips in an effort to forget my troubles—when this qualm, this terrible qualm shot through me. I mean, what do we know about the Dead? How do we know they're not looking at us? Well, I took this sudden fright, because if there was one time Leroy would be looking, it would be now, I mean with that glass of bourbon in my hand. Well, I confess, Reader, I cast a sneaky look around the room, and I whispered inside my head, *Leroy! Are you dead? Are you truly dead and in the ground?* Well, naturally Echo Answered (as Granpa Beesly would put it) and at that moment the doorbell rang, so the spell was broken, and I grabbed that drink and gulped it down, and scooted over to the couch and sat down, and the three of us just formed a Mourning Composition.

"Who's *that?*" says Saralizabeth, lifting her eyebrows. Well, it is this Nigra boy, this friend of Billy Black, who is passing through the living room in his white coat to answer the doorbell. But I am not really altogether alert, so I mildly say, "It is Lily's son, William, honey."

And Saralizabeth says that's not William because she remembers William, and that's not him.

So I recollect, and explain, but Lord, Saralizabeth is off again jawing at me, saying how I open the house to strange Nigras, and whatever will become of us, I don't even know who is working for me, I am absolutely hopeless in every particular from alpha to zed.

She is splashing away full midstream when the guests come trooping in, and Lord, she flipflops right over to the Welcome Noises without missing a stroke, a wonderful thing to see, and it makes me realize all my labors have not been wholly in vain. Well, we fall on their necks. I tell Cousin Bessie how sweet it is of her to come, and Saralizabeth tells Cousin Clayton isn't he the kindest thing. I tell Reverend Muncher how I simply adored the services, and Saralizabeth tells Mr. Beansbody (Peabody, I mean), the new sheriff, that she just didn't know how we would have managed without him and he was the very Rock of Gibraltar. I tell Judge Collie Meggs how his eulogy was just the most moving speech I ever heard in my life and how I knew Leroy was listening and was just so proud.

And in the midst of all this, Mother Sweet kind of sniffs the air and heads for the television like a dog to garbage, muttering "Sing Along With Bubba." Well, Saralizabeth says to me very loftily, as if it was all my fault, "Mothuh, Grandma is turning on the television." So I take the old creature very gently by the arm and say, "No, no! No television now, Mother Sweet."

Well, she just yanks her arm away in a fury and yells out "Sing Along With Bubba!" which is her favorite local program.

Saralizabeth says "*Later*, Grandma," through her teeth and pulls her away, and Saralizabeth's face is red and Mother Sweet's wattles are shaking like a furious old turkey. So I quickly fall on somebody else's neck as a diversionary tactic. "Oh Aunt Mary Louise, Leroy always said, in time of trouble—and Cousin Jim Slag as well! Dear friends and relations, come in, refresh yourselves. Have some iced tea and sandwiches and little cakes. Have some turkey and Pepsi-Cola and cornbread."

But Mother Sweet is making the most awful scene. She waves her arms and shakes her wattles and she goes up to one guest after another, saying, "Did you see that? Did you see it? They won't let me look! They prevent me!"

Saralizabeth comes after her, but she dodges away behind a guest. "They pull out the plug!" she hollers. "They hide the test tubes!"

"Some Doctor Pepper, and salad, and chocolate fudge!" I cry.

"They read my mail!" yells Mother Sweet. "They go through my bureau drawers. They steal from my purse. They're full of hate!" (Yes, yes, can you believe it? That's the way she carries on.) "Hate, hate, hate!" she hollers. "They're *jealous*, that's why," she bawls. "Jealous! Petty-minded vipers! Hate, hate, hate! Vipers, vipers, vipers!" And on like that. Well, Saralizabeth and I wanted to sink through the floor.

The guests rose to the occasion and pretended they hadn't heard a thing. They said what a grand funeral it was, solemn and fitting, and they just ignored Mother Sweet, who is sputtering about hate and jealousy and even sadism, yes, while Saralizabeth tries to quiet her and tells her she can have a Coca-Cola and a cookie if she works it right. So *that* blows over, but I tell you I am ready for the ash heap.

I manage to slip out into the pantry and pour myself an-other bourbon, which I surely deserved, from the bottle under the scrub bucket. I pour it into a nice big ice tea glass, and I put in a sprig of mint and a lemon slice and a spoon so nobody will know. It's practically the same color, and who could tell unless they had it in mind? I resolved to hold my breath and keep my distance, and I also popped a green mint candy in my mouth.

Well, I'm in the pantry and I can hear Billy Black in the kitchen talking to Mrs. Loomis's girl Carrie (loaned to us for the afternoon). This Carrie is giggling and squirming and she thinks he's just the most sophisticated young bachelor she's ever met. And she's a pretty little thing herself, if you can think of a real black Nigra girl as *pretty*—and personally I can. I can without any trouble. You see, it's just a question of imagination. Suppose the whole U.S.A. were Nigra. Suppose they'd never seen a white person. And Saralizabeth dropped down by parachute. Lord, they'd find her a regular freak that's what, with her hair so shiny and silky-yellow, disgusting! Like a snake-belly! She'd be so funny-looking and weird they'd make her the featured attraction in the Side Show. Jojo the Ghost-Faced Girl. People would come for miles and gawp and giggle. "Poor child, whatever could have *happened?* Whatever happened to her *hair?* Whatever happened to *her skin?*" And others would shudder and say, "Kill her, stamp her out!" It's all relative, I say. It's the Theory of Relativity all over again, and just because that was discovered by somebody with the name of Einstein, well *that* don't make it false. If Einstein had invented Coca-Cola, would we all get poisoned? (Lord, maybe he did invent Coca-Cola for all I know!)

I remember when I was a child, maybe six, I was mad at Lily—furious about something—did I say Lily? I mean *Alice,* my goodness, that was her name, *Alice.* Well, Alice was a darling good woman. At night when I'd say my prayers and finish up ". . . make me a good girl," I'd always hear Alice in the next room, "*Do, Lawd!*" Anyways, this time I was furious. Alice wanted me to do something, I reckon, and I was dead set not to. So I just turned on her, and I tried out my vocabulary.

Mean and hateful, I said, *"Alice, you're nothing but a nigger!"*

Yes, Reader, I said it. Well, Alice went into the kitchen, and my mother, she heard me and she came downstairs lickety-split, and she walloped me what I mean. First and only time I ever got hit. She walloped me, and shook me till my neck went crick-crack. "Don't you EVER say that again!" "Mama, I won't, I won't ever say it again!" Whooee. I felt lower than any worm. "Now MARCH in there and apologize." I went into the kitchen and there sat Alice at the table, with this hopeless, tired-out look, and she was crying her eyes out. I said, "I'm sorry," and I cried my eyes out too. "I'm sorry, Alice." Well, I never *have* got over it, not to this very day. Unforgivable. I still just cry to think about it.

Yes, my mama was never in her whole life anything but kind and good to Nigras. Naturally, she didn't let Alice use the same toilet or anything, but that was just in case. Mama was from an old Virginia family and she was a true lady, and I wish I took more after her, though some say I do. Maybe she was too busy to pay much mind to me, but whenever I got sick she'd sit by my bed and sing to me. Songs from operettas. I loved to get sick! Yes. She could have been an actress in musical comedy if it wasn't for having me. Well, I was nine years old when she got pneumonia and died. She got it from taking me to the zoo in Richmond. It was a windy cold day, and I was bad and wouldn't go home, and she took a chill. . . . Imagine what Mama would have said if she knew I married Leroy . . . ? But Lord, I didn't know how things would turn out. I vow I didn't. Leroy said he was going to study Law. He was sweet as pie back then, so slim and handsome, he just turned my head. How was I to know he'd wind up sheriff and all that? Mama, how was I to know? Oh my Lordy, oh my soul——

Well! Let me collect myself. I'm wandering far afield.

Yes. Billy Black was talking to Mrs. Loomis's girl. And I was eavesdropping, which I have a weakness for, and this is the moment I learn Billy Black is conducting a Nigra Registration Drive in Leroy's own house.

"Howcome I never saw you before?" says Billy.

"I'm from up yonder, up county," says the girl.

"Howcome you moved to town?" says Billy.

"My folks, they bought a farm, you know?" says the girl. "Paid the money, but the white man cheated us. He said we didn't pay it. So all us chillun had to move away."

"Girl," says Billy, "are you twenty-one?" And she says, uh-huh. And he says, "Then you register, hear? It's your right," he says. "You do it now."

She giggles and giggles, and I think she'll choke any minute, but she manages to say, "You Northern niggas come down here land us in the soup pot long with the onions."

Billy says, "Who's Northern?" He says he was born and raised right here in Cachattow County.

"You sho don't *talk* like Cachattow County," says the girl. And she is right, because Billy, like I said, has gone and got himself a Yankee accent.

"Well ah sho can talk Cachattow if ah wants to," says Billy. "Ah can talk mule, catfish, hawg and pone, anything you like."

She giggles even harder.

"You go to this address," says Billy. "Down by the African Baptist Church. They'll tell you how to register. You bring your friends too. Bring 'em all."

"What I want to register for?" she says, all flirtatious.

"So you can vote."

"What I want to vote for?"

Billy snorts and says, well, that's a good question. He says he personally don't think this voting is going to do one bit of good, but the idea is you got to start *somewheres*, making black folks think, and the idea is, you vote for some man going to be nice to up-county niggas like herself. You got to organize, you got to make a start, he says, and after *that*——

But Reader, he didn't finish, he must have acted something out in pantomime.

Well, my ears were stretched out like a mule's but just then Lily came through from the living room with an empty tray and she saw me and went into the kitchen and she must have given them the high-sign, for silence fell.

So that ended my eavesdropping. I know, Reader, that eavesdropping is not nice and no lady would do it, but I do it anyway. It is like an addiction to strong drug. I love to listen while invisible. It makes me feel—oh, how to put it!—all-powerful, all-seeing. Like God. That's it. "I know more than you think I do!" I have sneaked up on more half-open doors than you could shake a stick at, and cupped my ears at keyholes more than once. Well I did not eavesdrop on Leroy, no, I learned early on not to listen at *his* door because I wouldn't like what I heard. Why make it harder on yourself? But I have eavesdropped on Saralizabeth and her friends, and as a child I eavesdropped on my aunts and uncles, and I just especially love eavesdropping on the Nigras. It's like entering another world. The Nigras lead their life and we live ours, and they touch sometimes, but how do we know what they say when they're alone? In the midst of all my confidence that I completely understand the Nigra soul, there lurks this nagging doubt! Don't they always hush up when a white person comes around? And you know, they *act*. They're great actors, these Nigras, and we're the audience. And personally, I always did love to peek behind the curtain.

Well, Lily put an end to my eavesdropping. So I replenished my glass and returned to my guests, sipping at **my** drink and sucking away on the candy mint, sloshing the green juice around in my mouth, hoping nobody could tell. And they couldn't either. I was as dignified as I could be. I was the very figurine of mourning, yes. The very statuette of grief. And everything was fine, Reader, until——— *I saw that man.*

Lord have mercy, my heart simply stopped. My blood froze over.

Because there, by the sideboard, sipping a cola drink and eating a sandwich, talking with Cousin Clayton, pleased as punch and cool as brass, making himself right at home—*is* *Mr. Wimbly!*

That man!

Can you imagine, the brass of that man! I mean, bad enough he came to the cemetery, after I said he was not welcome. But to walk brazenly into my very house and home! The gall!

Well, he glances up and catches me with my mouth open and my eyes just horrified and ablaze, and over he comes, his head dipped to one side and his brow all furrowed up with that fraudulent sympathy and concern for the bereaved little woman.

"*Mister* Wimbly!" I said sotto voce as he came up, and my voice and my hands both were simply trembling with rage. "Might I *kindly* speak to you in private, and would it be *too much to ask* if you would step into the hall?"

So we stepped into the hall, and I prayed, *Lord give me strength! Lord give me strength to handle this without a scene! What is he here for anyway?* I asked myself. *And whatever it may be, I will not have him in my house!*

END THIRD INSTALLMENT

Mr. Wimbly
Smiles and Smiles

Reader, that last installment kind of rambled on, I do admit, and if I had any disease other than manic-depression, I might rewrite it. But who ever heard of a manic *rewriting?* The very thought is enough to make you chuckle.

I looked up *manic* in the dictionary, and it said *maniac*. So I presume I am a maniac, what else? But when I put it to Dr. Dimmer, and said, "Dr. Dimmer, a manic is a maniac, unless I miss my guess," he soothed me down, and said that being manic was just like being DRUNK all the time! A *little bit* manic is fine, he said, you feel great. Merry, giddy and gay. But too much is like a bad mean drunk, etcetera.

I said one of the patients told me that what manics *really* do is skitter madly around their problems, because they are too painful to look at. A manic just hops skips and jumps along life's path, nimbly avoiding the dog-do as she goes. I said that seemed plausible to me. He said well . . . And I said, anyway, here I was writing and writing, *all about my problems!!* So how could I be a manic?

"Whatever gave you the notion you are manic anyway?" he said.

45

I looked at him slyly, and said, "I read it on my chart when the nurse wasn't looking. Prelim. Diag. Manic-Depressive."

"Well," he hedged, "a preliminary diagnosis is only tentative."

"You mean I'm something else?" I said. "Lord have mercy!"

"Mmm," he said.

"A pinch of this and a dab of that?" I said.

Well, he laughed.

"Now, Dr. Dimmer," I said, "I've been told that manics are *obsessed with sex*, now is that true? I mean, I do tell a little off-color joke now and then to cheer up my fellow inmates, but—I mean, it's *other* people are obsessed with sex it seems to *me*," I said. "I am not obsessed at all," I said, "with anything—so far as *I* know—except that whenever I chance to see *that man* or even think about him, that Mr. Clarence Wimbly, *then*, I am obsessed all right. But it is not with *sex*. I am obsessed with *hatred*, and that is the truth!"

O Reader, ask me about Hatred. Ask me, I can tell you what it is, for I am its Victim. Hatred comes snarling up in me, out of the Nether Regions, and it shakes me in its teeth, for all the world like some great Dog of Hell shaking a small cat. I am that helpless in its grasp, all I can do is grind my teeth and clench my fingers, all I can do is to tremble and to shake. Well, Mr. Wimbly affects me that way. I shake with rage, and I only wish I were myself a Dog of Hell so I could RIP him into shreds!

And why? Because he is a brute. He is a mean and brutal man who never speaks a word of truth, the very Soul of hypocrisy, treachery, falsehood!

Yet I admit, hatred is mysterious. After all, my own husband Leroy, you might call him a brute. And yet I married him, and I didn't hate him, not the way I hate Mr. Wimbly. I only hated Leroy now and then, in normal wifely fashion. Leroy was a brute and Mr. Wimbly is a brute, and yet I hate Mr. Wimbly so bad that I could truly sit down and eat him for dinner. I could gnaw his bones, Reader, and I know it is not ladylike. I just feel that he is *everything* that's mean. Furthermore, he treats me like some little contemptible *idiot*. He just *denies* me. He denies I have anything whatever worthy of respect. And all the while, oh all the while, he's acting so respectful and concerned, butter wouldn't melt in his mouth, but you know in reality he wouldn't even spit on you, he wouldn't waste good spit. Yes!

And you can't get hold of him. That's the worst. Reader, that *is* the worst. When you're mad at someone, and you can make that person mad at *you*, well, you're satisfied. But Mr. Wimbly, he wouldn't dream of getting mad, or hating back, he just smiles and smiles, and talks in that smooth rotten-silk voice of his, all fraudulent respect. Unctuous!

And why does he despise me so? I ask you.

Because I am a woman! He is one of your woman-despisers. Why his whole life is made glad and happy because there are women and Nigras, to use, and feel superior to. I should like to ask, what would happen to Mr. Wimbly if by some stroke women and Nigras simply vanished from the earth? Ha! He would be in a plight! He would shrivel up and die!

God give me strength to master myself, for when I even talk about that man, I tremble and shake. Not with fear, Reader, not fear—it is the irresistible force of my desire to simply wrastle him down and trample him and put my high heels in his face. Yes. And that desire drives head-on into the cruel and bitter fact that I am not physically strong enough to do it. Well, since I cannot hope to master him and make him drink the cup of gall that he should rightly drink—then may God please give me strength at least to master my own self, and be more of a lady than to *harbor* such base desires. That is my constant prayer, and when I go to church I pray it at the altar of the Lord.

Clarence Wimbly is the kind of man whose favorite sayings are those about a woman's place. "Barefoot, pregnant, and on a farm"—you know the kind? "The only happy woman is knocked up and ground down." "A woman, a dog, and a hickory tree—the more you beat 'em, the better they be." But at the very same time, he calculates that he personally is just every woman's dream come true, a real Don Juan, and the women just fall fall fall (he thinks) like ripe cherries from the bough. All he has to do is open his mouth and bite.

Yes and I do mean BITE. The sacred sexual act is not sacred to that man, I can tell you. There used to be a story going around (and I personally believe it and would wager any amount that it is Gospel Truth) about one time when Mr. Wimbly visited a house of ill-repute in Jackson. Or maybe it was New Orleans. Anyway, he was squirming around in bed with this poor Godforsaken girl, showing off his manhood and everything, when suddenly the poor creature began to scream and scream, and came staggering out of the room hollering *Madam! Madam!* and streaming with blood! Yes!

And what had he done?

Bit her nipple off!

Yes! Bit it clean off. I ask you. Is that a monster? Why, they had to take two stitches and put her in the hospital for shock! And you know a nipple don't grow back like a fingernail. When a nipple's gone, it's gone.

Well, naturally, she SUED him, for mutilation, pain and suffering—not to mention wrecking her career. And Mr. Wimbly, did he pay? Ha. Of course not. He knew the sheriff and the lawyer and the judge and the district attorney, all the right people, and he got off scot-free. Not one penny did he pay that poor girl. And not only did he get off scot-free, but he won himself a great big reputation as a Devil of a Fellow. Oh! I tell you, I tell you, I would like to stick my high heel right into the *center* of his eyeball. I would. I would like . . . I would like . . . I would like to have him make some advance to me, yes, come at me with his big hands. And I would *pretend* to give in, you know—I would sigh and moan and carry on in lovesick fashion— and just when he was getting himself worked up—ha ha! Slip a knife right into his vitals.

Wouldn't that serve him good and right! Justice! Lord, Lord. Well, there isn't any. Not in this world. No. No justice, none at all.

And I would say to him, ha HA Mr. Wimbly, you think you're so much! Now you know better don't you, ha ha HA. And I would run skipping away, happy as a lark at dawning, scattering rosebuds, daisies, violets, barefoot in the morning dew, rosy as the morning, full of tender love and kisses for the world! Yes I would. Wearing a graceful Grecian chiffon gown caught sweetly under the bustline, and my hair cascading down the nape of my neck in silky curls and corkscrews, yes. And by that act, I would become the most loving woman in the world! the most beautiful! I would be Helen of Troy! Nineteen years old forever, virginal and pure and free! And pouring out, just pouring out, with love, love, love!

Well, even Mr. Wimbly will die in the end, I tell myself. He will grow old and feeble and go to the Old Man's Home. But you know, I take cold comfort from that thought. Because he will surely be one of your dirty old men who pinch the nurses and chuckle with their toothless mouths and leer from their watery eyes whilst they recollect their evil conquests. No, there is no comfort in this world! When it comes to Mr. Wimbly, I can't think, no I really cannot think what would satisfy me. He'll die in the end, but then, so will I. And what's gained? Nothing's gained. Some *other* Mr. Wimbly will just take over and carry the torch forward. And some other Prettybelle will wring her hands and gnash her teeth, I reckon.

And that poor mousy soul *Mrs.* Wimbly! So negative she just about disappears when you look at her. Had all her insides removed, plus one breast, poor thing is just tattered and torn, and I'll wager it's all she can do just to fix his precious dinner and totter off to church to pray the Lord will take her soon! She had four stillborn children, and no wonder they were stillborn, I say. He probably beats and bruises her, and bites her too, probably bit that breast of hers, yes, bit it most likely and then infection set in, and gangrene set in, and so she had to have it off. Lord, if you were married to Mr. Wimbly, you'd probably have one part or another bit off or cut off, beat off, operated off, drop off, until all that was left of you was just one suffering palpitating *trunk*.

Well, with thoughts like these in mind, I stepped into the front hall with Mr. Wimbly, who is a handsome man in his repulsive way.

"Mr. Wimbly," I said, "I do NOT recollect inviting you to this house." I said it right out.

"Why, Miz Sweet," he said, "I just wanted to pay my respects. You know I was one of your husband's most devoted and loyal friends."

And he looked at me with those electric blue eyes, all surrounded by kindly gentle lines, looking as trustworthy as your dear old country doctor, only handsome, and all the time thinking sex and evil in the back of his mind, about as trustworthy as a cottonmouth moccasin.

"I have to say, Mr. Wimbly——"

And suddenly I felt right weak, from anger I expect, and small stars and planets speckled the air all around me.

"I have to say, Mr. Wimbly—" I continued bravely, leaning on the banisters for support, "I have to say that you're not welcome in this house, not welcome at all."

"Why Miz Sweet," he said, all solicitude, "are you giddy?"

And if he doesn't catch me by both my hands and hold them fast!

"Mr. Wimbly!" I cried, and then, recollecting the guests, "Mr. Wimbly!" I whispered. "You take your *hands* off me!"

"Don't you carry on," he said, and he whispered something very low right in my ear which I could scarcely hear or understand, but it was something vile and insinuating about that wager, and I took it to mean that in his opinion I had the same interests *he* had, that I was some kind of sexual or fallen woman, prey to her own desires! Which was certainly as far from the truth as it could be!

Well, I couldn't believe my ears. I was that indignant my heart started going like a woodpecker, and I said, "MISTER Wimbly, this is Leroy's FUNERAL!"

Oh then you may be sure, he let me go and was all silky sorry and contrite, implying he just had terrible difficulty controlling his passion, etc., but that he was deeply guilty for such bad timing.

"But you know, Miss Belle," he said through those smiling teeth of his, "it's in the cards. You and I *know* that, don't we?"

"You leave this house!" I said, and Reader, I was so full of adrenalin, I vow if he and me had come to blows, I would have won the fight! Yes!

Well, suddenly he changed, and that's also Mr. Wimbly. He changes skin like a snake. Oh! To think that this is the man who teaches History to our junior-high-school children!

"Miz Sweet," he said, all pompous and official, "I'm here on business. I'm not trying to crowd my way into your social life." And he stopped smiling, and the kindly crinkles all relaxed and showed white inside where the sun had never reached.

"Business!" I said. "What business!"

"Those explosions at the cemetery," said Mr. Wimbly. "A Nigra boy was seen running through the streets, and a Nigra woman after him, and I have reason to believe they were heading for *your house*, and I got to know what help you have, and I got to step inside your kitchen."

"You will not step inside my kitchen at *all!*" I said. "And if you try to, I will make a scene."

He looked at me calculating if I would or wouldn't.

"Oh yes I will," I assured him. "Don't count on me that I don't mean exactly what I say! I'll scream right out loud. I mean it!"

Well, there's this long tense silence, and he wavers, but then he breaks into this mean sinister little smile again, which if you didn't know better would seem so kind and loving, tender and gentle, you would just give him anything he asked for!

"Well," he said, shaking his head as if I were just a cute

little willful naughty girl, "I reckon you might!" And then, sweet as dandelion fluff floating through the summer air, he says, "*You protectin someone, Miz Sweet?*"

Well, I have ears, and I could hear the menace in that one!

"Protecting someone," I said. "Whatever do you mean?"

"Miz Sweet," he said, "it may pay you to cooperate with me."

"With you!" I said scornfully. "I would sooner cooperate with a sick mule." I said that, Reader, but I was not as bold within as I was without.

"Yes, ma'am," he said, so sweet and tender. "It just might pay you. You not *hidin* anything are you, Miz Sweet?"

Do you know, I didn't think about Billy Black, all I could think of was—*he knows about the canceled check! Oh Glory, he knows!* And Reader, I will explain about that canceled check in just a minute.

"Mr. Wimbly," I said, smiling the way he did, or trying to, "are you going to leave my house? Or shall I make a little biddy scene?"

"Now, now, Miss Belle," he said in this soothing voice, like an owl soothing the baby rabbit he has in his claws, "I do see you're not yourself! I'll be going," he said, "and I'll be back later."

"Don't trouble yourself!" I said from the heart.

"No trouble, Miss Belle," he said from the doorway. And he then mouthed another one of those loathesome compliments which are really mortal insults if you know the truth, and he even had the audacity to refer once more to "our friendly little wager" and other things I couldn't even understand since he talked so low. And off he went! Smiling, humming a tune!

And leaving me with weak knees, I can tell you. For I was sure he knew about the canceled check!

You see, when I first inherited Aunt Millie Lou Ruffle's money, and discovered Leroy was going to let it alone, I sent off a nice big fat check to a certain organization beginning with the Initial N and ending with Initial P. N - - - P. Initials. Well I did it, and I was glad, and I posted the letter at the corner of Oak and Butternut.

I posted the letter, and the letterbox went clunk, and my heart went *clank!* For I suddenly thought of something. *Oh Glory, what about the canceled check!!!* I thought. *Leroy will find out!!!*

I tell you, I truly tasted terror on my tongue. Every day after that I rushed out in the morning and greeted the mailman and snatched up the letters and smiled and babbled until the poor fellow thought I was downright in love with him! I was waiting for the bank letter with the canceled checks, lest Leroy get to them first. I was a nervous wreck. My slipped disk got ten times worse, and my shingle pain came back, and my stomach was full of gas. I was so petrified, I jumped like a cat when anybody spoke to me, and I didn't sleep a wink for two weeks until that letter came.

It came, and I ran with it to the bathroom and I locked the door and I opened the envelope with trembling fingers. And there they were:—four canceled checks.

Now the first one was for Leroy's portrait in oil paints that hangs over the couch, which I most certainly did not order, though I had to pay for it. Saralizabeth got this Original Gift Idea one Christmas and answered an ad in a magazine, "Portraits Painted from Your Favorite Photograph." Well, she sent off a snapshot of her Daddy with his sheriff's hat and his silver star, and his hound dogs at his feet and his cigar in his mouth. And she told them his coloring and the color of his clothes and his hounds. And she wasn't content with the size they advertised. Oh no! She had to have it *huge*. Well, she read their answer wrong, and thought it would cost $25 when it really cost $250! So who paid for it? Reader, you are right. I did. And I cannot bear that portrait. Leroy looks so brutal and self-important—Lord, not to mention *lifelike*—he simply presides and domineers over the living room until you can't even get away from him. Well, anyhow, that was the first of the canceled checks, and it was a nice, clean-looking check.

The second was to Flower's Department Store for my mink-trimmed winter coat. And it was a perfectly respectable-looking good clean check. The third was to Saralizabeth for a new yellow satin formal. And *it* was nice and clean. But the fourth—!

Well, it surely had been handled, I can tell you. It was rumpled and finger-marked, and grubby at the edges. How did it get that way? Now you might say the dirt came from all those Northern Nigras fingering that check, but my Intuition told me otherwise. It was not the Northern Nigras. It was all those SOUTHERN BANK TELLERS! Yes! Passing my check from hand to hand, under the desk so to speak. "Looky here! Look at *this!* Look what Sheriff's wife is up to!"

Well, that was some years ago, and nothing happened, so I gradually quieted down and started sleeping nights again, only troubled once in a while by nightmares. You can really believe I burnt that check and flushed the ashes down the toilet and never mailed a check up North again. (Sent cash in the envelope, instead. Twenty-dollar bills. And if some Yankee Nigra clerk just pocketed the cash, well, that was all right with me. Whew!)

When Mr. Wimbly said, "*Are you protectin some-*

one?"—that could refer to Billy Black. But when he said, *"Are you hidin something?"*—that could only mean my canceled check! Lord, Lord, I thought. He knows about the check, he's going to *blackmail me!*

Reader, can you believe that once I was almost in love with him? That horrible, loathesome man? Lord, what errors can a woman's heart not make! Granpa Beesly used to say that "Love would just as soon alight upon a cabbage as a rose," and that is surely true. Only I would change it to say, "Love would just as soon alight upon a *nettle* as a rose." A stinging nettle. My own career surely illustrates that. Well, the time I refer to was long ago.

I was just a girl, and I was engaged to Leroy Sweet and pledged to marry him soon as he graduated Law School. (Ha! I'd have waited forEVER if I'd waited for that.) I was wearing his ring, all set to go. Well, at that time, I was also teaching Sunday school at the Tabernacle Methodist Church—not because I was especially religious or anything, in fact I wasn't even a Methodist! but chiefly because it looked good, and Leroy liked the idea and used to brag about it. He always billed me as a cultivated young lady from Virginia, and teaching Sunday school was to his mind one of those things true Young Ladies *do*. And who else was teaching Sunday school? Reader, you guessed it. None other than Clarence Wimbly. Yes, Lord. *Such* a religious man. To this day!

Well, he had an eye for me, and I knew it. A woman always knows it. And I confess, it spiced up Sunday school considerable, knowing Clarence Wimbly was watching for me, waiting round the corner for me, admiring me, thinking lewd thoughts about me, always ready with a compliment and a deep deep look into the Soul from those bold and intimate blue eyes—which had those kindly fatherly

crinkles started even then. Reader, I knew he was dangerous. I mean, I had evidence. I ran across a letter he had
dropped, and I read it, and it was from some poor child in
Peechuck, Alabama, telling him how she was pregnant and
her folks were kicking her out of the house, and
why wouldn't he marry her like he had promised, and how
could he write her such a cruel letter telling her it was all
her own fault!

I was horrified. Yes, I was horrified, but I also felt a distinct thrill simply coursing through my vitals. Love. Hovering over the nettle!

Oh, this is a shameful chapter in my life! Long ago and
far away, thank Heaven, and I was very young and surely
had no sense!

Sunday school picnic that year was held down at the
bend of the river, where there used to be a little tots' amusement park, with a wading pool and swings and a Giant
Stride, and a little carousel you pushed and then jumped
aboard, sand piles and such. Oh, it is a lovely spot, all wild
flowers and shimmering sunshine, with the muddy river in
front of you, and behind you the huge dark trees—almost
reminding you of Virginia, only the river was kind of small
and poorly by comparison to the noble Potomac! Well, Mr.
Wimbly was there with his class, and I was there with my
class, and where Leroy was I cannot for my life remember,
but wherever he was, one place he was *not* was the Tabernacle Methodist Annual Sunday School Picnic.

Oh, it was a day! Mr. Wimbly had his eye on me, and I
felt like Princess of the World. I had on a blue gingham
dress, innocent and sweet as it could be, and it exactly matched my eyes (lashes all curled and darkened).
I had taken a good hour to get my hair just exactly in the
most becoming way. The sunshine and the heat made me

all rosy (as I ascertained from peeking in my compact), and it curled up the fringes of my hair around my face in the most adorable damp way you can imagine. I was just breathtakingly pretty on that day, if I do say so, and I felt that Mr. Wimbly was simply gone and OVERCOME by me, and Reader, he was.

Well, as that beautiful shimmery day wore on, Mr. Wimbly and I we swung on the swings and we pushed the children on the merry-go-round, and we waded in the pool. Our classes met and mingled in the heat, playing, shouting, fighting, and he managed to touch my hand a dozen times or more, and I would slide it away from him, pretending not to notice, and once I felt the butt of his hand just as casual as you please against my thigh, and I was both thrilled and indignant, but he wasn't even looking at me, and it was a mere accident—or so he would have me fancy! Reader, I hate to say so, but my senses were fairly intoxicated by that man. I felt all-beautiful and all-desirable, and fairly intoxicated, I admit.

So back on board the bus, at last, and the children and teachers all ride back to the church, and the parents come for their children, and the day is over. I am feeling somewhat let-down—until Mr. Wimbly says he will drive me home. Now, Home is only five blocks away, at my late Aunt Millie Lou Ruffle's house, and I say, oh no, I will walk, it's just a step. But he says I must be tired, and he insists! Well, Reader, it *was* quite an afternoon, and I *was* tired, or told myself so, and with this same delicious and forbidden thrill chasing itself around my vitals, I got into the car with him. My heart going pitty-pat, and my conceit just preening itself!

Did he drive me home?

He did not!

Which I knew he wouldn't when I got in!

Well, the less said about the rest of that afternoon the better. Suffice it to say that, over my protests, he drove right back towards the amusement park (which he had observed from the windows of the bus to be completely deserted). "Why, Mr. Wimbly, wherever are you going?" said I. "Really, I DO have to get home. I have so many things to do."

Well, he pulls that old green Chevrolet with its Deathshead gearshift knob into a deserted road in the middle of those great dark trees aforementioned—a road no doubt well beknownst to him! And he stops, and turns off the engine, and commences his campaign. Let me tell you, in retrospect I see it was a beauty! But at the time I firmly believed myself in full control!

He was the weak one, I was the strong! HE not ME was the one who was huffing and puffing and begging and crying out with passion, and saying how he loved me, and couldn't he have one kiss, just one. Well, Reader, he had a dozen hands at least, that man, and I had only two, working with might and main to shove his away. And then I said to myself, oh all right, keep him quiet, do him a big favor, one little kiss . . . and I let him kiss me. Well, at that point he had sense enough to stop pawing for a minute and devote himself full-time to the kiss, which is getting more serious by the second, and I'm sinking a little, and his hand creeps to my bosom, and I push it away, and it creeps again, and I push, and so on a couple more times, and he breaks off the kiss, and cries. Real true sobs. Yes! He cries and carries on and leans on me and begs, and says oh please, please, and I think, oh well what's all the fuss about, poor fellow he is crying, and it's only the fabric of a dress! So I let him touch my bosoms through my dress, and pretty soon his hand is inside my dress! And I struggle, Reader, I do, but then he kisses me some more, and he's all over me, and I sink lower and lower, and by now the struggle I am waging, a valiant struggle, is as much against my own self as him. "Prettybelle, you must NOT, Prettybelle, you MUST not!" And I said, "Clarence, I might *want* to, but I *can't!* I'm engaged! Clarence, I can't. What would Leroy say?" And he says, "Oh to hell with Leroy, how is he to know? I WANT you!" And then all this puffing and burrowing and crowding and climbing on top of me, and "Please, baby, oh please, marry me, I love you, I can't stand it, I'm going to die, come on, baby!" and the like.

Well, his hand is crawling up under my skirt by now, and I hold it back, and I say to myself, Prettybelle, not one more inch! and then I say, Well, just one more inch, one tiny little inch, Oh Lordy, only one more inch, and Reader, I just sink underwater altogether, and I collapse and close my eyes, and even though it takes a bit of fumbling around with clothes and gearshifts and all—alas, he has his way with me.

Yes, I burn with shame to admit it, but he definitely has his way, and although at first I do not cooperate (still fancying I am the Mighty One, granting a favor to my humble, begging, pleading, crying Servant) soon—Reader, I blush and I stammer with shame to admit it—soon I am sobbing and crying out myself, and clinging to him, and kissing and rubbing, and generally carrying on like a Wanton Woman, and as I had NEVER carried on with Leroy —no never for Leroy, who had indeed recently deflowered me, but in a more reverent kind of way, with me kind of lying back dreamy-eyed and absent-minded during the transaction.

Just when I'm at my worst—Lord have mercy—bang!

It's all over! Finished! He lays back and pants a minute, then he picks himself up in a businesslike way, whilst I am still flabbergasted and in disarray—he picks himself up, zips himself up (or was it buttons in those days?), arranges his clothing, smiles to himself, looks at me coolly as you might look at a WORM and says: "You *are* a hot little bitch aren't you!"

Just like that.

Well, my heart fell into a true convulsive fit. And the blood simply drained out of my brain and I thought I would faint or die right there. Sometimes I wish I *had*.

"I knew I could get you," he said.

A vision of that girl in Peechuck, Alabama, flew into my mind, and I thought, *Good GOD, he took no precautions, and what if I am pregnant like that poor creature in the letter?* I have never felt so frightened and betrayed and mortally insulted in my life, bewildered and exhausted and in disarray. Well, I corrected the disarray as gracefully as I could (Lord, what an embarrassment, buttoning up and pulling down, straightening seams, stuffing my bosoms back into their brassiere), and I said,

"Leroy will hear of this! You RAPED ME," I said, "and Leroy will KILL you," I said, "and I hope he does."

Well, he only laughed this evil insulting mocking laugh. "Raped you," he drawled, sarcastically. "Leroy would believe that, wouldn't he, when I tell him how hot you were? Tell Leroy, go ahead! *You'll* be the one that gets it, not me."

"Take me *home!*" I said, on the verge of tears, as you may imagine. Because in my heart, I knew it was true. Leroy would believe Mr. Wimbly and not me.

So this Monster drove me home, whistling to himself, happy and bland and well-fed as any sunbaked reptile, and at my house he leaned across me to open the car door, and he said, all earnest again, all passionate and needful, "Prettybelle, when do I see you again?"

"OH!" I cried. I was never so indignant. I smacked that man as hard as I could across his face, and he smiled, and grabbed my wrist, and bent it till it hurt, and I squealed *ouch!* "I'll have you again, honey-child, whenever I please, and don't you forget it," he says, and he drops my wrist. "Give my regards to Leroy," he says. And off he drives, leaving me, Reader, alone with my Thoughts.

Well, after that, Reader, you may well believe I considered him my Mortal Enemy, and seized every opportunity thereafter to insult him publicly. I would mock him and belittle him and sneer (in a teasy, jokey way) in front of other folks at a party or gathering, so he couldn't do anything but smile! Yes I made sport of him, and it was a dangerous game, for the man could easily destroy my Reputation forever. But I could not stop. And after such a party, back at home, I would tremble and shake with rage, and cry, and tear my handkerchief, and bite my knuckles till you could see the mark.

Luckily I was not pregnant! Thank all my lucky stars. Though truth to tell, my sickness came upon me two full weeks late that month and I was in sheerest terror. Furthermore, it was kind of an eccentric one, I mean, half-hearted . . . just feeble enough to keep alive this little anguished DOUBT. Well, all I could think to do was praise and pet and pamper Leroy, and let him take as many liberties with me as he pleased, which was quite a few, as a sort of insurance policy against disaster. And by the next month I was *indeed* pregnant, and Leroy and me got married in a hurry. And during that doubtful time, Clarence Wimbly called me up quite a few times, asking me to go out with him!

And I would laugh and say, "Go out with YOU? Ha ha ha ha!" Yes, I seized every opportunity to insult him, and he seized every opportunity to catch me alone and make vulgar insinuating remarks or feel me up in private places, or pinch too hard, as I have described, like he OWNED me, like we had a SECRET PRIVATE relationship or pledge! Oh! Maybe he hated me as much as I hated him, but if so he never showed it on his face. Always smooth, unruffled, always smiling!

But now Leroy was dead. And I was standing in the vestibule alone, and Mr. Wimbly (who turned around as he went down the walk and waved at me with one finger in his mocking fashion) was threatening me with *blackmail!*

Do you know, I had my first true pang of sorrow for Leroy dead. I thought, who will protect me now? And for the first time it occurred to me that maybe Mr. Wimbly had been *held back* by Leroy's power and sheer size. I also thought, maybe everyone in town already knows what happened in that old green Chevrolet. Maybe they've been acting nice all these years because they didn't DARE say anything in front of Leroy. And maybe now Leroy is gone I will get snubbed and insulted. And if he told about the *check*—Lord knows what might happen. I might even get whipped by the Klan or something!

"Prettybelle," I said, there in the vestibule, "this way madness lies. Do not allow yourself such morbid thoughts. Folks in this town are kind, fine people! And YOU are being sick, neurotic, and paranoid."

But all the same, I felt as if a great black Pit had opened yawning at my feet. And at the bottom of the pit were distant little red crawling things, damned and bleeding souls, most likely, amongst whom I would soon be numbered.

But I fought back. I said, "Do not let folks mix you up,

Prettybelle Sweet. You sent that money because you felt it was only *right*. If *that's* the worst sin you ever committed you'd be a mighty pure and guilt-free female. Your true sins lie in the opposite direction." I said that, and it worked. The great black pit just shriveled up and dwindled, until it got no bigger than a prune pit. And I squared my shoulders, and I held my head high, and I marched back to the living room.

END FOURTH INSTALLMENT

Who Is My Daddy?

Yes I squared my shoulders, and I took a deep if shaky breath, and reminded myself I was the captain of my fate and had no cause to fear anybody. Put that man out of your mind, I told myself. He is no more than dog-mess on the garden path. Return to your guests, and hold them here, for night is on its way. I confess, Reader, I suffered from a dread of nighttime coming, which had nothing whatever to do with Mr. Wimbly but was that plain old-fashioned complaint Fear of the Dark, that primitive and antique panic at being left alone in the Cave by night. Yes. Especially this night.

So I rejoined my guests and they were busy reminiscing about Leroy, describing in fond detail how he could hold his liquor, orate, and shoot duck—which three things, Reader, are the very Measure of a Man down here, I reckon. I joined right in, and sipped my drink, and held my audience just fine till Saralizabeth gripped my arm like the iron maiden and simply hissed into my ear. "Do you know you're *laughing?*"

Well, in my opinion, laughter is perfectly permissible and appropriate at funeral parties. What kind of a De-

65

ceased would insist on gloom and sorrow everywhere? However, as I have said, down here they have these rigid and barbaric customs, and sure enough one or two faces plainly betrayed shock. So I bit my tongue and passed my hand over my brow, as if coming to my senses, and I said faintly, "Well, Lord have mercy, here I am laughing and joking, as if—as if——" And do you know, I didn't have to act at all, I simply sank down on a chair and burst into tears. I was so nervous, what with Mr. Wimbly's blackmail and Leroy dead and nighttime coming and Billy Black subversive in the kitchen, that I burst loudly into tears and took my lace handkerchief out of my sleeve to staunch the flow.

It was exactly the right thing to do! Even Saralizabeth looked mollified, though still somewhat sour and suspicious. I wept for fifty-five seconds and then (remembering one of Granpa Beesly's maxims, namely, *A woman's tears! Devastating for one minute, embarrassing for two, and a damned bore after three*) I hastily arose and blew my nose and gave those guests a big bright smile. I fear it was my flirtatious smile, but Lord, when you've been trained all your life long to be charming, scatterbrained, and cute, how can you turn it off?

"I do pray you will forgive me if I act strange this afternoon," I said. "Lord, twenty years of marriage down the drain! It's no secret, I reckon, that Leroy and I we had our little spats, *fights* you might call them——"

Well, I caught the echo of that one, and it didn't sound just right or appropriate to the occasion, so to take the curse off it, I gave a merry laugh and said:

"I mean, seemed like we hated one another, but——"

Well, that didn't sound much better, and there was Saralizabeth again, glaring and stewing.

"Leroy was not at heart a family man," I tried again. "He

was a man's man, and a dog's man. But do you know, he loved this daughter of his? My, he did love her. My me, he did. And I guess he loved me in his way. Thought I was crazy of course." I gave the Big Flirtatious again, though I truly tried to inhibit it. "Thought I was downright loco! Shamed to death of me—like this one here."

I pointed to Saralizabeth, who was making a terrible fierce face to scare me.

"Mother, you're *disgusting!*" she hissed in my ear. "You're *drunk!*"

"I'll say this for Leroy," I continued loudly. "He never fussed over money, and never said divorce. Never once did. And now he's gone, why it makes you stop to think."

And I did stop to think, but there was nothing in my head except more words. Senseless. Flapping in the Void.

And suddenly Billy Black stood in front of me holding a tray of sandwiches. Through a sort of haze or fog, I saw that watermelon face of yesteryear, only slimmed out now, longer and harder, but still the same "curly eyes and laughing lashes" (Granpa)—really a *cute* Nigra boy, same age as my son John lacking one month. Yes, they played together once upon a time.

Reader, if I have not mentioned my son John, there is good reason. Alas, he went to the bad. No use concealing it. Yes, at the age of seventeen he took himself one of Leroy's guns, and—Lord, it pains me to tell it, but I will. Johnny took himself a deer rifle, and he climbed himself a tree on Fairview Street, a butternut tree, and he shot and killed five people before they brought him down. He did. The victims were all men, save one, and they were all *big* men, Leroy-size, if that means anything (and Dr. Dimmer says it might mean something), and the exception was Mary Martha Riley, who was my own age and size. I haven't asked Dr. Dimmer what that means, because I am afraid to know, and all I can say in my own defense is, well, at least it was four to one, though whether that reflects Johnny's emotions or merely the condition of traffic on Fairview Street, who is to say, for he broke jail and got away before his trial, and never has been heard of since. Rumor had it Leroy fixed it so the boy could get away, on condition that he would never show his face or speak his name again, for he was good as dead to Leroy, but I doubt that rumor. Leroy would have wanted a show of vengeance for the Shame, not to mention the problem at Election Time. So there's the sad story, and I try to close my eyes to it, and only rarely do I remember that I have, or had, a son, and well, this Billy Black brought him to mind, and brought back floods of gloomy memories.

Anyway, there stood Billy Black, ex-watermelon boy.

"Is that William?" I said.

"Yes, ma'am," he mumbled.

"Why William, you certainly have grown up," I said, and I turned to the folks nearby and I said, "This is our maid's boy William," and they said, "Is that so?"

William appeared to be trying to speak, and he was coughing or choking.

"Our maid Lily," I explained to Cousin Clayton. "Do you know, Lily's been with us from the time I was a bride? That's twenty years ago. I swear, Lily cried as hard as I did at the funeral this afternoon. What IS it, William?"

For he made this loud gurgle in his throat, and then he simply bolted from the room, without passing those sandwiches at all.

"I bet ninety-nine out of a hundred Nigras would *choose* a strong hand like Leroy's, if you were to ask 'em," I said to the funeral guests. Reader, I said it, and a horrible sensation like a spasm ran down my tongue right into my esophagus, and an inner voice said, *Prettybelle Sweet, what on earth are you doing?*

"Excuse me a minute," I said, and I cut out to the pantry, breathing hard. Oh Reader, I hid there in the pantry thinking about Johnny. I remembered how for months I used to dream that Johnny was hiding out in Darkytown, in blackface or something, and I would go looking for him there, and sometimes I would find him, and sometimes not, but whenever I did find him, he would turn his face away. Deny me! And I'd wake up crying my eyes out.

Hiding out in Darkytown. Do you know that I myself have thought of doing that? Oh secretly, secretly! I myself have had the urge to run away to Darkytown. Yes, I have. Run away and live with the Nigras. I mean, when you were a little child, who was nice to you? Nigras. Day in, day out, rain or shine, who was nice to you? Nigras, and nobody else. So when I feel all weak and childish and unable to cope with Life (which is all too often, sad to say), I just automatically think inside myself, I'm going to run back to Mammy. Who is Mammy? Don't ask me! I reckon Mammy means Alice, though maybe there was somebody else before Alice. I don't recollect. I know I had a black wet-nurse—which is something you don't hear about these days. Times do change. Yes, I had a Nigra wet-nurse, and so did Johnny after the first two months. In fact, Johnny's wet-nurse was Lily Black her own self, because she had ample and plenty for her own son and mine. Oh she's a good woman, full of warmth. Lord, I declare, there were times, when I was weak and weary, I wouldn't have minded snuggling up to have a drink myself. Oh Lord, in the old days if wishes were bosoms, I expect every nice comfortable Nigra woman like Lily would have had six or eight, instead of two, and there'd have been white folks at each one of them, hanging on for dear life, yes they would, in the old days. Well, even now.

Now my own mama, rest her soul, was talented and beauteous, and I absolutely adored and worshiped her, but I can't say she pampered me. I can't really say she even NOTICED me much! I was a child who burned with love from a distance. A watcher. I watched her come and I watched her go. I watched her dress. Sometimes I got close enough to smell her and she smelled of yummy powder. She would powder her shoulders with a big pink puff. She had a beautiful black taffeta evening gown, off-the-shoulder style, that rustled and whispered. Pearls and diamonds. Her hair always shone, like the sun on daffodils, and she carried a little sparkly jet bag. Oh, Mama. When she looked in the mirror, she would purse her lips and pout her lips, and then smile at herself so warm and so charming, I yearned to lie down at her feet like a dog!

But! If I wanted to feel *good*, if I wanted to be pampered and comforted, oh, petted, praised, admired—Lord, I went to the black ones. Yes I did. Lucky I was to have Nigras in my life, I can tell you. Supposing I'd been born a Yankee child—why, I'd have been the loneliest most miserable mite alive!

Whilst I was cooling myself in the pantry, I declare, I heard Lily in the kitchen having words with her son. Or rather, he was having words with *her*.

"Mammy, you answer this. Did you *cry* at that funeral? Answer me!" he was hollering. "Did you CRY?"

Well, Billy's friend, the other boy, he was trying to soothe Billy and hush him up.

And Lily said, "I'm busy, boy."

But oh, he wouldn't let it alone. He was beside himself.

"Answer me the truth," he said. "You answer me! Did you cry?"

Well, just at that moment Saralizabeth bursts in from the living room with her Kleenex at her eyes, and she doesn't even see me lurking in the far corner of the pantry, she just pushes her way into the kitchen. She's running to Lily for comfort. Minute she gets into the kitchen she lifts up her voice and boo-hoos.

"Oh Lily, Oh Lily," she cries, just like she did when she was four.

I heard Lily murmuring, "There now, chile. There, chile." And I knew Saralizabeth would have her head on Lily's bosom, getting herself rocked and patted.

"I can't stand it," wailed Saralizabeth. "Lily, I just can't stand it."

"There now, don't you cry. Lily's right here."

"My daddy's dead," hollered Saralizabeth, like it was news.

"Now, now," said Lily. "Make yo pretty eyes all red."

I could just imagine Saralizabeth sniffling and mopping up her mascara with her Kleenex.

"And Mother!" screeches Saralizabeth. "She's drunk! Lily, she's just inebriated! Saying the most awful things— how she and Daddy fought! And how she hated him! Oh my poor daddy!" Well, things like that, she'd never have said in a calm state of mind. You just don't. Saralizabeth, so proper and so fussy! (In some particulars.)

"Poor Daddy!" she was sobbing. "Oh Daddy! What a horrible life he had. Between Mommie and the Nigras, he never had a mo—mo—moment's peace!"

Imagine? Saying that to Lily? Out of her head!

"Now, now, hush, hush," said Lily, and noises like that. Soothing.

Saralizabeth just sniffled and whimpered and blew her nose. Honk. She always had a noisy blow. (Imagine *her* criticizing Judge Collie Meggs.)

"The Nigras gave him *such* a hard time, Lily," she bawled. Now can you tie it? The Nigras gave him a hard time. Right in front of those four black faces.

"Nevermine, chile," murmured Lily. "Never you mine. He gone to his reward, honey, never you mine."

Saralizabeth bawls on. "He's in the ground, Lily. He'll—he'll—he'll decay!"

"Why, looky here!" says Lily briskly. "You taste THIS!"

Well, Saralizabeth snuffles in an interested kind of way, and says, "What," and gives a couple of windup sniffs and whimpers, and then she squeals, "Orange cake!"

Lily says, "Here's a nice BIG slice," and pretty soon, out comes Saralizabeth all cheered up, eating away at Lily's orange cake. Now how's that for psychiatry! This time she saw me as she passed through, but she just tossed her head, stuck-up and disapproving, and went back into the living room. Wouldn't say a word.

Billy Black waited till she was safely gone, and then he busted out again, full of quiet rage.

"Gone to his reward!" said Billy Black. "Now what's that reward? You tell me, Mammy, what you figure is the man's reward?"

"Boy, you trying yosef," sighed Lily, kind of sad and weary.

"Listen," said Billy. "I got something draggin my mind. You take a minute. Something I got to know."

"You knows too much already," says Lily. "Never should have sent you North."

"Who was my daddy, that's what I got to know," says Billy.

"Who is *what?*" says Lily, unbelieving. "What you talking about, boy?"

"I said, *Who was my Daddy!*"

"Lord, Lord," says Lily, impatiently, clucking her tongue. "What kind of talk is that? Who my daddy, who my daddy?"

"I don't dig this action," said Billy Black. "Come on, break it down for me. Who was he? You tell me. Who was my father? Tell me his name!"

"Boy, you know well as I do who was your daddy," says Lily. "Ole Jackson Black's your daddy and nobody else. Jackson Black, right now in New Orleans working in the railroad depot, and never come home cept to Lord it over us. Well, I prays to God a train run over him. Making big money, does I see any of it? Lemme praise the day. *She* get it. That yellow girl get every penny. But never you mine! That Insurance Policy is made out to *me.* I is the legal wife! And I prays on my knees every night the Good Lawd take Jackson on the tracks. Two thousand dollars that policy, all legal, and he can't change it. No sir. Last time he come home, he cut me with a razor and he try to poison me. Yes, yes. But I is living sanctified, and the Lord goin to answer my prayer."

Well, Billy, he kept trying to interrupt all this, and finally he just hollers. "Mammy!"

"I hears you, boy," says Lily, evenly.

"Jackson is a black man."

"The Lord see him," says Lily.

"If Jackson is my daddy, howcome I turned out so light? Answer me that. Howcome I turned out so light?"

Lily took a moment, and she sniffed, and said real lofty, "Oh, is you so light? Well now, that never catched my eye."

"I'm lighter than you *or* Jackson."

"Lord goin to punish the proud and the puffed up," says Lily.

"Proud!" spits Billy Black. "Proud of *what?* You tell me howcome my skin got lighter than my family."

"You favor Jackson's granddaddy."

"You're lyin, Mammy." And in a mean, mocking way, he says, "God is listening, Mammy. Jesus say, 'Lily? Tell that boy the truth!' "

Billy's friend says, "Come on, man. Lay off."

"I done tole you the truth," says Lily. "Ain't no mo truth I knows of."

"You come here to work when you were eighteen," says Billy Black.

"Long about," agrees Lily.

"And I was born a year later."

"Long about that. Maybe less."

"Well?"

"Well, yosef."

"Mammy," says Billy Black. "Don't play dumb. *Who was my daddy?*"

Well, I begin to get a glimmering of the point, at long last.

"Boy," says Lily, "I got work to do."

And the friend says, "Billy, for Christ's sake, will you cool it?"

But nothing is going to stop him.

"Black girl, white master," he spits out. "THAT'S the truth isn't it! I'm HIS SON! Tell me! You tell me——!"

Well, I'm just barely taking it all in. And it is truly unnerving. I hear this scuffle noise inside the kitchen, and it's the other boy bawling Billy out, asking what ails him, pushing him around. Away from his mother's throat, most likely! And this other boy says,

"What's the matter, baby, you WANT her to say yes? What's all this crap about your daddy? You got some kind of dynasty going? You special? You some kind of black-ass Hamlet?" And on and on like that, accusing him of being *middle class*, of all things!

Well, I am listening with twenty-seven ears, as you may imagine, and do you know, I actually cast my mind's eye over the face of Billy Black to see can I find some resemblance to Leroy! I think, the eyes? The nose? The chin? The forehead? Then I think, why Billy Black is *prettier* than Leroy. And I bite my tongue, I'm so ashamed of thinking all these things. I bite my tongue, I sip on my ice tea, and suddenly it strikes me funny. Do you know, I started to giggle? I just leaned against the freezer and I giggled. I thought, "Billy Black is my stepson!" Well, I giggled, and I chuckled, and I was having the best time, when I remembered my dignity, and I caught hold of myself. I said, Prettybelle, you are feeling your liquor and you had better watch it! What if somebody had caught you, laughing your head off and all alone in the pantry?

So I pull myself together, and I push through the swinging door into the kitchen, and I say,

"Lily, how about the cake and coffee?"

"Yes'm, *all* ready," says Lily, just as placid, in that soft soothing voice of hers. And I look around, casually, resting my hand on the table edge just to guarantee my dignity, and never have you witnessed such a scene of Peaceful Industry! Billy Black is putting cups and saucers on a tray. His friend is filling up the sugar bowl. Lily is arranging slices of orange cake on Granma Beesly's hand-painted china platter. Mrs. Loomis's girl is at the sink "rinchin out some dishes," as Lily would say. All those black heads bent over their tasks. All those black hands hard at work. I declare, if some scientist could harness all the human energy spent concealing our true thoughts, we could colonize the planet Mars in no time!

Well, I let those darkies know I'm on the job, yes sir, and I trot back to my guests. Maybe trot is not the word, but anyhow, I make it, safe and sound.

But Reader, wouldn't you know? The funeral guests are fixing to go home! One and all are fixing to go home. Panic!

"Wait now, don't go!" I cry out in alarm. "Coffee and cake are coming!"

But they're leaving anyway.

"Oh come on," I said. "Don't go."

But they kept going. Consternation!

"Wait," I said. "Wait, wait—I got something to tell you!"

Well, *then* they pause, of course, and listen politely. And Reader, I have purely nothing to tell them, but I open my mouth hoping for the best, and as I stand there I am suddenly stricken by remembrance of a dream. Yes. A nightmare. It just shockingly explodes into my mind in all its living color.

"Oh, oh!" I say to all my guests, putting my hands up to my cheeks. "Oh my glory," I cry. "I have just remembered this dream, this dream I had last night, this awful dream!"

They fidget, but they wait.

And Reader, here my memory starts fogging up, like the windshield on a rainy day, oh but I remember that dream all right, and it exploded out of me, just more or less as follows:

I dreamed I was a Nigra! Can you imagine? Oh, Lord. Most awful dream. I looked down, and there was my skin, all black. I mean, just *black*. I said, *Oh no! Listen here! There's some mistake!* I said to the Authorities, *This is ME, Prettybelle Sweet! It's me!* And nobody listened, nobody paid any attention. I kept trying to reach the king and queen, but they wouldn't listen, they didn't hear, I couldn't reach them! And I cried out, *It's me, Prettybelle. It's Prettybelle, don't you hear? I'm not a Nigra! I'm a blue-eyed blonde!* But nobody would listen, and they pushed me out the door. Well, I began to perspire! I want to tell you! And I thought, Oh my Lord, *what will Leroy say?* I began to shake all over and I never was so scared in all my life. I start looking at myself, and *everywhere* I'm Nigra. DARK Nigra. And the palms of my hands are pink, like theirs. And my nails are pink, and that's the last straw, and I scream! I pound on the door, and I scream, *It's me, it's me, it's me! Listen! Please listen! It's Prettybelle!* And I'm sobbing on my knees, and screaming out, *It's Prettybelle!*

Well, Reader, I felt this dream very deeply and my recitation was dramatic, I imagine, for along about now I vaguely perceive that everyone is motionless as death, their faces made of granite-stone. But how can I stop? That dream is eating out my insides and I am all aflame.

"Lord!" I cry. "I sweat to think about it! Look," I say to my guests, "I'm sweating even now. Feel my hands! All wet and clammy!"

By now I'm running down a little bit, and I realize I have done it again, and worse than usual.

"Well, I woke up . . . and it took me . . . the longest time . . . to realize . . ." I look from face to face, in mounting alarm, because those faces are COLD, those faces are HOSTILE. "To realize that I'm . . . NOT Nigra . . . and it was all a dream. Not Nigra . . ." And I smile sweetly and warmly as I know how, and I say, "which I'm not, of course." Well, that doesn't help. "It was all a dream," I plead. "That's all, just a dream!"

Well, I feel a sharp pain in my arm, and indeed I have been feeling it for some time back, and it is Saralizabeth digging all ten fingernails into me. And she now says to me between her teeth in a tone of absolute barely repressed FURY AND HATRED,

"Mother, I reckon you are all tired out. Why don't you just lie down a spell."

Well, I look from one face to another, bewildered, but the guests just simply plunge for their pocketbooks, and push out the door, all puffed up with this secret sense of scandal.

"You rest now," they say to me with big false smiles. "We'll just run on. See you real soon, hear?"

"Don't go!" I cry, wringing my hands. "Why, don't go, you all." And Saralizabeth insists I also said, "Party's just now getting good!" But I don't believe I said that, not for one second.

My heart was sinking like a great stone in the well, for I was being left all alone, just as I had feared.

Well, the guests went home, and Mother Sweet had also vanished somewhere, and Saralizabeth—you can bet she wasn't about to waste her precious saliva talking to *me*. She gave me one look, designed to wither up and kill, and flounced out the front door.

The house got quiet. After a bit the kitchen got quiet too, and Lily came in to say good night.

"Well, thank you, Lily," I said, not revealing my weakness. "Where is your son and his friend who helped out?"

"They's went," said Lily. "Carryin Miz Loomis' girl over Miz Loomis' house, and the big coffeepot."

"You tired, Lily?" For she did look poorly.

"Yes'm, reckon I is."

"Me too, Lily."

"Yes'm."

I waited hopefully for a soothing word, but it never came. So I sighed, and she turned away, and after a minute I heard the back door open, and I heard it close. And there I was. Alone in that big empty house and evening coming on.

END FIFTH INSTALLMENT

Alone And Unprotected

Yes there I was, alone, and no one to blame except myself. I was a plain dumb fool.

I went upstairs and took off my black dress and hung it
up. And I slipped on a fresh pink duster and a pair
of mules, and I came downstairs again, and poured myself
a drink. Well, I sat in one place and another, but always
there was Leroy in his portrait glowering at me, standing
there immortal through art with his damn hounds. I looked
at him, took a sip, and felt all itchy. I took another sip, and
gritted my teeth, and looked at him, and finally I boldly
said,

"Oh shut up, Leroy."

Now Reader, this was a fairly revolutionary thing for me
to say, and I automatically cringed and cowered, but nothing happened except Leroy kept on glowering at me from
his portrait. So I moved to the couch where I couldn't see
him, but such was my state of nerves that his presence
hung over my head like a weight of two hundred pounds
(236 to be exact)—and in some kind of rage I kicked off
my mules, and I climbed onto the sofa, and I wrastled that
picture down and stood it face against the wall.

Ha! I thought. That's that.

But it was not. What if someone should come in? What would they think? What about Saralizabeth, etc.? And that's the story of my life, Reader. Intimidated by others. Never true to my own self! Yes. Those lines we learned in high school,

> This above all, to thine own self be true
> And it shall follow as the night the day
> Thou canst not then be false to any man—

well, they may be fine for some people, but *I* would have gone over the hill to the Old Maid's Home!

So I put the blame portrait back. I wrastle the blame thing back onto its nail, and nearly slip my disk again in doing so, and I'm all out of breath, and dizzy from exertion or heat or else from bourbon whiskey, or all three, and I lie back panting and groaning on the couch, thinking morbid hostile thoughts.

Be reasonable, Prettybelle, I said. Those friends and neighbors who rushed out of here pell-mell, leaving you alone and Godforsaken, they are perfectly decent people, only scared. They have Inferiority Complexes, and cling to the Familiar with all their claws. That is why, I said, if somebody acts the least bit odd, they run like rabbits and buzz like a hive of damn-fool bees. ("That Miz Sweet, I declare, she surely is eccentric!")

Oh Reader, I swing back and forth! Between love and hate, I swing like a pendulum of some wretched old neurotic clock. One minute I think folks are basically good, but the next, Lord help me, it's the other way around, and what folks truly want to do is slaughter, torment, and EAT one another, and the only thing that holds them back is Social Custom.

God is Love, we're taught. But what if He is really Hate? I say it to myself. Yes, God is Hate. Hate makes the world go round. Love is nothing but a special kind of Hate. I mean, if you love somebody, that person has power over you, right? Well, love *desires* power, I say, and power is nothing but Hate. Power over others. Power to torture them, pull off their wings. In my opinion, everybody hates everybody. Wives and husbands, for example. They simply bloom on hate. Well, don't they? And look at History!

Dr. Dimmer, I have written a Quatrain on the subject and you can sing it to the Doxology if you desire, for it fits:

> Historians have tried to hide
> Man's greatest pride is fratricide.
> Our outside may be sanctified
> But inside is pure homicide.

And after that quatrain I hear a sort of chanting chorus starting slow and getting faster and faster:

> OH!
> God is hate and
> Love is hate and
> I am hate and
> You are hate. . . .
> Black is hate and
> White is hate and
> Sex all else a-
> Bove is hate. . . .
> Workers hate and

> Bosses hate and
> Infants they are
> Taught to hate. . . .
> Parents hate and
> Neighbors hate and
> Wives and husbands
> Thrive on hate. . . .
> Brothers hate and
> Sisters hate and
> Grannies keep a-
> Live on hate—

as I well know! And where to stop? One could go on, far
into the night. Well, Dr. Dimmer, I *try* to fight this morbid
streak in my nature. I say to myself, Think love, Prettybelle! Everybody, think Love!

> Although it takes a bit of time and labor
> With practice we can learn to rise above
> The blood-lust that we cherish for our neighbor.
> Think love, think love, think love!

Yes, I say that, and it's all very well in theory, but can you
imagine me saying, "I love you, Mr. Wimbly!" I would
rather die in torment.

Oh, I am so miserable.

I mean, I *was* so miserable—back *then*—with all those
evil thoughts in a ring around me like wolves, and
the guests gone, and Leroy dead, and the house getting
dark and full of creaking sounds, enormous and empty, and
heat lightning flickering outside.

I sat there all alone and said, Prettybelle Sweet, pull

yourself together. The time has come to *face yourself and your future. What are you?*

Well, when I said *What are you?* my scalp began this slow slow crawl, and shivers went down both thighs.

And the house creaked and sighed, and things moved in it, and I quick turned on a light, and nearly jumped out of my skin—seeing my own reflection in the black glass of the windows. I hastily pulled down the shades, shielding my eyes. Have you ever had that feeling? Scared to look into a mirror or a black window lest a Werewolf look back at you? Brrrrr!

When I'm alone in a house, I revert to a small child or primitive savage in a Cave. I'm not afraid of anything normal, like a burglar. I'm afraid of lions and tigers, monstrous Things that stalk you secretly, that lie in wait, biding their time, following, watching. . . .

Well, I felt *something* was in the house.

Lest I confuse or mislead you, Reader, I must explain that I am not presently referring to my husband Leroy Sweet, or any ghost of his. That will come later, in due time. No, this Thing in the house was not Leroy. It was worse than Leroy. Because it was . . . demented! Wild-eyed, with bloody fangs. Its hair in disarray. And it toyed with me, it stalked me, like a monstrous evil cat intent upon a mouse.

Now I had been dimly aware of this particular Thing before. Alone by night I would get this prickly feeling in the back of my neck. And around I would whirl, ready to shriek and faint—and nothing there! But this time I felt it nearer, right at hand, ready to show itself.

Well, I paced around the room terrified, whirling around, scared of mirrors, because the Thing *emerged* from mirrors like a horrible Alice-Through-the-Looking-Glass. As I paced around, I thought I could hear the Thing screaming, a horrible scream. I heard it echoing in my ears, and oh glory me, that voice, that scream, got more and more familiar. Yes. Because it was my own!

Reader, in a horrible way, the Thing was me, myself! Prettybelle Sweet, distorted and demented, with fangs!

Well, I ran like an antelope to the bourbon whiskey bottle, only this time it didn't help one speck. I don't reckon you've ever been afraid of your own self, Reader. I can well imagine it takes a Nutcake like me to accomplish that, but oh, there is no fear like it. I was turning into Dr. Jekyll and Mr. Hyde!

I said, Prettybelle Sweet, you cannot go on like this. March up to that mirror, look inside, and CONQUER this thing. So I took a deep breath, and whispered sickly and silently, "That's only me in there," for I dared not say it aloud, lest my voice be the scream of the Thing. And I marched up to the mirror, and looked deep into my own eyes, and Reader, the eyes were inhuman, like a reptile. Yes!

Well, I threw myself on the couch and I put a pillow over my head, and I cried and wept. Silently. I'm a good woman, I cried inside my head. I am not a banshee or a werewolf! I have been a good woman all my life! What did I do wrong? I come from a good family! Graduated high school! I was a virgin till I got engaged to Leroy! I was a virgin and I loved him! And when I stopped loving him, well I was faithful to him. Wasn't I? Didn't I give Lily money for her son? Didn't I? Didn't I do that? Yes I did! What ELSE was I supposed to do? Didn't I send money North? To all those black initials? What else, what else? Faithful, kept house, bore children. *I* couldn't help it Johnny went out of his head and shot five people from the butternut tree! I couldn't help that! I couldn't help Leroy's line of work!

How do *I* know he did wrong? HE never told me. And what could I do anyway? I'm only a woman. I was helpless. What can a bird do in the jaws of a retriever dog? Mama, what could I DO? Was it MY fault Leroy was famous coast to coast? Was it MY fault *Life* magazine called him the King of Hell?

The King of Hell. Yes! In great big type, with photos, on page 53, four years ago next month.

Well, I said to myself, the King of Hell. What can that mean? This must be Hell I'm living in. If Leroy was King, then what does that make me? The lady married to the King is called the Queen. What else? Oh glory, Mama, mercy! I could have left him, and I didn't. I could have fought—I didn't fight. The Queen of Hell truly IS me.

Reader, I felt bloodstained and evil. Dirty, full of ooze and rot. It was so awful, I couldn't help but wonder, WHY NOW? Why should I feel this NOW? I mean, isn't it ridiculous, with Leroy dead and me all FREE of him? Why do I feel so awful NOW?

I asked that question, and alas I got my answer. It was not an answer that I liked. I sorrowfully knew in one big burst that *Leroy himself, none other*, had kept me reasonably pure all these long years. And how? By meanness and abuse, that's how! Thanks to him, I was no queen of hell, I was a victim! *Look at this bruise! Listen how he talks to me!* I sorrowfully knew right then that I was going to miss my husband mightily. Yes, I would surely miss him. Though not for the customary reasons.

Oh, I had been a tightrope walker on the razor's edge! Whenever my heart was troubled, I could cure it in the twinkling of an eye. How? Just provoke Leroy, that's how. Provoke him to cuss me out, abuse me, cuff me around —Lo and Behold, I felt good again. Yes. Instant uplift.

See how I suffer from this man? I'd think. *Me and the Nig-ras, see how martyred and pure and helpless we are!*

But now.

Oh Lord, now what? Everything was changed. My balance was gone! My purity was gone! My status as a victim was snatched away! The razor would cut me to ribbons.

Reader, I couldn't stand it. I thought: I have to find some *other* way to suffer-and-feel-clean again. I have to find it fast. I have to cut my wrists, drink iodine, eat sleeping pills. I have to die. Oh Reader, can you understand? No doubt I was frenzied and hysterical and soon to become a maniac (prelim. diag.), but I felt I had to die. I could not bear to be the queen of hell.

At that moment, I was distracted by—a knock at the front door!

END SIXTH INSTALLMENT

Rape!

Now who might that be? I thought to myself. But, Reader, I was so glad and grateful at the prospect of rescue from my morbid thoughts that I simply flew across the floor to that front door, ready to fling it wide and greet whoever stood there with open arms, so to speak. I had my hand on the doorknob, when the idea came to me, *Whoa, now! What if it is Mr. Wimbly?* Well, I put on the brakes! I hesitated, and I vacillated, like a mule between two bales of hay, as Granpa B. would say, and at last I opened the door a tiny crack.

And who was it? Well, the very ultimate and last person that you might expect. Standing on the porch, looking all grim and determined, was not Mr. Wimbly at all—but Billy Black!

Well, I *was* taken off guard. I was plain astonished and startled. My jaw hung open, and I said,

"Why, why, William. Is that you?"

And when he did not reply (assuming no doubt that my question was rhetorical), I kind of stammered and I finally said, "Well, William, come in, what can I do for you?" You see, Reader, I was grateful for *any* human company, that's one thing, and another was just sheer embarrassment, I mean, hanging there at the door not knowing what to say.

So he stepped inside.

"Mrs. Sweet, I'd like a word with you, if that's all right," he said.

Well, I should have been forewarned. He came to the FRONT door, in the first place. That was already, you know, like a defiant act. I was not, as they say, unaware of this, but I pretended not to notice. By inviting him in and taking no notice, I thought to show him what a True Friend he had in me. Then in the second place, he knew full well that Nigras are not *allowed* in our neighborhood after dark without a Written Explanation. And in the third, observe that he said, "Mrs. Sweet." He did not call me "Miss Belle," which even white folks do as a sign of courtesy and respect. He did not call me "Miss Belle" and he did not call me "Ma'am." So right away, he served me warning, so to speak, that this was going to be a different interview from any that *I* had ever had, ever in my lifelong, and I do say for myself that I carried it well, and behaved in a gracious and kindly manner, at least at first, even though, underneath, I was growing somewhat jumpy.

Truth is, neither one of us knew exactly how to behave, and we both concealed our dismay rather handsomely, I thought, for although he had this stiff and sullen look, he held himself with dignity, even whilst standing on one foot and the other, and he acted nonchalant.

So I graciously led him into the dining room, and I graciously pulled out a chair from the table and sat down, and whilst he stood in front of me some distance off, I said to him,

"Well, William! Your mother and I are most certainly

glad to see you, and I would like to hear about your school-ing."

That was my contribution, don't you see, to set him at ease and give him a conversational hook. But the hook didn't hook HIM, as I had half an idea it wouldn't, and there was this awful pause. He had this stubborn look about him.

At last he said, looking at the carpet (worn thin by his mother's feet over the years), "Miz Sweet—" and in truth, Reader, he didn't even say MIZ Sweet, he said MRS.!— "Mrs. Sweet, I want to thank you for what you've done for me. The money," he said. "I am—uh—I am grateful."

Imagine, Billy Black, that little cute pickaninny of Lily's! there he stands taller than me, talking with this Yankee accent like some kind of Supreme Court Judge! Say-ing, "I am grateful!"

So I say, "Why William, your mother was not supposed to tell you where the money came from. But since you know, why, I will just say that I was glad to help you. Are you studying hard?"

Again this funny look came over his face, and he hedged.

"I'm studying," he said, and he frowned. "But I'm not— I mean I'm——" Well, he gets tangled up, and then he pauses, and quits being a Supreme Court Judge, and just blurts out, "I don't want your money no more!"

I should have got my back up and scolded him, but no, I just echoed in amazement like a parrot:

"You don't want my money no more? Anymore?"

He fidgets and strangles, and then he says, "No ma'am," and he got out that "ma'am" like spitting forth a frog, and you could tell no greater love hath any son for his mammy than to say "ma'am" to Prettybelle Sweet! "No ma'am," he said, "I appreciate what you did, and I'll pay you back." And he said all this nice and correct, obedient to his mammy's wishes, you could tell.

"Why, you don't have to pay me back, William," I said, kindly.

"I WANT to pay you back!" he said, quick and sharp. "And here's the first installment." And if he didn't put down thirty dollars on the dining-room table, counting it all out, mostly by ones!

I am astonished and nonplussed.

"Why William, I feel bad taking your hard-earned money," I say. "And what about school?"

"I quit," says Billy Black harshly. "I got other things to do."

"You quit! Does your mama know this?" I say sternly.

"She knows what she knows," he says, kind of impatient, but he mumbles it so that it won't seem *too* rude.

"William," I say, "you are making a big mistake. Why, you should get all the education you can. An education, for someone—of your race—can simply open all kinds of doors that otherwise are closed. Think of the boys who would *jump* at your opportunity!"

"I've *had* my education," he says, and he was just as restless and defiant as he could be. "I've got to go now," he says.

"Don't you dare to go now, William," I say, "we've got to talk this thing out!"

By rights he should have shuffled his feet and said, "Well, thank you kindly, ma'am, but etcetera."

Instead, he kind of heaved in his breath and showed his teeth a little, and looked longingly at the door, and mumbled, "What's the use, I can't talk to you."

And I said, "What?" for I couldn't really hear him. And

he said it louder, but not looking at me, looking at the wall.

My heart went pitterpat with nervousness, but I simply said, "Why not? I don't see why not. Haven't you known me all your life? Haven't I been your friend, William?"

"Look," he said. "I got to split."

"You got to *what?*" I said.

"I got to go," he said.

"William Black, you stop right there," I said, for he was walking out. "You just stop right there."

Well, Reader, I know what you are thinking. *What a fool* is what you're thinking, and you are surely right. Oh Lordy! If only I had let him go! Instead, I suddenly felt this guilty pang about bringing him into the dining room (which after all was next thing to taking him into the *kitchen*), and I wanted him to recognize me as a truly good-hearted person, who believed All Men Are Created Equal. I wanted to shake off Leroy Sweet, and put my high heel in Mr. Wimbly's eye, and so I said, momentously,

"Come into the living room, William, *and sit down.*"

Sit down. Can you believe it? That's what I said. Not only "come into the living room." But also "Sit down!" Right away I could have bit my tongue. What if Saralizabeth should come in? "*Sit down!?!*"

All right. We go into the living room. Gracious Prettybelle and Unwilling William, and Prettybelle sits graciously on the sofa. Unwilling William stands, and Prettybelle, waving her hand as if it's the most ordinary thing in the world, says, "Have a seat, William."

He sits down!!!!!

There ensues the most ghastly bone-cracking pause.

"Now William, I want to help you any way I can," I gulped, and that was true, for I really did want to help that boy, and felt, you know, protective-like and maternal. Anyway, I said, "William, I want to help you any way I can, but you are not helping yourself with that attitude. Now why can't you talk to me? I like to feel that you could always turn to me for help and advice."

"Mrs. Sweet," he said, "I'm not going to Uncle Tom it."

"Well!" I gasped and stammered, "I didn't ask you to Uncle Tom it. I only wanted you to be a doctor and a credit to your race!"

"Credit to my race?" he said, and his eyes just suddenly blazed and he said something terrible about being a credit to his race only if he committed certain acts of violence!

Well, Reader, just for a minute I got scared. Yes, Prettybelle Sweet felt just a hint of danger in the air, but she didn't let on. No. She just wondered if he could *smell fear,* like they say dogs can. I thought, well, maybe he can smell my fear and it will stir him up. As I have said, I am from Virginia and in Virginia we love and respect our darkies, except we do tend to exclude from our devotion those male Nigras between the ages of say seventeen to sixty, yes, about these we are somewhat skittish. In my white-and-yellow living room—Leroy's living room—those big black words he had just uttered kept rolling around and bouncing off the walls like cannonballs. Hate, kill, burn! Well, I thought, they're not new words, you know. They're good old homegrown words, white words, in a black mouth. That's all the difference! Hold on to yourself, Prettybelle Sweet. Confusion at such a time is unforgivable.

Well, I had to ask him. "William," I said, very serious and quiet, *"are you a follower of Ralph Abernathy?"*

Maybe it was my tone of voice. Anyway, I swear he looked at me and chuckled, and then he laughed outright, in some kind of amazement, and he shook his head.

And I felt hurt. I did, because after all I HAD given him all that money.

"Well, William," I said coldly, "I see you learned a few things up North besides medicine. I thought you were going to be a doctor and cure folks, not kill 'em."

What a spot I was in! Me, Prettybelle Sweet, why in school the children always called me nigger-lover! And truth to tell, I AM a nigger-lover in a kind of way, and I burn with shame at my own white race. Well, I swallowed a finger of bourbon neat hoping to kill the Smell of Fear, which by this time was so strong I vow I could smell it my own self, except it was just old-fashioned B.O. to me, whereas God knows what it was to him, a red flag to a bull for ought I knew. I drank that whiskey and poured more, and I calmed myself. Lord, it was only Billy Black after all, hadn't I known him from knee high, cutest little fellow you could hope to see and bright as a dollar? I sipped my whiskey and I had the strangest thoughts. Suppose I said to him, "Billy—" and put my hand out, gave him a little pat. "Can't we talk like two human beings?" Suppose I said to him, "Billy, let us shut our eyes and just become TWO VOICES IN THE DARK." Because do you know my soul yearned toward that boy in a certain way, just as it also skittered quickly to one side. Well, I thought how peaceful and homey everything could be if only he would do like Lily said—if only he, well, played the game. All right, *Uncle Tommed* it, I guess. Well, we'd have both been a lot more comfortable, I can tell you!

I sat down again and I couldn't ask him to close his eyes —it wasn't seemly—but the liquor started buzzing in my head and it got all dreamlike, so I closed my own eyes and tried out that reality which was a lot nicer than the open-eyed one. And there inside my head, with the liquor and the buzzing and all, the fear faded out and everything got very sentimental and warm and mushy. I thought of this and I thought of that, and I thought, *oh, Alice!*—remembering the time I made her cry, calling her a nigger. And I thought Lord, in this vast pecking order we call Mankind, Nigras surely are at the bottom of the line. When I was a child, everybody under the sun pecked me, except for Alice and the family cat. And I pecked *them.* Yes, I pecked Alice, made her cry. Me, little weak no-account me, I had POWER over somebody! Tiny and dependent and hard-pecked, just a yellow-haired bit of fluff, despised by my sister and ignored by my mama and abandoned by my papa, yes, I myself could pinch the kitty make her mew, say bad things to Alice make her cry. I vow, it made me dizzy! Dizzy and drunk with power. Undeniable power over cats and Nigras! At the same time, Mama and my sister had undeniable power over me. And Papa had power over all of us, having gone and died and left us uncared-for and alone! And this was as the world's way, dogs taking it out on cats, and cats taking it out on mice, and mice being the end of the line in the animal world, just as Nigras were the end of the line in the human world. For I could take it out on Alice, but who could Alice take it out on? Why, she didn't peck anybody, that's the truth. Alice did not peck one soul in this world. O Glory, thought I, sitting on the couch, what if I were Alice! What if I were Lily! What if I had no cat, no Nigra to be better than, and Reader, I suddenly felt so grateful, this burning wave of gratitude, that tears spilled out of my closed eyes and I wept. In my mind's eye, I hugged my childhood's motheaten old gray cat, and I hugged Alice, and I said, O thank you, Cat, O thank you, Alice, I love you and I will never forget you! I promise I will never hurt you, never make you cry! Oh, Lord, Lord, I thought, I am so indebted to cats and Nigras it is a debt I can never repay, though I will surely try. And Reader, to this day I can scarcely stroke a cat or talk to some poor hard-working Nigra cook without tears of gratitude flooding my heart and even oozing from my eyes. Somehow I feel they suffer their miserable existence—for me! For my sake! To make me braver and stronger, to give me courage to go on, to stand my own trials and pecks and abandonments. Yes. And so I kiss the hems of their garments, oh, I do, from my deepest heart, I kiss the very hems of their garments.

Well, in the midst of this warm moist orgy, I hear Billy Black clearing his throat, in some embarrassment. And I hear myself saying loud and clear and weepy,

"William, I want you to know I hated that man, that husband of mine, that Sheriff Sweet."

There is this long silence. I am paralyzed by my audacity and breach of etiquette. I keep my eyes tight shut like some poor ostrich fancying she is hidden safe away!

After while, I hear him clear his throat once more, and he says, tentatively, "You asleep?"

"I am not asleep," I said dreamily. "I am just pretending. I am living in a nice world where there is no skin color whatsoever. Why don't you try it? Close your eyes," I said, "it's nice." And I confess I probably giggled, or cried, or God knows what-all else that was foolish and stupid. And he said,

"I don't close my eyes. My eyes been closed too long. I keep my eyes wide open."

"Well, turn your back, then," I said. "Look at the wall. Try it," I said. "Come on! Pretend I'm Nigra," I said. "I'll pretend you're white. Come on!"

Reader, I don't attempt to excuse myself. I was just a

plain simpering idiot, and a revolting embarrassing spectacle, and I'd be the last to deny it. Everybody I ever knew would have been ashamed of me, and I'm ashamed of myself, clear down to the bone. I started babbling away, and I talked about my dead husband Sheriff Sweet and how I couldn't stand him, and I kept trying to convince Billy Black, or *some*one, how I had nothing to do with what Sheriff Sweet did, and suddenly I got this veritable spasm of joy. Wicked joy. Leroy dead only two days, and there I was, sitting in the parlor with a Nigra boy! I felt this BURST of joy and freedom, as if my little dried-up soul had suddenly felt the good rain fall, and was just soaking it up, coming to life, expanding, growing bigger, bigger, softer, softer, oh delicious! Leroy was dead, and Prettybelle was *free!*

Naturally, following that spasm, as the night the day, came the most awful pang of conscience, as if Leroy himself had come from the grave and stepped upon my little soft soul with muddy hobnailed boots. Pop went my poor little new soft soul. Splat. Mash! Hold tight, Prettybelle, I told myself. Slow and steady wins the race. So I rose and I crossed the room and poured myself another finger or two of bourbon whiskey.

Do you know, it actually flashed into my wicked mind to offer Billy Black a drink? Well, Reader, I do assure you, I did not go *that* far! Imagine, to sit in Sheriff Sweet's living room and drink with a black boy! I vow, if I had done THAT, the very fires of heaven would have rained down upon my head. Hold fast, Prettybelle. Steady on! And I tried to explain to Billy Black how it was with me and Nigras.

You see, Reader (as I explained to Billy Black), I simply FEEL for Nigras. My theory is that *everybody* feels for

Nigras, but most of us deny it. I say we all know perfectly well what it's like to be a Nigra in a land of mean snooty white folks. Howcome we know it? Because we've all been through it! Yes! Now I'll prove it to you. Isn't every little child a magical almighty Prince or Princess in his deepest heart? Reader, look back. Tell me your childhood tragedies! Or rather, don't tell me, I'll tell YOU. For one and all, those tragedies are the same. Some mean old sister or friend or parent came up to you and said, "Hell, YOU ain't no prince or princess! You are only dirty miserable YOU!" Right, Reader? Somebody made you realize you couldn't Command the Sun to Shine, Bring Back the Dead, or Kill Your Enemy with One Glance!

Now take a pretty little girl (I said to Billy Black), all golden curls and Ruler of her daddy's heart. First her sisters and her friends work her over. Next her kitten dies. Then she grows up, marries a man who knocks her around; she cooks the dinner, washes the dishes, does the laundry, gets fat, and her children tell her how dumb she is. You mean (I said), you mean that erstwhile Empress of the Seven Seas, Goddess of Life-and-Death don't understand the Nigra's story? Ha!

True, hers may be but a cup of gall, whilst his is a veritable ocean, I said. But gall is gall.

> Brother, Sister, gall is gall.
> The taste's familiar to us all.

Well, do you know, I told all this to Billy Black, and he simply snorted at me? Yes he did, I vow. And the harder I tried to explain, the harder he snickered and sneered! I declare, the watermelon boy that I remembered, wistful

and merry by turns, his loving little heart a-burst with gratitude, had simply vanished in thin air.

Leroy's portrait doubtless did not help. I mean, I was
sitting right under it, and I noticed that Billy Black's eyes
kept sliding up there, fascinated and furious, and he'd kind
of grind his teeth. Then he'd shake his head and maybe
mumble something like, "It's no use, I can't talk to you."

As for me, I was a mass of crosscurrents, clashing tides,
and eddies. One minute I was all vast limpid compassion,
the next, I was ruffled and indignant, and still next, I just
felt awash in a Sea of Muddy Confusion. Billy Black kept
on mumbling how it was no use, and he couldn't talk to
me, but all the same he DID keep sitting there, as though
he had something further on his mind. Well, I should have
answered him. "You're right," I should have said. "And I
can't talk to you! And so good-bye!" But no, he sat there,
and I kept babbling. I had this compulsion to reach
through to him.

"I always used to think you LIKED me, William," I said.
And Reader, he DID, before he went North. Why, he used
to think I was the prettiest kindest white lady in the world,
and when he was a little boy he used to think and dream
about me, how I was magic like a fairy godmother, and I
would make things come out right. Like magic. And I bet
when he was in Chicago learning his new Way of Life, how
to hate people and all (and I mean, who can blame them?),
why I simply wager that he would say to himself, "But what
about Miss Belle?" Yes, he would say to himself, "The
white man is a devil all right, amen! But what about Miss
Belle?" And I bet he had to fight and squirm against that
thought. I bet he went all weak and sentimental every time
he thought about me. I don't bet, I KNOW it! Why, he

used to look at me with those soft shiny eyes, just full of love and worship, and I would hand him one of Johnny's old shirts, and he would say, "O thank you, Miss Belle!"

Well, you know, that kind of love makes you feel GOOD! Why, it practically made me the Mighty Empress once again! All Kindliness and Love!

Reader, I reckon I just simply wanted him to love me once again. And when I saw he wasn't about to, why, I tell you, I was discombobulated. Well, I told myself, it HAS to be there somewhere!

Reader, when you get used to that kind of love, oh, it is hard to give it up. It leaves a gap in your life. And if it is roughly snatched away from you, well, you try to get it BACK!

So I said, "Now William, you got to go back to school. You do it for ME, for nice Miss Belle who always used to give you toys!"

Well, this new William, he just reared back like I had said a filthy word! And he acted restless, like he wanted to go, but something was holding him. And his eye wasn't soft and shiny but had a film across it, behind which Lord knows what thoughts were hidden. Sarcastic and disagreeable ones most likely. Why that boy, he had the sweetest smile you ever saw on a little black fellow in your life, and if I smiled at HIM, why he would squirm and laugh and be embarrassed and thrilled, and it would simply MAKE HIS DAY!

As I replenished my drink, this Billy Black at last begins to talk, by fits and starts. He tells me how black folks got to have nothing to do with white folks anymore. How they got to make their way alone. How they got to rise up on their feet and tell OFF the white man. How he used to be shamed of his black blood, and how he was now shamed to think he might have white blood. Some white man, somewhere, he said. Some white rapist in his blood.

Aha, I thought to myself. He is working around to that question, that's what he's doing. That Question which is eating at his mind, as I know full well, having heard him in the kitchen.

"William I was always fond of you," I said.

Well, he answers like a shot.

"And why was that, Miss Belle?" he says.

"WHY?" I said. "Well, I don't know WHY."

"Did you owe me something, Miss Belle?"

"Owe you something! I declare, William, whatever could I owe you?"

Well, he put on an act, a kind of mocking Uncle Tom act.

"Miss Belle," he Uncle Tommed, "I puzzle in my mind. Why'd you give me that money? I jus ask myself that, over and over. That was sure a mighty lot of money. White folks don't give black folks that kind of money less'n they got a reason. I reckon I'm jus askin you that reason, Miss Belle."

Truly, I was not at my best, Reader, and I was not quite up to this kind of thing, and so I say,

"Why, William, why I, I just——"

And now he leans forward, and he speaks very sharp, without the Uncle Tom. "Don't say you did it *to be nice*," he mocks, "cause I don't buy that. There's got to be a reason, and I *want to know it!*"

Well, Reader, I declare, I sat there in my foggy foggy dew, and I thought to myself, well, now, what WAS the reason exactly. Why DID I give him all that money?

"You're a mighty foolish boy, William," I said bravely, "looking a gift horse in the mouth, that's what *you're* doing."

"I don't want no gift horse," he said. "I want to know your reason. I want to know howcome you got SUCH A BAD CONSCIENCE!"

Yes, he said that. He did! Lord have mercy!

"Bad conscience!" I said indignantly. "Why, I've never done ANYTHING bad to a member of your race, William Black." And I was getting huffy.

Then he decides to play a big bluff card, and he stands up and puts his hands low down on his hips, and he looks me right in the eye, and he says,

"Miss Belle, I happen to KNOW the reason you gave me that money."

"Well, if you know, it's more than I do," I said, "and I wish to heaven I never HAD given it to you at ALL!"

Well, he pursued it.

"And the reason is—the REASON is, that I'm——" and he stopped and struggled for a moment, "I'm—RELATED to your husband."

"Related! You? First I heard about it!" I said.

"Kind of CLOSE related," he said.

"Is that the case?" I said.

"Sheriff Sweet's money sent me to school, and why?" said Billy Black. "Because I'M HIS SON, THAT'S WHY!"

"Well!" I said. "Well! Well! Well!" And I said, "So that's it. I declare, you're BAD-TEMPERED enough to be his son!" I said. "And I suppose you're MY son too?"

He brushed that off, and said I knew full well what he was talking about.

Well, Reader, I got huffy and indignant. I told him I had no such knowledge whatsoever, and that the money was MINE I sent him, and was not Sheriff Sweet's money at all, and he was NOT Sheriff Sweet's son in any way what-

soever, and if there was a White Rapist on the scene it was
not my husband, and he Billy Black ought to be ashamed
of himself.

"I HEARD you bullying your poor mama in the kitchen,
which was a shameful thing! What's SHE ever done to de-
serve that kind of talk, and you better just put in your pipe
and smoke it that you are NOT Sheriff Sweet's son, or any
other white man's son, far as I know!"

And I said, "I declare, you act like you WANT me to say
yes, so you can Huff and Puff about it, and feel all mean
and sorry for yourself." At least I considered saying that,
but possibly I did not actually say it, not wanting to stir
him up any further. But I did say,

"Sheriff Sweet no doubt has done bad things, William
Black, but not THAT bad thing, and I can prove it."

"How can you prove it?" he said.

"Why," I said, "if that had happened, do you think we
would of kept Lily on? In our house?"

I said that, and his eye glittered. I said it, and it started
echoing in my ears, and the more it echoed, the worse it
sounded. Reader, a statement like that, though true, is absolutely an awful thing to say out loud. I mean, if you think
it through. And Billy Black was thinking it through, I can
tell you.

"You mean," he said, slow and drawly sarcastic, "that
naturally if my mother had been raped and impregnated
by your husband,—*naturally* you would have fired her."

"That's right," I said. "I admit it don't sound very fair.
But don't act like it comes as a surprise! You know the
score, William Black. You know how things are as well as
I do, and that's how they are."

Well, he studied for a minute.

"But what if Sheriff didn't tell you?" said Billy Black.

"HE's not going to tell you! And SHE's not going to tell you."

"In that case," I said, "I am blissfully ignorant. And not a word can I say to convince you. Only the money, that was MINE. He didn't even know about it, and if he HAD, he'd have raised the roof."

I see him calculating, and I see he doesn't believe me. I see he's got it just fixed in his head he's Sheriff Sweet's black son and nothing's going to root it out. So I take several more sips of my drink, and I close my eyes again. And what was the point? I thought. I mean, what is he AFTER?

"William," I said. "Supposing you *were* his son," I said in a dreamy way. "I mean, what difference would it make? Sheriff Sweet is dead and gone."

"Don't I know it," he said, low and bitter. "I got here too late."

I keep my eyes tight shut, which is the only tactic I can think of to maintain a slight remove.

"What would you have *done?*"

"No need to talk about it, Miss Belle. He got away."

"Would you have shot him or something?"

"No need to talk about it now!"

"To avenge your mama?"

Silence.

"Is that what you been hatching in your head? You came back to avenge your mama?"

"I came back for the Voting Drive," he growled.

Well, I sat up, and got brisk for a moment.

"That reminds me!" I said. "I will thank you, William Black, to conduct your Voting Drive some place other than my house. What you do elsewhere," I said, "is your business. But I absolutely do not care to have my house the center of the Nigra Voting Drive."

"Mrs. Sweet," he said, "I will conduct my part of the Voting Drive wherever I damn please, and I will take the consequences."

"Yes," I said. "You will take the consequences, and what about me? I tell you," I said, "I have been warned and threatened!"

He just smiled. "*You* been warned," he chuckled, like to say, What they going to do, slap you on the wrist? Like whatever I had to risk was little or nothing!

So I sat back with a sigh of misery and I closed my eyes once more and sipped at my drink.

"William," I said. "Sheriff Sweet is dead and gone. And I don't know what you can do to get revenge. He's dead and gone," I said. "Hard to believe it, but he's dead and gone."

I say this in a kind of dreamy way, and in this shut-eyes world, and Reader, I confess, I am suddenly decidedly woozy. Things start going around just a wee bit, and they get—well, I'm ashamed to say it, but they—get kind of woozy humorous.

After a little bit I said, "I tell you, William, why don't you shoot Mr. Wimbly, he's a good man to shoot."

And then a little later, I said,

"William, I mean to say, that's just a wonderful idea! I mean if Mr. Wimbly didn't rape your mammy, it was only because he didn't think of it."

And I said, "I truly RECOMMEND Mr. Wimbly, William," and I giggled.

"Big joke," came his voice into my flesh-colored whiskey-dewed private bower. "Mighty funny, isn't it, Miss Belle. You sit there with your eyes shut pampered as a baby."

And then, Reader, I really tied it.

"Well, you could rape ME," I suggested. "William, you could always do a tit for tat." And I just giggled and chuckled away. "You could rape me, William, and impregnate me, and then it would be a REAL happy mess!" I giggled and sipped my drink with my eyes shut, and it seemed the funniest thing I ever heard of. "Now WHO on earth would that child be?" I said. "It would be Leroy's stepson, and his grandson, and Saralizabeth's brother or her nephew, and my own stepgrandson, I declare—it's too much for me——" and Reader, I got the giggles and hiccups at the same time like any teen-age schoolgirl. "And you could rape Mother Sweet," I suggested. "Now there's a tit for tat!"

Well, I giggled and hiccuped until tears came out of my eyes, and I kept on giggling and crying until I got plain exhausted and overcome with sleep, and I snuggled down on the couch, still giggling now and then, and I said (or think I said), "William, can't talk to you anymore now, run on home."

Well, Reader, since we are now approaching the Rape of Prettybelle Sweet, which was to have so sad and tragical an Aftermath, I want to be as accurate as I can under the circumstances. I just rack my brains, trying to remember every detail and report it as accurately as I can, only, truth to tell, much of it happened in a kind of Twilight Sleep like having a baby. Well, I will pierce that Sleep as best I can.

First, Time Passing sense. (Which is foolish, because Time couldn't have passed at all.) Jumbled dreams. A quick snitch of this and a snap of that, none of them finished or satisfying, because by now I'm beginning to feel poorly. My stomach, you know. Head aching. Like possibly throwing up. And I think I hear Saralizabeth saying, "Honestly, Mother!"

And then, I had a truly Vivid Dream. I dreamed this nice old man with a white Vandyke beard and courtly airs comes up to my couch, and says, "Miss Belle, I want to crown you Queen, and place upon your head the Crown, and upon your shoulders the Mantle of Empire!" And I was pleased and happy, but couldn't seem to get up. So I said, smiling graciously, that I was right pleased and honored, but could he just please put them on me lying down? So he gets this darling big sparkly crown, with rubies and diamonds and wrought gold and velvet padding, and he kind of gets it on my head, which is bobbling about. But he has trouble with the velvet mantle, since I am dead-weight, flat on my back, and he keeps struggling and struggling, and it is like trying to dress a great big bloated infant who won't cooperate. And he struggles harder and harder, pushing me this way and that, and lifting up my buttocks in order to spread the velvet mantle there (scarlet, with an ermine collar, it was a darling thing), and I realize he is losing patience, and is getting ROUGH! This courtly old man, yes, and he is saying how much he likes me and always has, and how I should just keep quiet because I know I'm crazy about him too, and won't I get up and dance the first waltz with him? I know it sounds silly! And I say, I'd *like* to dance with you but not now, later. And he bursts out laughing, and twists my arm so hard it hurts. And I say, "Why, whatever are you doing, you are hurting me, I will wear the mantle later!" And his face has changed, and he is showing teeth like a terrible wolf! And I try to fight my way out of sleep and I realize something terrible is happening!

Something terrible *is* happening, and what it is, is I am being RAPED!

Reader, I am struggling in the dark. All the lights are out, and the dark is exploding stars. My legs are spread-eagled, and I am bruised and battered and I have no clothes on.

That is, my bosoms are absolutely nude, and my dress is wadded up around my middle somewhere, and I try to scream and moan, and I feel this, well, great . . . organ . . . right inside of me! And I shriek NO NO NO! And I really struggle like a mad woman. And he says, "HOLD STILL, YOU DAMN BITCH!" And other things—I declare, nobody except Leroy has *ever* called me names like that (unless you count Mr. Wimbly that time). Then, Reader, there is this TERRIBLE PAIN. I mean a piercing frightful pain somewhere in my body, and I really shriek, and fight, and my strength is as the strength of ten. I keep on shrieking and shrieking and kicking and biting and scratching, and I get clouted hard across the face twice, and suddenly——

It is all over!

It is all over and I am moaning, Oh, oh, and HELP HELP, and the room is empty, and the lights all out, and no one is there, and I am bruised, battered, raped, and well, I am overcome. I am a mass of pain, and my ears are ringing! Reader, I am wet with blood, my hair has all fallen down, my clothes are tattered and torn!

There is no doubt about it, I have been thoroughly horribly RAPED! On the very day of Leroy's funeral!

END SEVENTH INSTALLMENT

The Paradox

Well, I stumble out of the living room from table to chair, clutching myself and trying to call out for help. I hear this kind of weird whooping sound, and I think, there is a small child whooping in the shrubbery. But it is not a small child, it is *me*. Lord have mercy, I am whooping in the strangest fashion.

Through the whooping and the ringing in my ears, I also hear *music*. I hear Rock and Roll music coming from Saralizabeth's room upstairs, and I hear Hillbilly music coming from Mother Sweet's room upstairs, which means that somehow they are home and awake. So I stagger to the staircase and I hang onto the banisters and I croak,

"Oh, help, rape. Oh, rape, help."

The music plays on.

And I think to myself, "O Prettybelle, fat lot of help you will get from THEM! Best run over to the neighbors."

Well, Reader, I was in such a state of shock, I scarcely remember what happened next. But I do know I kind of pull down my pink duster and I straighten my poor torn stockings, and I stagger to the downstairs lavatory to staunch some blood and wash it off, and apply bandages, and I discover that my bra isn't busted after all, but the straps are pulled out of their buckles, and so I fix them and conceal my body as best I can, for I surely am not going to display myself to the neighbors naked!

Not that I have anything to be ashamed of, no sir, I do not, for my bosoms are as good as the next lady's and better when you consider my age. (Which is crowding forty.) No doubt they are a MITE less firm than Saralizabeth's, but I will match them against ladies of my age any day, excepting movie stars, naturally, for Lord knows how much assistance they get—pushed up here and padded there, not to mention downright surgery!—whereas I wear nothing but a simple bra and what I show is all my own.

I search around by the sofa for my pink-feather mules but I can only find one. However, I put it on, and I run out the door, which is standing wide open, or rather I *hobble* out the door, and I am just that dazed and bewildered that as I go I start moaning and croaking, *Help, Rape*, and then I whoop a little, and I screech *Oh Rape, Rape*, and I find myself beating on Mrs. Ludie Lindley's door. And when she opens it, if her face isn't a study!

"Why, Belle Sweet!" she says, and her eyes fly open.

She draws me inside, and I mumble, *I been raped, I been raped, raped, raped!* and I sink on the floor in a perfect swoon. I remember thinking, on the way down so to speak, O Lord, do not let me *urinate* whilst in this swoon! as I have heard it is a common occurrence.

Well sir, when I come to, I am on the sofa in Ludie Lindley's somewhat threadbare living room, and a regular *crowd* is all around me. "Where am I?" I say in classical fashion, and they feed me coffee and a bite of cake (not up to Lily's, I can tell you), and some lady has lavender smelling salts in a little fat bottle which bite my nose something fierce, so

I push them away. Truth to tell, I do not object to all this attention. I kind of lie back, weak, faint, and I hope attractive, and I let it all soak in. I cry quite a bit—partly from nerves, but mostly from sheer *gratitude*. Nothing like sympathy to start the tear ducts flowing.

I hear somebody whisper, "Poor thing, been through so much!"

And I think to myself, oh yes, it is true. I have been through more than flesh and blood can bear! Beginning with what I do not think about, my son Johnny up the butternut tree . . . then my nervous attack and being carted off to Pummicami (the FIRST time) . . . then Leroy dropping dead, and the shock of *that* . . . and the arrangements, and the funeral . . . then Mr. Wimbly sniffing and threatening around . . . and now, THIS! Raped and dishonored! Oh, it was too much.

"Where is your daughter, Miz Sweet?" says fat Mrs. Peggy Thompson from down the block. "She's got to be TOLD."

"In her room playing Rock and Roll music," I say faintly.

"You mean—she was *home*——"

There are gasps of surprise. "At home!" "Her daughter was at home!"

"I don't rightly know," I moan. "I don't rightly know. When she plays that Rock and Roll music, why the house could fall about her ears."

Clucks and gasps of sympathy and fellow feeling. They knew how it was, yes, yes. POOR Miz Sweet, too much to bear! Oh, Reader, I declare, I just wanted to hug and kiss them all, every one of them, except maybe Peggy Thompson, who I observe shaking her fat powdered jowls and exchanging sour looks with Jemma Bagler. Jealous, that's what *she* was. But the others were just as sweet and nice, and also shocked and dismayed—they couldn't do enough. Well, as I said, I was that tired and worn out, I lay back like some infant child and received it. I secretly yearned for a finger of bourbon whiskey instead of all that black coffee, but alas how to ask in a ladylike way.

Now on the fringes of those kind ladies, stand the men in small knots. They are muttering and growling and making gestures. Well, I blocked them out of my consciousness, Reader, for I simply did not care to hear what they had to say. Not that it was something bad against me! Oh, far from that. But whatever it was, I didn't care to hear.

After a bit, old Doc Cunningham sidles in with his scuffed-up old black bag, and he shoos everybody out of the room. And do you know, his famous bedside manner just got the best of him, and he didn't act appropriate at all, he only cooed and gurgled and mock-scolded. And out came the stethoscope, and he said he guessed he'd better examine me.

"Oh, Doc Cunningham, I just simply CAN'T be examined right now, I can't, I can't, I can't." And I started this new whooping noise of mine, which was very impressive, and impressed even me. Truth was, for some reason, I could not BEAR to undress in front of him at that time. I was simply too tired to undergo the strain, and have him poking about in my insides and fingering my poor bosoms.

"Oh, Doc Cunningham, have mercy. Just give me a calm-down pill, give me a nice feel-good calm-down sweet-sleep pill, and I promise I will come into your office in a day or two and undergo examination."

"Miss Belle, you ought to check in the hospital," he said.

I said, "Oh no! No hospital for me! I have no major wounds, I have only these couple of bruises and this place on my lip." For I had peeked in a mirror and indeed I was swollen and cut on the left side of my mouth where I got clouted, and a bruise was puffing up under my left eye.

"But Miss Belle," said old Doc Cunningham, "surely this is blood upon your robe, a *lot* of blood."

"Oh is that blood?" I said. "Well, most likely it is HIS blood then for I surely kicked and scratched him mighty hard!"

"Well, well, well!" said Old Dr. Bedside. "Aren't we upset! Now we'd just better calm down," and he pulled out his syringe and filled it with something, and he gave me a shot of something in my arm that soon began the nicest warmest glow.

"But no examination," I begged.

"Miss Belle, there is a risk of Contact."

"Give me a douche and I will take it. Oh, Doc Cunningham, indulge me just this once."

"Now little lady," said he, "what about those mean old police? They going to want a report."

I said, "Mercy, the police! Why, just make up anything you like." And I smiled at him—a sort of confused blend of the Big Flirtatious and a new one—you might call it a Tremulous but Brave.

"Well," he said. "Let me see can you get up and prance around."

So I got up and walked, and I vow, except for this one strange pain it wasn't too bad. And in my hysterical condition, I just pretended that odd pain did not belong to me. Yes, I simply turned it off, like you turn off a spigot!

So he pursed his lips and said "Mmm," for all the world like a psychiatrist (Dr. Dimmer, that's for YOU) and at last he patted me on the head and put his stuff back into his dilapidated old black bag, and he wrote out a prescription, and handed it to Ludie Lindley on his way out.

"Let her rest," I heard him say. "Clear out these people." But even so, a veritable swarm returned and clustered round, and soon before my bleary red-rimmed eyes swims the face of Saralizabeth. Somebody had found and fetched her.

"MOTHER," she says. "What*ever* is this all about!" And she looks daggers at me, as though to say (like her father before her), *What have you gone and done NOW!* "Are you all right?" she manages to ask me grudgingly.

I open and close my mouth weakly a few times, and I smile upon her in motherly fashion, but very wan, and I give her arm a feeble pat of reassurance.

"She's exhausted," explains Ludie Lindley under her voice to Saralizabeth.

"But MOTHER," says Saralizabeth. "WHEN did this all happen? And WHO DID IT?"

I point to the swollen place on my mouth, and mumble, "Hurts to talk." The lovely medicine was working and I began to drift and float downriver in a rosy pink canoe with birds singing and fishes playing just for me. I declare, if it hadn't been for that weird turned-off pain, I would have been downright . . . content.

A commotion at the door, however, melts my happiness away, for the police are clumping in. There are two of them, large tough State Troopers, but even so, I was thankful to have *them* rather than Sheriff Peabody, for in my nervous condition I vow I might have laughed at him—the thought of him being Sheriff instead of Leroy strikes me so funny— and that Adam's apple of his! And needless to say, merry laughter under the circumstances would have caused another scandal.

Well, they clump over to my sofa in their shiny boots, all mean-looking and extra-large in size, but clean-shaved and neat, I have to say. They all pull up chairs and open their notebooks and fetch out their ballpoint pens. Everybody pushes close and holds their breath, to hear the dirt at last. And those troopers clear their throats, and settle their legs and scratch their enormous chins, and one of them says:

"Well, now Miz Sweet, who did it?"

Just like that. And Reader, my heart constricted like you squeezed it in your fist.

Because I realize, Glory come to Jesus, I have not yet made up my mind to tell on Billy Black!

Well, I wished with all my heart I had had sense enough to pretend to be in the Land of Dreams, all drugged by the doctor floating down the Rosy River, but instead I was caught there looking at them, if not bright-eyed and bushy-tailed, at least awake.

So I just goggled and said, "Huh?"

Reader, to tell or not to tell. I was torn in two. If that isn't a fix to be in!

Oh, I was not upholding crime, no sir. I truly do believe in Law and Order. But I was so confused. On the one hand, I had been raped, dishonored, called names, and clouted on the head. But on the other hand, there in my mind's eye stood Lily Black, wringing her hands. Oh poor hard-working and long-suffering soul! And nearby in his Sheriff's hat lounged Leroy Sweet with his dogs at his feet and his Star on his chest and God knows how many bloody crimes upon his head which, although I did not commit them myself personally, and indeed do not know for sure that he committed them himself, and furthermore prefer not to think about them *at all*, nevertheless simply pulsate in the mind's eye, GLOWING IN THE DARK. Oh, Reader, I do not attempt to *defend* myself, I'm only reporting how I felt!

HOW CAN I TELL ON BILLY BLACK!
The issue is not between me and Billy Black at all, but somehow between *Lily and Leroy*. Or *me and Leroy?* I declare, I can hardly say.

Well, the tears start oozing out again, tears being the Weapon of the Weak at Granpa Beesly always said (only he included *cunning* and *deceit* as well in the arsenal, and I surely wished that I could dredge *those* weapons up), and I croak a little, and the only idea I get is to pretend I've lost my voice.

Naturally, those two State Troopers are not precisely MOVED by this feeble-minded strategy. "Don't worry, Miz Sweet," they say. "Just pull yourself together. Take your time. We'll get the varmints whoever they are."

They! I thought. More than one!?

It soon becomes clear that these Shiny Boots and Whipcord Knees are going to stay and wring it out of me, if it takes forever. And I need time to *think!* I weep and croak and I point to my throat, and I pantomime how exhausted I am. And Ludie Lindley backs me up. But nothing budges them, oh no, they settle in for the night.

Well, I am saved from these policemen in the most amazing way!

In the very midst of all these questions, I detect a flurry of excitement near the front door. Buzz, buzz! News Bulletin! Flash!

It seems that *somebody* had the bright idea to go looking for Mother Sweet. And they found her all right, at home in the bathroom taking a bath. Well, they fetched her out, and told her what happened—and Lord have mercy! SHE WAS RAPED TOO! Yes!

At least, so she said.

And maybe she WAS, for all I know!

And maybe NOT.

Yes, maybe not. For Mother Sweet (as well I know) is a jealous old soul, and not quite right in the headpiece. I can just HEAR those old wheels wheezing and rattling: *Pretty-belle got herself raped? Prettybelle? Why, she can't get away with that! Because I was raped too. Yes sir. I'm the widow around here. I'm the one that got raped around here! Yes sir, I was raped, raped, raped! Don't listen to that Prettybelle, listen to me! I'm Leroy's mother. Pay attention to me! Me, me, me!*

Well, it's pathetic, poor old soul. And so I said to myself, "Prettybelle, do you begrudge a moment's fame to that poor old foolish creature?" And Reader, I did not. I managed to be gracious about it. Yes. I managed to mouth out (remembering I couldn't talk), "Lord have mercy! How IS she?"

And they told me she was in surprisingly good shape, though a little disturbed in her mind.

And I silently mouthed out, "Oh, yes, my, my," and I clasped my hands and looked all worried and alarmed, and I gestured to those gawping State Troopers that they'd best trot right over and question Mother Sweet. Which is exactly what they did! Yes! And if *I* didn't heave a sigh of relief. Whew!

(And if I didn't also chuckle up my sleeve, imagining that interview! Lord, Lord!)

Having thus gained time to collect my wits and solve my dilemma, I indicated that I wanted to sleep, and Mrs. Ludie Lindley was right sweet, insisting that I stay with her, and I was willing.

Well, with much ado, they got me out of the living room, and just in time, as more people kept arriving, and newspaper reporters and Lord have mercy, even TELEVISION cameras! So I fled away and into Ludie Lindley's daughter's bedroom (vacant since the child ran off two years before) and all I remember of it is the bed with a big darned place on the pink candlewick bedspread, and on the wall this faded daisy wallpaper and two tacky pictures of an Indian chief and a Scottie dog. Linda Lindley was that child's name and she was a pretty, fragile thing. And everybody HOPES she got married, for she's another one, like Johnny, that hasn't been heard of since, and who can blame the poor creature, considering how her father used to whip her with a knotted rope! He did. Mr. Emmet Lindley. He would whip her with a knotted rope and then make indecent advances. So I have heard it said. And I myself have heard the child shrieking in the distance, in a muffled way behind closed doors. Well, he was *warped*, you know, that man, Ludie Lindley's husband since divorced. He was warped since childhood on account of his truly awesome appearance. Why he had half of one ear and none of the other. And he had a glass eye and his face was stitched and sewn together! Yes! All on account of a wolf. Can you believe it? He lived in Alaska as a child with an aunt and uncle who had a pet wolf cub. And that wolf cub grew up tame and loving as any dog. Until one day the child sneezed in his ear. Yes, Mr. Lindley, age of four, sneezed in that pet wolf's ear, and the creature reverted! Tore him to shreds! Tore the child to shreds before he recollected himself, realized what he had done, and started in a-whining and kissing him on the cheek (though whether he was apologizing in his way or simply lapping up the blood is a moot point to my mind). Well, Mr. Lindley had about a hundred operations, and his life was saved. And then what? He winds up whipping his daughter with a knotted rope and making indecent advances. Oh Reader, Reader, I declare, in this life how can you say WHO is the victim? I ask you that. How can you SAY?

But to return.

They put me to bed in Mrs. Lindley's daughter's bedroom, and they turned out the bedside lamp and tiptoed out and closed the door, and at last I was in a position to collect my wits, but Reader all I could do was see pictures.

I saw Lily sitting heavily at the kitchen table, grieving for her children, her two bad boys, Billy and that other one, that Skeeter, of whom less said the better. There she sat, all wore out, not even complaining. Just a-choke with all the misery of her race, misery and grief and that kind of hopeless patience. Then Leroy muscles in, and starts jawing at me, ordering me around, and I began to squirm and perspire. And to tune him out, I changed channels, so to speak, and started imagining that "interview" those big smart Troopers were having with Mother Sweet, and I could not help but chuckle. For if there is anyone who can immobilize the State Police, I tell you it is Mother Sweet.

Well, the medicine was still glowing nicely, and pretty soon I just abandon the effort to collect my wits, and I let myself relax, and feel all comfy-cozy.

And Reader, as I lay there, a most delectable happiness stole over me. From nowhere! As if my whole body was full of singing birds, and just expanded and expanded until it filled the whole room. I felt enormous, strong and good. I felt benevolent and self-satisfied and kindly toward all creation. Oh it was the sweetest feeling in the world.

(And here, Reader, I should like to interrupt with just one brief remark by way of clueing you in. I want to say that, no matter what happened later, it was definitely Billy Black that raped me and nobody else, and no matter that Billy Black denied it. Of course he would! No matter that

Lily denied it, she's his mama. And that young lawyer from the Civil Liberties, he also said Billy hadn't done it. Well, do not be thrown off by that, for it is nonsense! I mean even though it was dark at the Exact Moment and I may not have seen the face right then, I may not have said Howdy-Do, but I surely know who raped me, I should hope to think! And who raped me was *Billy Black*.)

Anyway, I had this heavenly indescribable feeling, and I thought, what is it? Why is it? Why do I feel so deep-down happy and full of joy? And I thought, Prettybelle, I must say, you surely feel things at the wrong time. This is surely one mighty peculiar time to be so happy. I felt I never again would know sorrow or misery! I was just blissfully pure! Yes. I was a babe again. I was a virgin! (In a manner of speaking.)

Now if that isn't ironical and paradoxical, I'll put in with you.

Soiled and dishonored—and yet I felt all clean and virginal! The queen of hell was gone and trampled under foot. Prettybelle was pure! Well, it was a kind of ecstasy. For I had paid. Yes, I had paid and expiated. All my sins stamped Paid in Full. Reader, it was heavenly bliss.

And although I frequently do not believe in God, I surely prayed to Him this time. I prayed, *Dear God, please let it last!* For do you know, I was already addicted to that feeling? Like a Drug Addict with his morphine fix. I HAD to keep that feeling. I would lie and cheat and steal to keep it!

END EIGHTH INSTALLMENT

Return of Leroy Sweet

I slept like a warm baby, and dreamed of sipping lemonade on someone's lap. Yes, I slept like a baby, but alas, awoke. For when I awoke, I felt no ecstasy I can tell you. I had a head like a giant Boil and a stomach like the Sewers of Jerusalem. Aches and bruises and that weird sore pain. I felt like Job himself, beset by woes on every side.

Is my strength the strength of stone? or is my flesh of brass?

So I said, Lord, do not test me further at this moment, for I am a weak vessel and the poison of Thy arrows drinketh up my spirit. I am sick and weary and I know not where the bathroom is. I know not where the aspirin is. And I fear more tribulations lie ahead of me. And I must say, I was surely correct in that.

Well, day was dawning, breathless and already promising its heat. And like a sick animal my soul and body yearned only to crawl inside some dark familiar hole. So I decided to sneak out of Ludie Lindley's house and go back home to my own room and my own bathroom and my own medicine cabinet. Since it was barely light, all the town was asleep. I struggled upright, and I groaned and winced and held my head and managed to get dressed with frequent rest periods, and I found a pencil and paper and I left a note of thanks to Ludie Lindley on my pillow. And I started to make my bed like a good guest, but I confess Reader, my stomach just rebelled, and so I only pulled the spread to show my good intentions. And I tiptoed down the creaky staircase and out the front door, barefoot, wearing my bedraggled duster, carrying my torn stockings and my one pink mule.

Well, the cicadas were already tuning up in the trees, and far away the dogs were barking, and it was that spooky light of dawn which by rights ought to look like twilight played backwards, but mysteriously does NOT, is altogether different, being ghostly instead of familiar and nostalgic. Now why is that, I wonder. In the movies you can always tell when they cheat, and shoot some scene at dawn in order to avoid the crowd, and then pretend it's sunset in a City of the Dead. You can always tell that spooky light.

Well, as I said, the distant hounds were yelping and the cicadas were revving up, and lo and behold a great television truck is parked in front of Ludie Lindley's house, but luckily no sign of life about it, so I just crept on down the block along the gray sidewalks past the gray flowers and hedges and houses, under the gray trees into my own gray house, and I locked the door behind me, and I took the phone off the hook, and I put some Kleenex in the doorbell, and I went upstairs to bed.

My head was like a light bulb breaking and my stomach was like the great gray green greasy Limpopo River, and trials and troubles lay on every side.

But even so, yes even so, I remembered my ecstasy, and I figured it was still there, somewhere, hiding, biding its time, ready to take over, just give it half a chance.

I took six or seven pills of various descriptions and they kept me asleep a fair good while. But at last a strange noise awoke me, and there tottering about in my room in her orange pongee wrapper with her hair up in three curlers poking around in MY bureau drawers, was Mother Sweet.

Poking in MY bureau drawers and humming a song. Just as happy and busy as you please.

My first impulse was indignation, but I soon regretted that, as it made my head ache. I looked over to see if Leroy was awake, and Reader, as they say, recollection flooded back.

"Well Mother Sweet," I said. "Good morning! I understand that you were raped last night. Mother Sweet? Do I understand correctly?"

She just yanked open my bottom drawer, stirred it all around, happy as a lark, and burst into loud song.

> Give me oil in my lamps,
> Oil in my lamps,
> Give me oil in my lamps I pray,
> Hallelujah, Lujah!

"Well, honestly, Mother Sweet," I said.

She held up a pair of my pink panties, shook them, smelled them, dropped them on the floor, and kept on burrowing.

So I said again, "Well, *honestly*, Mother Sweet!" And I added, "Hadn't you better go back to bed? I mean, here we are, after all, raped and dishonored, and sick, and also BEREAVED, Mother Sweet, and you walk around singing and gay, messing up my bureau drawers."

Well, she began throwing things out right and left, but I was too plain exhausted to get up, and then she lifted her head like an old hound from its rabbit.

"Where's Leroy?"

I declare, I just heaved a sigh.

"Where is my son Leroy," said Mother Sweet, suddenly all prickly and indignant. "I'm going to tell him," she said. "This time I am surely going to tell him, because I have kept silent too long." And she started in about how I opened her mail and hid it, how I stole her things, and her silver thimble, and she wound it all up yelling in this spiteful old voice just a-tremble with fury, "And where is my BRASSIERE, I should like to know!"

"Well, it is NOT in MY DESK," I said rather irritably, for that was where she was heading. And indeed she started yanking at the drawers thereof.

"Not a drawer in this house that works," complained Mother Sweet. "Take a—STRONG—MAN—to open 'em," and she is just pulling and yanking every whichaway. "SHE jams 'em!" said Mother Sweet, addressing the wallpaper.

Well, that "she," Reader, referred to yours truly.

"She jams 'em," said Mother Sweet, "in order that I won't know what she's stolen. Lily too. You can't trust Lily. Dark skin, light fingers, that's an axiom. My son Leroy gave me that silver thimble!"

Well, I felt weary, weary. My bones all ached and my joints creaked like a rusty gate. That old hymn went through my mind,

Art thou tired?
Art thou weary?
Art thou sore opprest?

"Oh, Mother Sweet," I groaned. "Surely you have not forgotten."

Mother Sweet lifted her head a little suspicious bit. Wattles swinging.

"Leroy—passed away," I said. "He passed away. We went to the funeral, don't you remember?"

"We did?" she said thoughtfully.

"Of course," I said.

"Well that was nice," said Mother Sweet.

"And ALSO, Mother Sweet, we were RAPED," I said. And I said it somewhat acidly, I confess. "Don't you remember?" I went on. "We were raped. At least I was most assuredly raped, and you said you were too."

"At the funeral," said Mother Sweet.

"No, no, no. Not at the funeral! Right here. Last night."

"Now, is THAT what happened!" said Mother Sweet. "Those boys last night. They raped us, yes they surely did." Well, she took out laughing, and she laughed until she had to wipe her nose. "He, he, he!" said Mother Sweet. "Serves them right, I say! My, my, if that don't take the brass ring."

I just moaned aloud.

She stopped laughing and gave me this shrewd look from her little gray eyes, and sniffed, and said, "You're surely in the fog THIS morning, my dear."

Well, I closed my eyes.

And when I did so, I realized that noise I'd been hearing wasn't in my head at all, but it was voices, outside, and it was the doorbell buzzing away (though not ringing, because of my clever notion with the Kleenex), and it was *lots* of voices, and folks banging and knocking at the door. Buzz! went the doorbell. Bam, bam, bam, somebody knocked.

Great Lord, I thought, there is a veritable army in the yard outside my door!

Well, Mother Sweet was now standing at the window looking down. And the weather was very dark and ominous out there, fixing to storm, and the wind was picking up the leaves and branches, most unusual for ten o'clock in the morning. Mother Sweet is peering out in an interested kind of way, and she says,

"Why, who's all those people in our yard?"

I say to myself, Prettybelle, get up, you have GOT to get up.

"Just masses of people," said Mother Sweet. "Looking in our windows. There's Granpa Merihew."

Well, Reader, that did it.

"Granpa Merihew passed away in nineteen hundred and twenty-seven," I wailed. And I simply burst into tears and lamentation.

"OO-oo, Granpa!" yelled Mother Sweet, waving her hand.

Well, they spotted her, naturally, and started calling and asking questions, and I jumped out of bed and ran to pull her away, and I took a quick look myself, and Lord have mercy, everybody in town was there, practically. And TWO television trucks, and cameras, and police cars, and Lord knows what-all.

How can I face it? I cannot face it at all!

I pulled her away, and got my hands slapped for it in true Mother Sweet fashion, and I was nervous lest she might even bite me with her old false teeth, so I dropped her.

"Mother Sweet, pay attention, this is serious," I scolded.

"Serious, poo!" sniffed Mother Sweet loftily. "What's so serious? They were only niggas."

I tell you, Reader, a conversation with Mother Sweet is like standing on your head to eat prunes.

So I said primly how a Woman's Body was her Citadel of Virtue. And Mother Sweet snorted and sniffed and said,

"I have many a sin on this old head, dearie, but I am surely not going to fret about THAT one."

"WHAT one?" I said.

"Why that rape one," she said. "I am not going to fret about THAT one."

"Mother Sweet," I said, "nobody I know of is accusing you of sin."

"I should hope not," said Mother Sweet. "They were only niggas."

"I truly fail to understand you, Mother Sweet," I said. "Did you DO something to those Nigras?" Now, Reader, you know and I know there was only *one* Nigra, but by this time I am so confused I scarcely know if it is winter or summer.

Well, old Mother Sweet, she chuckled in this evil way, and started in telling how powerful she was, and how she could just destroy any man that came along. How she noticed this Power of hers when she was real young, just a girl. How a man would come to her all full of piss and vinegar (her words Reader, not mine) and when she got through with him—POOF! "Just like a sorry old balloon!" chuckled Mother Sweet. And she told how it worked every single time, like a charm.

Well, at first I was somewhat foggy as to her meaning,

but it came through eventually, and I simply felt ill at my stomach with embarrassment. But Mother Sweet just nodded her head proudly and smiled this happy triumphant smile and I vow, expected me to praise her!

"Oh my goodness," I said. And outside, the wind blew and the sky was black and a crack of lightning came.

"Your trouble is, you're hung over," said Mother Sweet. "Too much Old Crow! You've got a headache, that's what you've got."

Which was surely true, and shrewd of her to notice. And BOOM came the thunder, right on top of my poor electric light bulb head. And Mother Sweet, glancing out the window from behind the curtain, declared in a conversational tone, casual as you please:

"There's Leroy now."

I tell you, my scalp crawled. I clutched my lavender duster to my poor dishonored bosom, and I actually asked her, "Where?"

"Coming in out of the rain," said Mother Sweet, approvingly.

By now it was indeed pouring down rain in torrents, and the limbs of the trees were madly tossing and twisting and whishing and whooshing, like the end of the world, same kind of storm I used to love to scamper out in as a child, but no longer, Lord. And all those folks outside began to scatter, and some few still bammed at our door, but I was not about to answer, and most of them ran away to their cars, and I was right grateful for that thunderstorm, giving me a respite so to speak.

So I dressed, and took more pills, and I went downstairs to the kitchen where I managed to consume a little nourishment. Vanilla ice cream, with a middling-size glass of Southern Comfort poured over it, and topped **with**

Brewer's Yeast. Don't laugh till you've tried it. Lily had
not come to work, which was disturbing, and even ominous. It meant she had to know, and how could she know?

Saralizabeth was in the living room talking away a mile
a minute to some girl friend on the telephone, very melo-
dramatic, and paying no mind whatsoever to all the racket.
And I notice three sopping-wet photographers on the back
stoop so I quick pull down the blind. And there were more
on the front stoop, and I felt besieged and beleaguered. I
took my ice cream, and I fled down the basement stairs to
Leroy's private den, with all the guns and pictures of
hounds and dead ducks, and I stepped inside, and I shut
the door, and I sat down. No windows, don't you know,
cozy as could be, all private, pine-paneled and secure, and
100 percent Forbidden Territory to Prettybelle Sweet only
four days ago. ("Prettybelle Sweet, you stay the Hell out
of my den, hear?") Well, there I was, all the same, and
there I lounged, very Camille, and ate my ice cream. And I
liked it. (I mean, the den. But I liked the ice cream too.)

Well, I turned on the radio for some soothing music, but
what did I get, midst the static of the storm, but NEWS
OF MY OWN RAPE!

Yes!

Reader, I learned to my surprise and dismay from that
news broadcast I learned my rape was known from coast
to coast. I, me, Prettybelle Sweet, I was a national crisis in
race relations! I was a veritable international sensation. I
crowded Peace and the Monetary Scandal right off the air!
Yes. Can you believe it? *Raped on Funeral Eve. Widow
of Widely-Known Sheriff. Resting under Sedative in State
of Shock.*

Well, I practically had to pinch myself. It was the weirdest sensation! To hear news about your own self coming

over your own radio. Hiding in the basement yet the center of all eyes! For a moment the delicious ecstasy came humming back—a hint of promised joy. But it faded. For, Reader, gradually bit by bit, I came to realize that . . . well, events were moving in a way that . . . boded only ill.

Search Underway for Rapist, said the radio. *Retaliation Feared against Negro Community.* And, *Son of Family Cook Sought for Questioning.*

Oh, Lord! I thought. Why can't they let it alone? Isn't it enough that I've been raped! Already they suspect Billy Black. Now how could that happen? They want to question him. Whatever does that mean? To question him. Oh Glory, I thought, and it flooded over me:—could they *lynch* him? Yes they could.

I confess, Reader, and you may doubt me if you will, this was the first time that thought entered my mind. Lynching! Oh! I thought. What can I do!

Well, the Governor came on the radio. Governor Colship himself, yes, and he appealed for calm and order. He said any citizen who took the Law into his own Hands would be severely punished. He said our great State would show the Nation how fair and judicial it was. He reminded everyone that under the Law, somebody was innocent until he was proved guilty. (Which was a surprise to me, I always thought it was the other way around, didn't you?) He said Mrs. Sweet's own testimony had not yet been taken, because of her condition, but that she would shortly name or describe her assailants, and the Law would swiftly take its course.

Shortly she would name her assailants.

Oh Lordy.

Well, I snapped the radio off, and I sat there in the dark and I sweated and shivered, and felt ill, and wished I could die. Reader, if I am manic now, I surely was depressive then. I looked at Leroy's guns with a longing eye. What to do, what to do. Some dogs were barking and howling, and I thought, Oh what if those dogs are tracking Billy Black! He is running, panting, sweating, and the dogs are coming closer, catching up! Well, it was only Leroy's dogs out back in their kennel, scared of the thunderstorm—but all the same!

I shrank smaller and smaller. I wished I could shrivel up and disappear forever. Oh where was my Purity now? My Happiness? Instead of purity, there was evil once again, and rot. Reader, there was evil at the very fountain source of Prettybelle Sweet. In the marrow of the bone, damp rot, with maggots crawling.

Come on, I said. Don't you believe it. You are a victim, not an executioner. You are a soft furry animal, not the trapper in great boots! Do you hear me? Victim, victim, victim!

But the words merely echoed about, poor tinny things and meaningless, midst all that angry, booming thunder, those torrents of ferocious blowing rain. And I got more and more morbid, and then, Reader, you may believe this or not, as you please, it's all the same to me, but *I heard Leroy's voice calling me. I did.*

"Miss Belle!" said the Voice. "Miss BELLE! Miss Pretty . . . Belle!"

Do you know, I was that miserable, I couldn't even bother to be scared? All I could think of was, *Oh no, what now, what next?*

"Miiisss Be-e-e-elle!" he said. And it was no imagination, I can vouch for that! It was Leroy Sweet himself, and furthermore, he was trying to scare me, making his voice all hollow and ghostly, coming from here, and now from there.

"Miss Pretty Belle!"

Well, I was in no mood. So I just said,

"Oh come on, Leroy. Honestly!"

And then I saw him. I did. He came glimmering out of the dark, dressed just as natural, if somewhat colorless and pale. He stood there in front of me on the braided oval rug, casting a bluish glow like a television set. And he put his hands on his hips, and he spread his legs apart, and he just looked me over, witheringly, and he shook his head, and he said, real slow and drawly,

"Prettybelle. . . . . . . you . . . SLUT."

Now, Reader, I ask you, would I make that up? Those were Leroy's opening words to me, and true to the man. "Prettybelle, you slut," he says, and right away, I'm on the defensive. That's Leroy's gift. He is charging me with being somehow to blame for my own rape, and he is furious.

"But Leroy," I whined. "I couldn't help it. I couldn't *help* it, Leroy."

"Couldn't help it," snorts Leroy, and I tell you, he chews me out. "At MY FUNERAL!" he hollers. "AT MY OWN FUNERAL you let that boy into the house. My own funeral. Prettybelle," he says, "I can't turn my back on you ONE MINUTE."

"But Leroy," I hear myself squawking. "I couldn't know he was going to rape me. How could I know he was going to rape me?"

"Rape YOU," spits Leroy, scornful and furious. "You think he raped YOU? Puh! It was ME he raped. ME."

Well, that was an odd thing to say.

"Leroy," I said, "that's an odd thing to say. It was surely me he raped!"

"ME. Leroy Sweet," says Leroy, stubborn as a mule.

I mean it was ridiculous, and I was not about to let him get away with it.

"It was ME," I said.

"Me, Leroy Sweet, Sheriff."

"Me, Prettybelle Sweet, widow." I kind of emphasized that "widow" in just the slyest way. And I added, "After all, I surely ought to know!"

"You were so damn drunk," said Leroy, "you don't know anything. And anyways," he said, "in the whole damn deal, you were the LEAST of it. You were totally unimportant."

"UNIMPORTANT!" I cried. "ME? The whole United States of America has been trying to get inside this house. To see ME. The new Sheriff and the troopers and the television and the radio and the reporters and the photographers and the doctor and the preacher and the neighbors and everybody, coming to see ME, because *I* got raped. Not you."

I was that indignant, I really was.

"Well now, let me tell you something," says Leroy. "It was *me* that boy was after, and YOU were no more than my possession. You know what that rape was? It was the merest act of vandalism. Like letting the air out of the tires on my TRUCK."

"Your TRUCK!" I hollered.

"My PICKUP truck," he snarled.

Well, Reader, fortunately I happened to have with me a polished silver cream pitcher filled with fine bourbon whiskey, and having no glass I just poured a drop discreetly into my ice-cream bowl and sipped it from the spoon in a ladylike way, Leroy or no Leroy. And I smiled at him.

"Leroy honey," I said brightly, in a conversational and friendly tone. "Isn't there anything you're supposed to be

DOING? I mean, shouldn't you CHECK IN someplace?"

It stood to reason, didn't it?

"You just let ME worry about that, Miss Belle," said Leroy. "And lay off the liquor."

"Leroy, I'm SURE there's something you ought to be doing. You're not going to be—I mean, you're not going to be just—hanging round the house——?"

As Leroy is about to answer, the storm slacks off a bit and he pricks up his ears and turns and scowls, listening, and then he simply YELLS,

"DID YOU FEED MY DOGS?"

Well, I was that distracted and upset, I simply passed my hand over my brow, and murmured, "Did I—? Did I *what?*"

Leroy paces around like a caged madman, and says, "That's Rex out there crying! That's Prince! Those dogs are HUNGRY!"

"Why now, Leroy honey, they're only scared of the thunder," I quavered.

"God DAMN you, Prettybelle!" busts out Leroy. "Can't remember ONE DAD-BLAMED THING! Won't even FEED MY DOGS!"

Well, I wrung my hands.

"Leroy," I said, "is that what you came back for? To see if I fed the dogs?"

"NO IT IS NOT," said Leroy.

"I'll feed 'em Leroy, I promise I will!"

"It is not the dogs!" said Leroy.

"I'll feed them every day. You don't have to worry, sugar. I'll just feed 'em and feed 'em. I'll feed them right this minute!" I said and I started to get up.

"YOU SIT DOWN," said Leroy.

I sat down, making soothing noises.

"Poor thing," I said to him. "*Poor* Leroy, worrying about his dogs! I don't blame you, honey, not one bit. But it's all right now, because Prettybelle will take care of it. Yes, sir. You can just go on back where you came from, and rest in peace, honey. Because Prettybelle going to take GOOD care of those dogs, and——"

"Prettybelle, SHUT UP," said Leroy.

Well, I thought, it has to be *something* worrying him, and please God let him *not* have read my Will and Testament! So I said,

"And I'll clean your guns, Leroy, I will. Keep everything just as nice. Polish up your boots, and shine your badge, and wash the wagon good, and——"

I declare, he raised his hand to me.

"Leroy," I faltered, cowering back. "If you're going to act mean—maybe I just WON'T feed your dogs!"

And I covered up my head real quick, expecting him to hit me. Which he didn't, so I peeked out, and he is simply standing there with a funny expression on his face, frustrated and perplexed, and Reader, it did occur to me, in passing, Can a ghost hit people? Very likely he just can't! and I thought, Hmm!

Leroy looks at his hands in a perplexed way, puts them behind him and clears his throat, business-fashion.

"Prettybelle," he says, reasonably, "you act like some two-year-old pickaninny. Pull yourself together," he says, "because I'm here on business."

"On business," I repeated, thinking, well now, if those were not Mr. Wimbly's own exact words as well.

"That's right," he says. "Now you just march over to that table and open the drawer."

Well, I struggled over, and I opened the drawer, and waited for instructions.

"Take out one sheet of paper, one envelope, one ball-point pen," says Leroy. "Close the drawer, pull up a chair, sit on it, and write what I tell you."

Well, in a daze, I obeyed him, and sat down at the table, holding the pen, waiting. Do you know, for an instant it almost felt *good*, having someone do my thinking for me? And he stood there, scowling and thinking, whilst I waited helpless and walled-in.

"Leroy," I said timidly. "Is it—the rape?"

"Quiet," he said.

"I couldn't HELP it, Leroy," I whimpered. And when he didn't answer, I just wailed out loud and clear, "Oh Leroy, I just couldn't help it, how could I help it, Leroy?"

He clicks his tongue in exasperation, and shows his teeth, and tells me to shut up, and that the rape was just a God-send Straight from Heaven!

"WHAT!" I exclaim, unable to believe my ears.

"It couldn't have been better if I'd set it up myself!" says Leroy, and he starts in to chuckle, and he starts in to laugh, with his hand to his mouth like he always did to cover up that missing tooth on the right side he never would see the dentist for. And he said all the liberals and agitators were squirming like a nest of hog-nosed snakes. He said my rape was just what the doctor ordered. He said it was an Educational Opportunity without Parallel. He said the whole damn South was knuckling under and caving in, and this would stop it. Well, he started quoting imaginary headlines, and laughing, rocking back and forth, until he started up a rattling choking coughing fit, and had to stop.

"Leroy," I said very stiffly when he had recovered himself. "Do I understand correctly you are GLAD this happened?"

"GLAD!" shouts Leroy, outraged, turning on me. "MY

WIFE? Go no farther, Prettybelle! Now if id been Old Jackass Beansbody's wife—!" And if he didn't break out chuckling again, and wiping his eye.

Reader, somehow I was just revolted. And I just automatically cast about in my mind for some way to get back at him, yes I did, but all I found was to defend poor Peabody, so I said,

"Well, jackass he may purely be, but who named him deputy, I should like to know? Who named him second in command? You named him your own self!"

"Well, aren't you the smart little trick," said Leroy, very ugly. "Yes I named him, and why did I name him? Because his daddy just happens to own the brick works and the button works and the sweater factory, that's all, and is the richest man in the whole damn county, that's all, and the biggest contributor to my campaign. That's ALL, Prettybelle, but you can't be expected to understand THAT. Because all YOU got in your pretty little head is S-E-X."

"ME?" I said. "Sex? Why that is not true! I am not interested in sex AT ALL," I said. And then I had my clue, and I saw my way, and I said, very innocent and puzzled:

"Leroy . . . I'm just the least bit foggy about last night. I mean, it WAS rape, wasn't it? I mean, Leroy, I—oh my me!—I surely didn't cooperate, did I?"

Ha, ha, ha! THAT set him back! Oh, one thing I've got to say for Leroy, he was HUMAN, yes. I mean, unlike Mr. Wimbly. You could always get AT Leroy, with a little effort.

"Prettybelle, you are purely a slut," said Leroy. "Even to think that way. You were foully raped."

I nodded my head, all innocent and obedient. "That's right I'm sure," I said demurely.

"You fought and kicked and scratched and yelled till you were hoarse."

"That's right!" I exclaimed. And I cleared my throat and hacked a little bit.

"You're covered with bruises from head to toe."

"Oh," I said, "am I?"

"Possible grave internal injuries," said Leroy.

"Lord, Lord."

"Shock, loss of memory, emotional exhaustion, and hysterics."

"Well now," I said, admiringly, "if that isn't JUST the way it is. And Mother Sweet too."

"That's right," said Leroy. "AND DON'T YOU FORGET IT."

"Oh, I won't," I said.

"Idiot female," said Leroy, from the heart. "Between you and Peabody, you going to foul it up some way. Now listen. We don't want no lynching, hear?"

I tell you, Reader, my heart bounded with joy at THAT.

"We want simple justice done in a law-abiding community," said Leroy.

"Like the Governor said," I added.

"That's right," said Leroy. "Now. Question Number One: *Howcome you didn't name them boys last night! Howcome you wouldn't talk?*"

"Well, Leroy," I said, "I started to. I did. And it was the craziest thing. I just opened my mouth and instead of talking I just went SKKKKKKKK."

"You were plain stone drunk, that's why," said Leroy.

"Me?" I cried indignantly. "Whatever are you saying? That's not so! I just opened my mouth," I said to Leroy, "and it was like somebody pinched my tongue with a pair of pliers. Yes!" Reader, I said that, and as I spoke, why I felt the words were true. "It was the strangest most amazing thing," I said. "I purely COULD not talk. I just went SKKKKKK."

"Well, let THAT go," said Leroy. "Cause sure as hell if you'd of talked last night, you'd of got it wrong. Now!" he said. "Prettybelle, take that envelope."

I took the envelope.

"Write on it, *Names of the Boys that Raped Me*."

"But Leroy," I said.

"Shut UP," he said. "Just write it."

So Reader, I shook my head, and I wrote it.

"Now take that piece of paper," said Leroy.

And I took the paper.

"Write down these names," said Leroy, and he pondered a minute, and then he rattled them off. "WILLIAM BLACK. ROYAL COVINGTON. RUFUS SMITH. EVERETT CLAY. MORTON CALHOUN. CHARLES JOHNSON. ZEKE FLOWERS. RUNT PICKALILLY. You got that? Now sign your name."

Well, I'm scribbling away in some kind of trance. And I say,

"But Leroy!"

"You got that?"

"I got it. But Leroy—"

"Well, what," growls Leroy in sulky fashion.

"*I* don't know all those boys! I only know Lily's boy William."

"Well, take my word for it," says Leroy.

"But Leroy!" I say. "That Everett Clay, he's the Nigra preacher, isn't he? Why, HE wasn't here last night!"

"Miss Belle," says Leroy—he always calls me *Miss Belle* when he wants to be sarcastic— "Miss Belle, if id been Jesus and the twelve apostles here last night, you wouldn't have knowed it. So just fold that list, and put it in that envelope, and seal it, and don't worry your pretty little hungover head."

"But Leroy," I said.

"What now," says Leroy.

"There was only ONE boy. You got EIGHT."

"Just do like I tell you, honey," says Leroy, in a soothing way.

Well, by now the storm had blown itself out, I reckon, because you couldn't hear it anymore, but you could hear somebody going BAM BAM on the front door, and so I listened, and I heard old Peabody's voice, hollering,

"MISS BELLE YOU ALL RIGHT? MISS BELLE, OPEN THE DOOR!"

"All right, Prettybelle," says Leroy, briskly. "Get your tail upstairs and answer that door, and name those boys, and hand over that envelope."

Well, Reader, it crossed my mind that I sure would get some sympathy if it was eight boys raped me instead of one, but one thing I am *not* is dishonest! And so I said,

"Leroy, there was only one boy."

"Like I told you, Prettybelle," says Leroy, very sweet and controlled. "You were a wee mite under the weather."

"But sugar," I said. "There was only one."

"You're mistaken, honey-pot," says Leroy. "You just can't remember right."

"One boy, sugar. One boy. I DO remember. One boy, and——"

"JUST name the boys on this list, honey," says Leroy, swelling up his chest to make himself look enormous. "JUST do like I tell you. Don't fret yourself. HEAR?"

BAM BAM goes Sheriff Peabody. "MISS BELLE?"

"But Leroy," I said, "there was only one."

"GOD DAMN LITERAL FEMALE!" bellows Leroy, exasperated beyond endurance. But he checks himself, and controls himself heroically. And he says, all gentle and kindly, "Prettybelle, sugar-baby. Those boys on that list, they are all bad dangerous boys. Mighty dangerous bad boys shouldn't be loose. Understand? Corrupting all the good boys. Understand me?"

BAM BAM BAM they're knocking. "MISS BELLE," hollers the new Sheriff. "WE'RE COMING IN, MISS BELLE!"

"GET on up there!" says Leroy. "Jesus Christ in his nightgown! GET on up there and do your duty."

Well, I scurry out and stumble up the stairs, and I call out, "I'm coming, I'm coming, wait a minute!" And I think, Will Leroy *follow* me upstairs? Will he go back where he belongs? Is he going to hang around *forever*? What to do, oh what to do? And Reader, I still had no more idea in my head of what to do, than a lamb being led stiff-legged to slaughter.

END   NINTH   INSTALLMENT

Prettybelle,
Name Those Boys!

Well, Saralizabeth had already answered the front door
and hordes of men in wet shirts were pushing and pressing
in. Saralizabeth simply took one look at them, backed up,
and fled away upstairs. As for me, I barely had time to ar-
range myself upon the sofa, and pull up the afghan over my
feet and knees. Heaven knows it must have been 90 degrees
of heat in there and well-nigh 99 of humidity, for if the
storm had cooled it off outdoors, it surely had not pene-
trated my living room. There was a crushing heat. Nevertheless I pulled up the afghan, to indicate that I was both
modest and under the weather, and they all came piling in,
damp and sweaty, with cameras and microphones and
wires and floodlights. And Beansbody in the lead.

I mean *Peabody*, and I will never again call him Beansbody, for ever since Leroy explained how he got to be deputy only because he was a rich man's simple son, my heart
just opened up to the poor fellow, all nervous, trying his
best to make good on the new job, and no talent, no talent
whatsoever. I resolved never again to laugh or sneer. Well,
in he rushes, saying, "Oh Miz Sweet, that you Miz Sweet?
You home Miz Sweet? You sick Miz Sweet? You all right

Miz Sweet?" He is all upset over me, which was surely a pleasant change from LEROY, and Lord if he didn't have a little present for me from his wife! Can you beat it? A little rape present. Peppermint tea and wine jelly! Now if that don't show how old-fashioned and hopeless he was, I'll put in with you! Well, I was touched. He was just aburst with compassion and sympathy and distress and you could read it right in his big muddy green eyes, in those innocent wet strings of gray and yellow hair sticking to his receding forehead, not to mention in his Adam's apple which was working away harder than ever, bless his poor old impossible heart!

"Oh, POOR Miz Sweet!" cries Mr. Peabody, and he practically wrings the rainwater out of that big hat of his.

Now up to this point, midst all that jostling crowd, I hadn't spotted hide nor hair of Leroy, nor had I heard his voice amid the din of those reporters' shouts and questions. So I figured no doubt he was not allowed in. No doubt he could materialize only in his Den, or else he didn't thrive in crowds, or had to obey some fussy rule or other. But alas, Reader, the very instant our new Sheriff says, *Oh, poor Miz Sweet,* I hear Leroy very clearly. His voice soars above all the racket, and what he says is: "JACKASS!" And he is referring to Sheriff Peabody, who is being nice to me—reason enough!

"JACKASS!" says Leroy.

Well, I heard it, but nobody else did. And when I glanced around, uneasy, I couldn't spot him anywhere. Audible (I thought) but not Visible. Hmm. So I rearranged myself, and smoothed my hair, and smiled wanly.

"Oh, don't worry about me, Sheriff," I said.

"What say ma'am?" said Sheriff Peabody, cupping his ear.

"Don't worry bout me," I shouted. "I'm all right. Just a bit Light-headed and——"

"What say, ma'am?" says Sheriff Peabody.

"LIGHT-HEADED," I shout. "AND CROAKY IN THE VOICE."

"Oh, ma'am!" gulps Peabody, all choked up, and swallowing hard, and shaking his head. You can tell he feels like Lee at Appomattox. And he only wishes he had nerve enough to go down upon one knee and kiss my hands. Yes! Well, I hope Leroy is taking it all in.

"Forgive me, ma'am," he says, "I surely——"

"What?"

"Oh, ma'am!" he shouts, "I surely do hate to bother you, so soon and all, but—I'm sheriff now—and——"

Well, I nod at him for encouragement.

"—and ma'am, I got to question you." Up and down bobbles that old Adam's apple, and I thought, dear Lord, DON'T let me get the giggles now, in my miserable and hysterical and desperate situation. Furthermore, the flash bulbs are popping and a television camera is looking at me from its great snout.

"Well, not with all this racket going on, I hope," said I, because the poor simpleton I swear barely seemed to notice that everybody was talking at once, reporters shouting questions, shoving in, and photographers pushing up close for pictures.

"What say, ma'am?"

I simply wave my hand weakly to indicate I can no longer shout, and I lie back, and blink what I hope are big blue pathetic eyes, wan with suffering but very brave. Snap, crackle, pop, go the flash bulbs.

He bends down close to hear me.

"All this racket," I whisper. "All these people."

Well, he galvanized into action. And to my surprise him and his big young deputy, they actually manage to clear the room. "All right, fellows," he says. "Break it up now. She'll talk to you later. That's all, that's all now." Him and the big young deputy boy just start shoving them back, talking them back like two lion tamers.

Then he turns to me, and pulls up a chair.

"Whew!" I say. "Peace and quiet."

And he fetches out his notebook, sober and serious.

"I declare, Sheriff," I say, patting my lip and brow with my lace handkerchief and fanning myself. "I just don't know if I'm up to it."

Well—BAM!!

Somebody has slammed his fist onto the table, and I know who it is. This time the others hear it too, and old Peabody scowls at his deputy, and growls,

"Hell you doin, kickin the furniture?"

Then he realizes he said *hell* in front of a lady, and if he didn't start to blush! I vow, I thought to myself: This Peabody is too good to be true! Why, he would eat from my hand, if I so desired. He would sit up and beg! Reader, you can sense these things. I thought, my, my, his mama surely did a fine job of raising HIM! And I began to feel brighter. I did. And I admit it crossed my mind to wonder what it might be like MARRIED to a man like that, and I tried to recall any recent news of *Mrs.* Peabody—her health and welfare—but without success, which had to mean her health was robust, and I wouldn't have married him anyway, not with that neck of his. Lord! It would have haunted my very dreams. Still, I felt brighter. A little taste of power is sweet now and then, yes, mighty sweet and relaxing. A woman truly needs it now and then, to tone up the muscles and unwind the nerves.

Well, to pick up the thread.

Leroy hits the table, Peabody says, "Hell you doin, kickin the furniture," and blushes, Deputy looks sulky and put-upon and says he didn't do nothing, and Prettybelle smiles as brilliantly as she knows how, showing every pearly tooth for Leroy's benefit, and says,

"Oh THAT's all right, it's just the plumbing."

And I hear this distant muttering rumble, which might have been the thunderstorm retreating, but far more likely was Leroy growling away in fury. *Plumbing!* he was growling to himself. *Plumbing!*

Well, I gloat over that one, until I notice the peculiar way that Deputy Boy is staring at me. Morbid fascination is the only way to describe it. He's a moronic-looking boy to begin with, but extremely large and yellow-haired and handsome—it's not the features but the expression that's moronic. Troubled with adenoids, no doubt, or else postnasal drip. Anyway, his mouth hangs open, and he has a fresh red sunburn and a fresh haircut on his sun-bleached yellow hair—for you can see the pure white skin all round the edges. His little bitty ears are neatly tucked into his skull. And he is looking at me, he can't take his eyes off me! I wonder, is my blouse unbuttoned? Are my legs apart? What the Sam Hill ails this youngster?

"I reckon I better speak to your daughter too, ma'am," says Peabody, humble and reverential. "And old Miz Sweet as well."

"Oh Sheriff, do you have to?" At that minute out the corner of my eye I see Mother Sweet steaming in from the kitchen, carrying a sack of cookies and a bottle of Coca-Cola, with her head lowered and her nose aimed true, looking neither to the right nor to the left, heading straight for the TV.

"Poor Mother Sweet is just hysterical," I say.

Well, Peabody, he intercepts her, or tries to, and asks her kindly to sit down. "Step aside, Leroy," she snaps, and turns on the TV. "Mammy's busy, Leroy."

And it's a fine question, Reader, whether she saw or sensed that Leroy was present in spirit, or whether she was talking to Peabody in the confused notion that HE was Leroy. I personally vote that she truly heard the ghost of Leroy, for I have no doubt he was haranguing her like he did me, saying, "Mammy, you back up Prettybelle, hear? You back her up now, when she names those names!"

Whilst Peabody calls up the stairs for Saralizabeth, the Deputy Boy kind of circles around me and continues his fascinated stare. So I say somewhat acidly,

"Something troubling you, son?"

He steps forward and his eyes get eager, and he says, kind of avidly, "What-all did those boys DO to you, ma'am?"

I can tell you, he is reenacting that rape inside his head and enjoying every minute of it . . . a pastime I will not encourage.

"I mean, what-all did they do? Like, uh, what-all kinds of things?"

I thought, stick with your Imagination, son, for it is no doubt better than Reality.

"What-all?" I echoed vaguely.

Saralizabeth comes thumping downstairs, cross and disagreeable, but pretty as a picture, radiant with rage as you might say. She spots the telephone and says,

"Who left the phone off the hook! No wonder I haven't had any calls!" And she flounces over and slams it back.

"I can't imagine," I reply, "because you're the only one has used it."

She glares in my direction, but finds me, Reader, so loathesome that she will not deign to cast her glare upon my FACE but casts it instead upon my lower quarters, thus withering my feet and knees.

"Mr. Beansbody," she says, tossing her golden hair, "I TOLD you people all I know."

"Peabody, ma'am," he corrects her, modestly.

Well, the Deputy Boy has transferred his affections in a hurry, and now he's licking his chops over Saralizabeth.

"You got raped, too, ma'am, didn't you," he says to her. "My land," he says, "I reckon YOU sure got raped!" And inside his mind just know he's saying *Hot dog!* etcetera.

Saralizabeth, all twitchy and prickly and touch-me-not, nevertheless takes in this boy through flickering eyelids, for he *is* handsome, sure enough.

"You think I'd be so CALM if I got raped?" she says. "It was—my *mother* got raped." She curls her pretty lip and flares her little nostrils. "And my—*grandmother*," she drawls.

The Deputy Boy looked surprised at that, and shook his head. I vow, with that yellow hair, blue eyes, and red face, he looked like some kind of national flag.

"Now Miss Saralizabeth, according to the Time Element," says Peabody, flustered but pompous, "you came in whilst the rapists were still here."

"So I'm told!" snips Saralizabeth.

Deputy Boy edges forward. "Wha'd they look like?" says he.

"Like Nigras, I sup*pose*," says Saralizabeth loftily. "I never saw them. They were hiding."

Deputy Boy looks puzzled, tips his head way over to one side. "Well, I mean," he says, confused. "Howcome they didn't rape YOU?"

Peabody says impatiently. "I'll ask the questions, son." He is trying to get everybody settled in a proper circle and he wants to do it all just very correct and official.

But the Deputy Boy giggles and shakes his yellow head, and says, "My land, that sure is crazy. My land, I sure don't understand that. I mean, my land, to pick your grandmaw and not you?"

Well, Saralizabeth flushes and tosses her head. "No accounting for taste," she snips, "as the old lady said as she kissed the cow."

Well, old Peabody is fussing around, nervous and important, and he says, "Miss Saralizabeth, would you sit here," and he gets the Deputy Boy sitting down and he tells him to fetch out his notebook, and he gets me all settled and comfy, and he tries to ride herd on Mother Sweet, and manages to extract her from the television set, and he gets us all in our Family Circle, and he fusses and stalls and arranges, and——

WHAM! BAM! Leroy can't stand it another minute. BAM! He is fit to be tied! "Horse manure!" I hear him say (only worse). "Oh HORSE manure!" Well, thank Fortune nobody but me heard it, unless it was Mother Sweet. "GET ON WITH IT!" snaps Leroy. He is addressing Peabody, trying to reach through, trying to place thoughts in his head. "Get ON with it, jackass!" snarls Leroy. "Ask for the NAMES. It's so EASY. Just GET THE NAMES. ASK—MY—WIFE—FOR—THE—NAMES!"

Poor Leroy, poor soul, he did sound that frustrated.

"NAMES," rages Leroy. "NAMES! Oh, GOD!"

Mother Sweet puckered her lips and raised her eyebrows, and sang out loud and clear,

"Leroy, calm yourself."

Well, everybody simply stared at her, except for Saralizabeth, who took a deep breath and rolled her eyes to the heavens in saintly martyrdom.

"I always told him one day he'd drop dead," said Mother Sweet to Peabody, chewing her false teeth like a cud. "I told him. I said, You'll drop dead, Leroy! From sheer bad temper! I told him that. You behave yourself now, Leroy," she said, looking into space. (My Lordy, can she *see* him, I did wonder, for I assuredly could not.) "You'd be better off standing up for your old mother, and telling this Miss Snippet to keep her sticky fingers to herself," said Mother Sweet, in one of her customary references to ME.

"Oh God," wails Saralizabeth, whether to herself or Him, who is to say.

"I'm robbed blind in this house," says Mother Sweet. "Never should have moved in. I haven't got one brassiere left to my name. Leroy, not one to my name. *Look* at me," she yells. "LOOK at these old dugs just flopping and flapping——"

"GRANDMOTHER!" screeches Saralizabeth. "You be quiet, or I SWEAR I WILL PINCH YOU SO HARD——!!"

"You see?" says Mother Sweet, mumbling her teeth, sniffing and nodding her head with satisfaction.

Well, Beansbody and the Deputy Boy are simply dumbfounded.

"Grandmother is not precisely with it," says Saralizabeth, in a cold rage. "And I personally have answered all the questions I intend to!"

And up she gets and flounces over to the TV set which is already warmed up by Mother Sweet, and she settles down on the love seat in front of it, twisting a lock of hair and sucking a fingernail. Mother Sweet trots right over and sits down beside her, but Saralizabeth snarls and shoves.

"Grandmother, you are such a PIG," says Saralizabeth, shoving. "Sit in your OWN place, you don't have to sit on ME."

The TV just blares on, loud as can be. (*Sports in Review*, by Geritol and Fasteeth.) Mother Sweet sips her Coca-Cola and commences a cookie. Peabody and the Deputy Boy seem hypnotized.

And Leroy, oh poor Leroy! "NAMES!" he croaks.

Peabody recollects himself, alas, and turns to me, poises his ballpoint pen, and opens his mouth to speak.

What to do!

"Oh!" I screech.

Peabody jumps forward. "What *is* it, ma'am?"

"I feel faint. I just feel so faint!"

"NAMES!" bellows Leroy, like the voice of Jehovah.

"That is NOT Granpa Merihew," says Saralizabeth crossly to Mother Sweet. "The man at bat is RON SWOBODA."

"NAMES!" yelps Leroy.

"Ma'am," says Peabody.

"I just feel—so dizzy," I say.

"I don't suppose you'd care to go with me to the show tonight," says Deputy Boy to Saralizabeth.

"NAMES!" pants Leroy.

"BASE HIT!" says the television set.

Well, Leroy is drumming on the table, the hounds are howling, the telephone is ringing, and somebody pokes a television camera right through the window screen!

"Look!" I screech, pointing at the nozzle of the camera.

"GIT outa here!" shouts the Deputy Boy, glad of some action, I reckon. And together, him and Peabody just shove that camera out, slam down the window and the blind.

I hear Leroy keening. "Let them IN, you fools," bays Leroy. "Let 'em back in! Confounded jackasses!"

"Hey! Mary Hester!" sings out Saralizabeth, having answered the telephone. "Honey, let me tell you! I just can't tell you! It is horrible beyond words!"

"Now, ma'am," puffs Peabody. "You did recognize those boys, I understand. If you'll just name them, I can let you be."

I wet my lips in nervous terror.

"I'll take those names now, ma'am," says Peabody.

"Will you KINDLY HUSH UP," says Saralizabeth to everybody, but especially to Mother Sweet and the television set. "I cannot hear a THING."

"Uh, those names, please, ma'am?" says Peabody.

"What say, Sheriff?" says Prettybelle, fanning herself.

"All those big buck Nigras, that's *right!*" says Saralizabeth. "I mean, Mothuh just invites it, and do you know we have television people here, and radio and newspapers and magazines, and they are simply standing ten deep outside in the yard, well you know Mother, I mean, oh Lord. She simply BLURTED it right out—NO she isn't hurt! She never looked better in her LIFE. I mean, the shame of it just never enters her head. I mean, she could have kept it quiet. She could have called the doctor and told the police quietly. But no, she has to run all over the NEIGH-BORHOOD in her dressing gown! Oh my poor daddy, I reckon I should thank God he's gone," and she went on and on in the same vein.

Until Peabody at last shakes himself and says,

"Please ma'am, could you identify those boys?"

"Why, I couldn't DEFEND myself, Sheriff," I replied. "I'm just a woman."

"No ma'am," says Peabody, "I didn't say that. I said,

could you please give me the names. It was William Black, wasn't it, ma'am, didn't you say that, and——"

"You mean, who were they? Who were those boys?"

"Yes, ma'am," says Peabody, happily.

"Those boys last night?" I said.

"PRETTYBELLE I'M WARNING YOU! GIVE HIM THAT LIST!"

"They must have had a key, ma'am," says Sheriff Peabody, "because no windows was broken. Doors and windows all okay. So they had to have a key. Now the onliest one could get a key would be your maid's boy, William. You listening, ma'am?"

"Why, I think so, Sheriff."

"NO!" says Saralizabeth. "No, no, no, not ME. I didn't get raped, thank heaven! Well, I don't KNOW howcome. Why does everybody ask me that? How do I know howcome?"

"Ma'am, what I said was, Was one of them William Black?"

"What say, Sheriff?"

"PRETTYBELLE, I'LL BREAK YOUR NECK. I WILL."

"I mean, one of those boys WAS William, wasn't it?"

Well, I suddenly shrieked softly, because I had the weirdest feeling in my neck. The same as at the funeral party, when I told how happy the Nigras were with Leroy. "Oh!" I said. "My tongue feels so funny! My jaw is all peculiar! Oh, mercy me!" And I half rose up. "Oh Sheriff I feel awful!"

Well, he looked alarmed.

"Oh Sheriff, I'm about to THROW UP!"

I declare, people do recoil when you threaten to throw up.

"Oh! I am!" I said, holding myself. "I am going to throw up! Right HERE! Right NOW! Go away! Please!"

I moaned and leaned over the edge of the sofa, and Peabody jumped to his feet.

"Oh my stomach!" I holler. "Oh my tongue! Forgive me, Sheriff, you have got to run along. Run on, Sheriff, see you later. Oh. QUICK!"

Well, they retreated in consternation, Peabody and his Deputy Boy, but alas only to the doorway where they stood dismayed but undecided. So I double over, and run into the kitchen, waving them out behind me.

In the kitchen I lean on the sink to catch my breath a minute. Those men are still lounging on the back stoop and I overhear them talking—about Billy and Lily! How Billy is being hunted high and low, and how Lily is—well, Lord, they say she is sick and in the hospital! They say she has had some kind of *stroke*. I declare, when I hear that, it is the last straw. How could Lily be sick? Tears come into my eyes and like a small baby I wail. "I want Lily!"

In the living room Peabody is trying to persuade Saralizabeth to come after me and help, and Saralizabeth is fighting back gamely. But soon I hear footsteps, or think I do, and I cannot STAND it, and I flee down into the basement into Leroy's den and close the door and collapse upon the couch, and I think, if there's anybody in this world *should* have a stroke, it is ME.

I know I am likely to see Leroy again down there, but heaven help me, I would rather cope with Leroy than what's going on upstairs. Yes. The known rather than the unknown. Well, nobody comes after me, and I get the feeling Leroy is working himself up to Visibility. I cover my eyes, but when I peep through my fingers, sure enough, there he is, glowing away with his blue light over in the corner. I heave a sigh. No rest for the weary. Yes, there he is, pondering and scowling, not making a move, just studying.

I close my eyes tight, hoping against hope that he is only nerves or indigestion. But when I peep again, he is standing right in front of me, looking me squarely in the eye.

"Prettybelle," he says. "You have no intention in this world of throwing up."

So I sigh sheepishly, and I say it is true my tummy *has* improved somewhat, but I have a bevy of other symptoms if he cares to listen. "For example—" I begin, but this cold blue Leroy is glaring at me in such a manner that my voice trickles away. And then, remembering upstairs, I simply suddenly had to snicker.

"Oh Leroy," I snicker. "You surely were a caution! Lord, Lord! Carrying on like a maniac, and nobody could hear a word you said!" Well, I laughed and laughed and Leroy stood there, and I thought, whooey, I better watch it. One thing you don't do to Leroy Sweet is LAUGH at him.

"You going to break my neck, Leroy?" I said.

He stands there, glimmering and glaring, and I think, well Lord have mercy, what can he do?

"Why, Leroy," I said. "I don't think you can break my neck. I think your hands would simply sail right through my neck like a breeze through a rose garden. In my opinion," I said, "you are nothing but ectoplasm or whatever it is!"

Well, he did not reply and I warmed up to my subject.

"Now what you ghosts can do," I said, "is groan and thump around and lead people. Scare 'em and lead 'em. Like, in the night, you call me out of bed. 'Follow me!' You lead me right to the river's edge and wave your arms and say, 'Oooooo Prettybelle, jump in, jump in, honey!' Or you could say, 'Oooooo Prettybelle, take that nice shotgun and put it in your mouth!" Like that, Leroy. But you cannot break my neck, I do not see how you can break my neck, and you might as well FACE UP TO IT!"

Well, I vow, poor Leroy, his cheeks kind of sagged, and his chin quivered, and he looked dejected. He did.

"I never thought," he said, all emotional, "I never thought the day would come when my own wife . . . my own WIFE . . . would talk to me like that. I always thought . . . a wife . . . was supposed to HEP her husband, not . . . tear him down. But then—" he says, turning his head sorrowfully, "you never DID love me. Oh, I know it. You never did."

And he chokes up, and struggles manfully with his emotions.

"Well," I said. "I did. I did love you. Once."

And my heart beat pitterpat, because it's the first time I have dared own up that I do not love him anymore.

"Well," said Leroy, heaving this brokenhearted sigh. "You're a big lady from Virginia, and I'm just a red neck. That's all. Just a red neck. You always did look down on me and that's the truth."

"Why I did not! Come on, Leroy," I said.

"Oh, I know, I know the truth," said Leroy.

"Leroy!" I said.

"All I wanted," says Leroy, humbly, "was to ask you this one little question. I didn't want to bother you. I didn't want to force myself on you. Just one little question."

"Well," I said, generously. "Go ahead, ask it."

And in the same humble way, he says,

"I just wanted to ask howcome you didn't hand over that envelope with the list of names. I mean, what was the thinking behind it?"

I clicked my tongue and shook my head. "Leroy," I said.

"I *told* you the only boy I recognized was William. Now you wouldn't want me to fib, would you?"

"But Prettybelle," says Leroy, still humble, "could I just ask you one more question?"

"You just go ahead ask it," I said kindly.

"Howcome you didn't name William?"

Well, that was a good question, and I shook my head. "Leroy," I said. "I vow, the only answer I can give you is this. Every time the name WILLIAM comes into my mouth, ANOTHER name simply takes over in its place. Now that's the truth, and it's a funny thing."

"And what name is that, Prettybelle?" says Leroy.

"Well, Leroy," I said, "that name is SKEETER. You remember him? That's Lily's OTHER boy."

"Lily's other boy," says Leroy.

"That's right," I said. "Whenever I might try to say WILLIAM all I can think of is SKKKEEETER. Well," I said, "I surely can't name Skeeter, because he's dead."

"That's right," says Leroy. "He's dead. Got drownded."

"Mm," I said. "Got SHOT," I said.

"Drownded," said Leroy.

"I'm only quoting what you *told* me, Leroy!" I said. "Got shot, you told me. Got drownded—that's what you told LILY."

"Well, damn it, he did get drownded," explodes Leroy "Got shot, and then got drownded. Is that all right with YOU? I mean, he got drownded in the god damn river."

"Got CHASED into the god damn river," I said.

"Prettybelle," said Leroy, irritably. "That boy got chased into the river by a Law Officer doing his duty. That boy stole. Stole a bun right off a bakery truck."

"Standing *alongside* a boy that stole a bun right off the bakery truck. That's what you TOLD me, honey."

"Well, I don't know WHAT the hell I told you," says Leroy, trying to hold on to himself. "But I ask you this, Miss Belle. How the hell is that officer going to tell one nigger from another nigger in the dark of the night?"

I just didn't say a word.

"Oh for the love of Pete," says Leroy. "*I* didn't do it. Way YOU act, you'd think I did it!"

"Oh Leroy," I said. "I know you didn't do it. All you did was laugh."

Leroy clicked his tongue. "When I *laughed*," he said patiently, "I did not know that it was Lily's boy. Shu!" exclaimed Leroy, shaking his head. "How about that! If that isn't a woman, for you!"

I just sat tight-lipped and poker-faced.

"Prettybelle," says Leroy, "I am not going to stand here and BICKER. Wasting precious time! Reasoning with a woman," he said, for all the world like Granpa Beesly, "is like reasoning with the Four Winds and a Mule. I am not going to ARGUE, Prettybelle. I am going to TELL you. And you just TRY to take it in. But if you CAN'T take it in, then just take my word for it. Hear?"

"Mmm," I said.

"There is a Land of Dreams and there is Dirty Reality, Prettybelle," says Leroy. "And you live in one, and I live in the OTHER."

"Is that so," I said, interested and cordial. "I mean, you *still* do?"

He ignored me. "In the Land of Dreams, Prettybelle, everybody's nice and everybody's got money and a job and a nice house, free and equal, all that jazz. The flowers are blooming and the sun is shining and the dogs don't catch rabbits anymore."

"A-men," I said. "Speed that day."

"Oh, is that so?" says Leroy. "Well, if the dogs don't catch rabbits, the rabbits going to multiply and eat up all the crops, and folks going to starve. What do you say to that?"

Silence seemed the wisest argument.

"That is called ree-ality, Prettybelle, and you don't like it, that's too bad, all I can say. Cause it sure as hell ain't going *away*. You with me so far?"

"I follow you, Leroy."

"That's the way the good Lord arranged it," says Leroy. "And now we get to Nigras."

Well, I fetched a sigh. "Leroy, I don't feel good," I said. "I don't feel good at ALL. Can't we just chat some other time?"

"The time is NOW," says Leroy. "And we will go from the general to the particular. We will move from my point of view to your point of view, and I will prove to you that you are wrong even from your OWN point of view."

"I declare, Leroy, I'm not up to it. I have this awful headache," I said, "and anyway, I truly KNOW all that stuff, I have heard it since I was in the cradle. I mean, how they are naturally inferior, and smell bad and first cousins to the baboon and no I.Q. and statistics show and the Bible says and evolution proves, and on and on, the Glory of Ancient Greece, and what-all," I said. "And also, in Cachattow County, they outnumber us, and do I want a nigger sheriff, a nigger government telling us what to do? do I want to be a washerwoman in a Nigra family, and have Saralizabeth marry one? Might as well save precious time, Leroy, like you said."

And when he opened his mouth, I interrupted him once more.

"I also know, Leroy, how *happy* they were till Washington and the Reds and *The New York Times* stirred them all up. And the riots up North. Give em an inch and they take a mile. It's us or them. Right, Leroy?"

Well, he WAS disconcerted, I can tell you. And he stuck out his chin, and said, "Well, what you got to answer to all that? What's your answer? What's your answer?"

"Well, my answer is very simple!" I said, shrugging my shoulders. "My answer is, *Fiddlefaddle.*"

I vow, I was well-nigh overcome by the extent and daring of my newfound courage.

"Fiddlefaddle," echoed Leroy.

"All of it," I said. "Just fiddlefaddle."

"My wife," said Leroy. "My WIFE!"

"Widow," I said. And Reader, I was so dazzled by my courage and audacity that I did not stop. "FURTHER-MORE," I said, "*I am leaving all my money to the N Double A C P, and it was ME sent William to school up North!*"

Well, Reader, I had gone too far. There was a roar and a rush and the air turned all blood-red. Leroy swelled up until he filled the whole room, and I was being suffocated and crushed to death! And I uttered this terrible loud cry of despair which they must surely have heard upstairs, and started throwing things. I knocked over the gun rack and kicked the guns. I threw everything off the desk. I threw an inkwell and a heavy glass ashtray. I threw a silver golf cup and a bronze pointer and a souvenir aircraft carrier. I pushed over the chairs and the lamp and at last I hit him squarely in his vast soft swollen face with a decoy duck, and he disappeared.

He did. But at that moment, Reader, a convulsion or electrical shock seized me and my body shuddered and shook and convulsed itself and it fell down thump! upon the oval braided rug. Yes. I lay sprawled out in the most peculiar and unnatural position, my head thrown back and my arms askew, frozen and paralyzed. Yes. And it scarcely seemed like me at all, but it was. And I thought, *I have had a stroke, I have had a stroke. Like Lily, I have had a stroke!*

As I lay there on the floor, I heard or thought I heard the thunder and the wind come back, and I remembered when I was little how I loved the spring and summer storms, and how I would take off my dress and run outside in just my panties and my barefoot sandals. I would run in the wild rain and wind, and my heart would swell, and I would run under all the mighty trees with their great strong limbs madly tossing and swishing, raging and swirling amidst the terrible crash of thunder and the fierce merciless swift lightning, and I felt I was a part of it, I just absorbed its power into ME, yes, running in the storm all unafraid and mighty. Oh, I did love that. And then I would run home all wet and shivering and spent, and Alice would scold me and wrap me in a big warm towel and dry my wet bedraggled hair and declare she didn't know what I was thinking of. I would stand skinny and shivering and naked on a newspaper, sucking a wet string of hair, while she rubbed me down with a big soft towel and scolded, and then she fed me good hot soup.

Yes I lay there on the braided rug, Reader, and my brain was mushy and delirious, and it kept saying over and over like a stuck Victrola, *Lily, pick me up, why don't you pick me up?* And it said, *Lily, Lucy, Dessie, Pearl—Alice, Queenie, Lucy, Lil.* Maid names and cook names, like in a rhyme. My brain simply stewed and simmered in a kind of twilight state. *Oh, Alice, were I but a babe again* was its main theme. Yes. Were I but a babe so I could sleep upon your lap once more, fussed over and scolded! In a nice warm kitchen full of good smells from the oven. *Oh, Alice, Lucy, tuck me in,* my foolish brain kept saying. Put me to sleep and hear my prayers. Make me a good girl. (*Do Lawd!*) Lily, put me to bed and tell me what to do. I wish I could sleep and never wake up. I wish I had never grown to woman's estate. Yes, oh yes. I wish all things were different than they are. Oh sleep. Yes, slumber and sleep, under soft warm covers. Hear my prayers, Lily. Singing in the kitchen, that high wild voice. Whoever heard those hymns before? High wild hymns. Singing, ironing. Ironing, singing. *Apologize,* said Mama.

If I should die before I wake, I pray the Lord my soul to take. And God Bless Mama, Sister, Granpa, Aunt Millie Lou Ruffle and Papa in heaven. And my doll and my teddy bear and my cat Lady. And make me a good girl.

Do, Lawd! said Alice.

Make me a good girl.

Alice Lucy Dessie Lil, bless me now that I am ill.

Get down, Miss Belle. You too big to climb up on my lap!

It's just a game, Lily, can't you see? Lemme up on your lap, it's just a game.

You too big, Miss Belle, too big.

And I lay there on the braided rug until they found me, and there was a fuss and they carried me off to the hospital which by this time I was in no shape to object to. In fact, it was all right with me. Peace, Lord. Just to sleep in peace.

END TENTH INSTALLMENT

Billy Black Is Captured

Reader, I interrupt my narrative briefly to report that, in the opinion of Dr. Dimmer, I have not been writing exactly what he had in mind. He says can't I just write some simple pleasing verses that would *stand alone* so that the *Pummicami Gazette* could publish them?

Well, I told him the *Pummicami Gazette* would have gladly published my whole story, verses or no verses, had not *someone* vetoed it. "What's the matter?" I said. "Isn't it lively enough?" He said it was lively enough, and possibly too lively, it might upset certain patients. Well, I told him Mrs. Ethel Wilcox liked my story fine, and she is Fiction Editor of the *Gazette,* and despite her warfare with the C.I.A. she is a gifted, highly educated lady, who taught English at three different colleges. Her plan is to quit the *Gazette* and found a *Pummicami Literary Quarterly* of poems, stories and politics. Mrs. Wilcox may be somewhat paranoid but she is on friendly terms with countless famous writers and calls them by their first names, and they owe her money, and she says she will have no trouble at all getting MSS from all over! And even in such brilliant company, she says she will start publishing *my story* right away! First issue! She says it is rough but it has quality.

Well, Dr. Dimmer hears this and true to form pulls this long wet face, and starts tearing down the whole project, all the while *pretending* benignly to approve! Well isn't that nice, he says, but all the same . . . if he were me . . . he wouldn't count *too* far on Ethel Wilcox.

I said, "Dr. Dimmer, you don't know Mrs. Wilcox if you say that. Is she your patient?" And he said no, she was Dr. Gamely's patient. And I said, "There, you see? Mrs. Wilcox will publish that magazine if she has to write out all the copies longhand!"

And I fetched my hand from behind my back, bursting with pride, and I showed him what I had been hiding, and it was VOLUME ONE NUMBER ONE of the *Pummicami Literary Quarterly*, done underground on a hospital Xerox machine. And on its cover it said in big letters:

Beginning this Issue:

RAPE OF THE
SWEET WOMEN:
MY STORY

by Annabelle Sweet!

Well, Dr. Dimmer's face was a study. He looked it over carefully, and I swear, he was put out.

I said, "You see, here is a poem by Robert Lowell and a poem by Allen Tate and an article by Paul Goodman, *as well as* autobiography by me."

"That's very nice," said Dr. Dimmer. "How very nice. But are they not simply copied from other magazines?"

And he said, "Are you positive it was Ethel Wilcox produced this magazine, and NOT PRETTYBELLE SWEET?"

I had to twinkle, and I said, "Well, Dr. Dimmer that's for us to know and you to find out, but you will observe Mrs. Wilcox has her name on the masthead and a lovely short story in the Faulkner manner beginning on page 17."

Reader, I vow, I am fond of that man, but he is not easy to get along with. He has this true disagreeable streak, and it simply permeates our conversations. I mean, I try and try to please him, and I NEVER succeed.

Now, for example. He says he wants a poem to "stand alone." So I bring him in the following, which I started before coming to Pummicami. I work on it real hard and polish it up and bring it in. And it is called "Ballad of the Black Prince" because it is about little Nigra children before they learn what color they are. I hear it sung to a guitar, all broody and sad and lonely.

BALLAD OF THE BLACK PRINCE

Long ago in another world
Now sunk below the sea
A child was born—a boy—a prince!
And they held a jubilee.
They held a jubilee.

Oh the leaves never dropped in those days,
The river was full of fish.
The frost when it came in those days
Was gentle as you could wish.

The boy grew handsome, proud and kind,
His body straight and strong,

And everybody applauded his bright sayings
Whether right or wrong,
Whether right or wrong.

Oh the leaves never dropped in those days,
The river was full of fish.
The frost when it came in those days
Was gentle as you could wish.

His daddy brave rode off to wars
Of conquest and of glory
And then came home with wondrous gifts
To tell the prince his story,
To tell the prince his story.

His mammy was a stately queen,
So beautiful and wise.
She smelled of cinnamon and sugar,
Black stars in her eyes,
Black stars in her eyes.

Oh the leaves never dropped in those days,
The river was full of fish.
The frost when it came in those days
Was gentle as you could wish.

The sun shone down and the prince would play
In the dirt beside the grass
When he slept the stars were crisp and cold
As bits of broken glass,
As bits of broken glass.

Daring he was, and unafraid,
He knew not Grief but Hope.
He breasted the wind on a silver tire
That swung from a golden rope,
That swung from a golden rope.

Oh the leaves never dropped in those days,
The river was full of fish.
The frost when it came in those days
Was gentle as you could wish.

In the warm weeds of the backyard
He played and dreamed of a day—
In the warm weeds of the backyard,
As he played, it vanished away,
His world, it vanished away.

A bitter storm blew down the sky
As cruel as man's contempt,
The silver tire turned to black,
The rope was only hemp,
The rope was knotted hemp.

Oh the leaves always drop in these days,
The river is running with blood,
The frost when it comes in these days
Is cruel as any god,
Is bitter as any god.

But long ago in another world
Now sunk below the sea
A child was born—a boy—a prince!
And they held a jubilee.
They held a jubilee.

Well, Reader, I bring this Ballad in to Dr. Dimmer, I
hand it to him, and I breathlessly await my morsel of
praise. For personally this Ballad simply brings tears to my
eyes, especially when I hear it sung in my mind's ear, so to
speak, in some lovely pure voice to a lonely sad guitar.

And what does Dr. Dimmer say?

He says, "Very nice, Mrs. Sweet. Very nice indeed. I think the *Gazette* might publish this." So far so good, until he adds: "But of course, it is NOT about Nigras."

Well, I ask you. Can you make that man out?

I laughed and said, "I wrote it, didn't I, and it IS TOO about Nigras."

He says it is not about Nigras, but secretly about me myself. Implication:—kind, unselfish thoughts and deeds simply do not exist upon this earth—only mean and self-pitying ones in various disguises! Well, I deny that, and I always will, to my last breath. And I told him so.

Well, he says, had I by any chance observed that the *outset* of my Ballad and its *rhythm* bear a striking resemblance to a certain poem by Edgar Allan Poe? And the NAME of that poem (he says portentously) is ANNABELLE LEE. Which of course happens to be my own first and middle name. Well now, that was supposed to PROVE something, I reckon! (Not to me!)

And so—back to my story.

You will recall, Reader, that Prettybelle in some kind of stroke or fit had fallen, twisted and askew, upon the braided rug in Leroy's den, having been *hounded past endurance* by one and all, including her late husband. And they found her there and whisked her off to the hospital in an ambulance. I refer, of course, to the regular or normal hospital, not Pummicami where I presently reside and where Dr. Dimmer hacks away at my various and flourishing complexes and manias after his fashion—which is surely an inefficient fashion to my mind, being nothing more or less than weekly chats, about as therapeutic as a tea party.

The name of this normal hospital is Merihew General, and yes it is named after kin of Mother Sweet's own beloved Granpa Merihew. I am taken there in an ambulance, and Doc Cunningham appears, out of breath, and he pokes and prods me and he comes up baffled, haunted by the painful notion that Prettybelle Sweet is playing possum. But Reader I am not playing possum at all. My right arm and hand are truly paralyzed and so is my voice! Prettybelle Sweet cannot utter a word.

I am put to bed in a delectably comfortable and air-conditioned semiprivate room, where I am waited on hand and foot, and where I sleep, sleep, sleep.

Well, next morning, Doc Cunningham wakes me up and sits down beside my bed with a quizzical look on his face, and says, "Now Miss Belle! Let's have another look at you."

Well, I yawn and stretch and snuggle into the covers, and yearn for more sleep, but I reluctantly and obediently sit up on the edge of the bed as he directs me to. Then he tests all my reflexes, and I have to admit I jumped, twitched and tickled in fine fettle, which he pointed out.

And then, suddenly, he lets out a holler, and says "OH LOOK THERE!" pointing behind me, and I turn with a start, and I look, but of course I cannot talk, so I turned back to him and with my lips I formed the word WHERE?

And he frowned. Reader, he frowned, and I realized he had set me a trap. Well, it hurt.

"Miss Belle," says Doc Cunningham, "I got to tell you something. Your neighbor here in this bed, she says you talked in your sleep all night, she says you talked and carried on so much she couldn't hardly get a wink."

Well, I declare. Now why would anybody tell such lies?

With my left hand, I pushed back the white curtain that shielded me from this neighbor of mine, whom I had indeed scarcely been AWARE of, and there she was, all fat and flabby and white-haired, reading *Good Housekeeping* magazine, and was she embarrassed? She was not. She just looked at me and waved. Yes, she waved. Well, I dropped the cloth in a hurry, for this lady had a sarcastic and malicious eye, and how could I defend myself? How could I denounce her, voiceless as I was?

Well, I shook my head, and looked at old Doc Cunningham reproachfully, and the tears came up.

"And your right hand," says Doc Cunningham, "all those fingers and nerves are fit as a fiddle. Why you could knit me a pair of Argyle socks," he says. "Miz Sweet, all's wrong with you is strain. Now, move that arm. Come on, move it."

But Reader, I could not move it. Doc Cunningham kept scolding me in a fatherly way as if I were two years old, and I just sat and pouted and the tears coursed down my cheeks. Too much!

Well, he scratched his nose.

And after a bit, he took out a big needle, and said, "Miss Belle, I'll take a blood sample." And he held my right hand, and he stuck that needle right into the back of my hand. And he scrunched that needle here, and he pushed it there, and he said, "My, my where IS that vein?" And he looked at me sharp.

And I sat there cool and sorrowful, because it did not hurt me one bit.

Well, after that, he called in two other doctors and they all three test me, and wire me to machinery, and poke me and prod me and take my blood and measure this and measure that, and finally they determine that I have indeed had a small stroke of some sort, which I could have told them to begin with. And they let me go back to sleep.

Outside a cruel wind was blowing, but I would think about that tomorrow, and I went back to sleep. Sheer cowardice, Reader.

> *The coward sleeps and dreams of heaven;*
> *The brave man sets his clock for seven.*

I was not about to set my clock for anything, and I woke up only with the greatest reluctance, hours later, to the blare of television.

My friendly neighbor lady had rented a hospital TV and she had turned the news up very loud and naturally that news was all about my rape. Well, I closed my eyes and put the pillow on my head. I activated an internal jamming system and garbled all the words. But one thing did come through: *Billy Black had not been found!*

The manhunt had not found its quarry. Well, that was music to my ears. I jammed the rest, and I felt my heart at peace. I thought, he is far away in Chicago by this time! Soon everything will blow over and be forgotten, and Lily will come back to work. So I went back to sleep.

Next time I woke up it was morning, and a sweet little red-haired nurse persuaded me to eat a morsel or two and relieve myself, and she showed me all the flowers. There were flowers from just everybody, all the neighbors and Sheriff Peabody and from my own daughter Saralizabeth. And Lord, I even got two dozen roses—yes, two DOZEN red roses—from that repulsive Mr. Wimbly with a note about what a brave and noble little lady I was and how I had his sincerest admiration and sympathy. Well, I tell you, my speech almost returned at that, and I told my nurse in pantomime to GET THOSE ROSES OUT of here, which she did, in the apparent belief I was allergic. Which indeed I was. And I went back to sleep.

The third time I woke up, the nurses were shaking me and saying brightly, "Miz Sweet, you got a visitor!"

Well, I looked up from bleary sleep-filled eyes and there in the doorway holding his hat in his fist was Sheriff Peabody with a great big hopeful smile. And at the sight of *him*, Reader, I simply FELL back asleep with a clunk, and all their efforts to arouse me were unavailing.

Reader, I slept, and they let me, for three days. Oh sleep is an amazing phenomenon, and I would surely write a good long poem about it, save that certain other poets have beat me to it, including Shakespeare. Yet, Reader, it is foolish to be overawed. I mean, there is room on this earth for all, thank God. Even the ant is perfect in his antlike way. Yes. And the roar of the yellow lion does not deny the ant, nor does the mighty computer or the great jet plane deny one single small soft pussycat preening and licking itself in a patch of sunshine vain as she can be.

Therefore I present this, Reader, not as a poem, but as a passing Thought:

> *Sleep is where you can always go*
> *When it's raining rain and snowing snow.*

Is it not curious that of two human beings with the same afflictions (GUILT for example) one will suffer from insomnia and the other sleep around the clock? I mean, Macbeth on one hand, and Prettybelle on the other?

I vow I would have spent the rest of my life abed, but alas Merihew General Hospital had other ideas. After three days, the nurses routed me out, forced me to exercise and walk down the hall, even though everybody was peeping out at me with the most intense curiosity. All those pallid faces in all those pallid beds, raised up on stalks, so many mushrooms. Lord! And on the fifth day they told me I had to go home. "You'll be better off at home Miz Sweet, with that lovely daughter nursing you."

So they said; and they put me out into the heat. Well, I thought, it could be worse. At least—voiceless and para-lyzed as I am—folks will leave me alone and not plague me with their blame questions. . . . And willy-nilly home I went to be nursed by my lovely daughter. Yes.

But Lord, what did I find! Without Lily and without me, the house had simply fallen to rack and ruin. Papers and dirty dishes all over the living room. Bathroom basins sticky with dirt! Clothes lying here and there, furniture out of place, the dogs starving. Saralizabeth had been living happily on peanut butter sandwiches and scrambled eggs, and Mother Sweet on Coke and cookies and tomato soup. Well, I was not about to surrender to that kind of slovenly approach. But how was I to cope, one-handed?

Reader, can you wash dishes one-handed? Can you open a can one-handed? Can you skin a carrot? Without cans and carrots, what hope for a balanced diet? Well, the dishes were piled up in the filthy sink, and cockroaches had sprung from nowhere, and garbage was oozing out of three waxed garbage bags, and in the backyard the dogs were howling with hunger like the voice of *doom, doom, doom,* to the House of Leroy Sweet.

Those animals!

Well, I found Saralizabeth and tugged her by her dress into the kitchen, despite her protests, and I pointed to the Dog Food.

And with my lips I said to her (and she understood me too), I said, "You may starve your *mother* if you will, but at least go out and feed your *daddy's dogs*."

And she said, like they do, "In a *minute*, Mother." And then naturally, she went off and never did come back. Well, the dogs were howling so loud that at last I simply one-handedly stabbed a hole in a great sack of Dog-Meal, and I dragged and hauled that great sack outdoors and over to the pen. And Lord you have never heard such barking yelping howling, or seen such dashing leaping struggling. I vow, I was petrified of those great hounds. Well, I set the sack down and with my one poor hand I managed to open the gate a crack, intending to somehow shove the Dog-Meal inside, thinking, Well, with their sharp teeth they surely can rip the bag apart, for I cannot! But the minute I got the gate ajar, Lord, OUT they came, the whole pack of them, tumbling and rushing and snarling and raging, they burst right out of the pen and they knocked me flat into the dirt. They knocked me flat into the mud and they stepped all over me, and I thought my hour had come. They found the bag of meal and began fighting over it and snarling, and I managed to roll out of their way, covered with muddy footprints, as well as scrapes and scratches. Oh I cannot abide those dogs. In my opinion they are killers. I mean, like Mr. Wimbly they will wag their tails and act all loving and respectful but they would tear you limb from limb given the slightest opportunity. Well, the Dog-Meal went scattering to the four winds amid that struggling seething knot of hound-flesh, and I simply burst into tears. Reader, I sat there in the mud and wept, and then I crawled back into the house tear-stained and filthy, and went upstairs to take a shower.

But Lord, can you take a shower one-handed? Can you undo your skirt, take off your blouse? It cost me seven minutes by the clock to undo my brassiere, and could I ever get it *on* again? Could I pin up my hair? put on the shower cap? Well, at long length I did, and got into the shower and it was too hot and then too cold, and inside the shower curtain was an enormous hairy spider looking at me. Well, that spider was the end.

I leaped out of the shower, slipped, burst into more tears, and I said to myself, Prettybelle, you are *going* to move that arm. And I tried and tried, and grunted and sweated, and it moved a bit, and a bit more, and Lo and Behold, I could move my arm! Well, I was so encouraged that I said to myself, Prettybelle, you are GOING to recover your voice. And I tried and tried, and I husked, and I whispered *cat*, and I croaked *cat*, and then I said it right out, "*Cat!*" And Halleluja! Whew!

Thank the Lord that is over with, said I.

However, I did determine to PRETEND to be voiceless and one-handed—until everything blew over.

Reader, I was so sure everything would blow over! Just hold out a little longer, I thought. Billy Black is one thousand miles away, and soon it will all blow over. Lily will come back, and I can find my purity again.

So I believed. And Billy Black COULD have escaped back North if he had really tried. Oh I knew they set up roadblocks and all, but he could have done it if he'd tried. He could have spared us! Well, it was not to be.

That very evening as I crept downstairs after my nap I heard the voice of Huntley Brinkley discussing my rape, and there upon the screen was me myself! I tried to turn my eye away, but I was held. Great God, I thought, it's me, on Huntley Brinkley coast to coast! And I sank into a chair. I sank right down beside Saralizabeth and Mother Sweet who were already rapt with attention, and I watched from start to finish.

There on the screen was Prettybelle Sweet her own self,

tottering out of Merihew General Hospital! So *that's* what I look like, I said to myself. And I looked pretty good! I mean, not so old and beat-up as you might expect. I looked somewhat sad and spiritual, but I vow I looked right *young!* All that sleep, no doubt. Well, I disappeared into the car, and we watched me drive away.

And then, Lord, we see our street, our very house, and there's some neighbors, and police, and the courthouse, and Darkytown, and something or other is on fire, and then we come back to our own living room. Well, do you know, on television, our living room looked downright tacky. Leroy's portrait was all askew, and that sorry old brass lamp I've been vowing to throw out for the last ten years, oh it showed up in all its glory, wouldn't you know. And they showed Mother Sweet, who was absolutely hilarious, chewing her cud the way she does, and looking very wise out of her little old gray eyes. And then an interview with Saralizabeth, and you could tell the cameraman liked HER all right, for he did her more than justice, closeup and full-figure both, and she surely did look cute, but as for talking, she hadn't much to say, except the usual, how she surely was *lucky* to escape when both her Mama and her Granma, etc.

And then, Reader, oh then to my horror, they showed this big police car drive up through the darkness to the county jail, and out pile some policemen, dragging with them three captive Nigra boys. And one of them is surely Billy Black. I peer at that screen. And it is!—Oh Lily! It's him all right, Billy Black has been captured. My womb contracts into a stone. He has not escaped up North at all, he is captured and in jail.

As the policemen shoved and hurried those boys inside, the camera zoomed up real close, and Billy Black kind of turned his face toward it, and looked out of the corner of his eye, and Reader, he was looking square at me. He was. Oh my heart jumped. Of course, he was looking at the camera and not at me in reality, but the way it felt, he was looking directly in my eye.

Reader, I did not have time to take this in before Mrs. Loomis's girl Carrie appeared on the screen, and poor ignorant little creature, she was terrified and trying not to cry. And I guess she must have turned him in and betrayed him, or else somebody claimed she had, for she kept on denying it, saying how she *hadn't* told on him, that he *wanted* to give up, that he himself *made* her go out and get the police.

And next a nice-looking well-dressed young white man came on, and spoke for Billy Black, and said he was a lawyer and there was no case against Billy Black. He said it was a plain obvious political frame-up on account of the Voter Registration Drive. Well, I declare!

But Sheriff Peabody came on to deny that, and his Adam's apple bobbled coast to coast, and he said about Billy Black: "Oh he's the one, all right, him and the others. Oh we got 'em now, all right."

And then in a twinkling we are back in New York, where Chet Huntley comments that Mrs. Sweet has still not told *her* version of events since she was still in shock, and that her testimony was considered crucial. And we move on into a commercial for trapped stomach gas.

Oh, I was left gasping and horror-struck. All I could see was those leaping flames in Darkytown (was it a church?) and those three handcuffed boys hustled quickly into jail, past a hundred hostile white faces, and how small they looked, small and surrounded, and their heads all bloody, and then Billy turning round like that, just as they shoved him in the door, and looking at me in the eye.

Well, I crept on back upstairs and into bed again, and I pulled up the sheet. I thought, *I should be* GLAD *they caught him.* And I thought, *I am, I'm glad. I'm* GLAD *they caught him.* Yes, sir.

And then I thought, Well, I could shoot myself with one of Leroy's guns. I could put it in my mouth and pull the trigger with my toes, and I bet I could do it if I tried.

And I thought, Oh shame on you, Prettybelle, trying to weasel out. I remembered the time I poured the pitcher of water off the porch roof right on the lady with the fancy hat, and how the lady came and rang our doorbell all furious, and nobody was home but Alice, and Alice came looking for me. And I hid in the clothes hamper, and Alice looked everywhere but she didn't think of the clothes hamper, and she went back and said, "No ma'am, that child not home, can't find her no place," and the woman's furious voice about her hat as if Alice had done it, and Alice saying, "Yes'm."

Make me a good girl.

Now listen here, Prettybelle, I told myself. Just calm yourself and steel yourself. They've got no case against those boys unless you talk. What case have they got? No case! They need your testimony. They need YOU. Isn't that what Huntley Brinkley said? Isn't that what Leroy knew? Why else would he come back from the grave tormenting you to tell? All you got to do, Prettybelle Sweet, is hold your tongue. And everything will STILL blow over. Yes! Hope is not lost. Just hold your tongue. Do not let them trap you. Do not say one word. Hold tight. Hold fast.

END ELEVENTH INSTALLMENT

The Trial,
or,
A Wound in the
Side of the South

Reader, I did hold fast. Day after day, one day at a time, I held on, I held fast. But Lord, do you think it was easy?

Besieged and bombarded by questions, morning and evening, day after day, not only from Sheriff Peabody but also from lawyers, policemen, reporters, neighbors, relatives, and delivery boys? Why, hardened criminals break down under pressure like that. I mean, who was I to fight off single-handed all the Armies of the Law? The best brains in the county were working and plotting day and night to outwit poor Prettybelle. Nobody cared at all how sick I was, and from every side I felt these ominous dark forces gathering. For if they couldn't outwit me, well, they could force me, couldn't they? That was my nightmare. They could seize and overwhelm me, throw me down. Force open my mouth and jam a microphone right down my throat. They could *make* me talk. I dreamed about it night after night. And how I fought them in my dreams, like a tigress. And every morning I would wake more weary than the last, and closer to despair. Reader, one little slip and all would be lost. My lovely feeling, my purity, my virginity (which only *came* as a result of that rape anyways) would vanish forever, all Accounts would be Unpaid again, and I would die die die of misery. Oh Lord I was confused. I mean, who was the victim? And victim of exactly what? Like we said in second grade, *Button button who's got the safety pin?* That's how it was, Reader, all dark confusion and ominous gathering storm.

Yet somehow I held fast. Somehow by miracle I did hold fast, and Nature aided me in its mysterious way. For everytime I forgot myself and started to answer a question, I got that spasm in my tongue, which simply froze and locked in place! And everytime I slipped and started to give the game away by pointing to a photograph the way they wanted, or by nodding my head yes, that spasm seized my *neck* and froze and twisted IT. Yes. And Old Doc Cunningham said there was a name for that, and it was a true disease called *torticollis.* (Latin for twisted neck.) And other people have it besides me.

Thus aided by nature, I held fast. And I tell you, it baffled them. It did. It baffled and stymied them. And in the Jail, Billy Black also kept silent. Try as they might, they could not persuade that boy to confess his crime, nor would his friends confess. But even so they held them, they charged them with my Rape, and they prepared for trial.

Lord, I could not help but think: if only things were as they used to be! Bad as that was, it was better than this. Was Leroy right? Leave Well Enough Alone, he said. Preserve the old, beware the new, lest doom and disaster fall upon your head and house—and everybody else's head and house. I remember him pointing out those first little Nigra girls who integrated the school. Two darling little good girls, so clean and neat in their starched and faded dresses, and their hair all neatly braided by their mamas, oh those good little dear little girls brought up so neat and proper, told by their mamas *you be nice and folks will treat you nice!*—and they believed it and trusted in it—and then got sent to integrate the school. How could they understand what happened? Hated, spat on, and despised! What had they ever done, the bewildered little things? All they'd done their whole life long was love their mamas and be good. Yes, Leroy pointed out those little girls, and said, "Now see? See how they *suffering?*"

Oh Lord, if only Leroy hadn't died, none of this would have happened. If I'd watched his diet, counted his cholesterol! Did I? I did not. Did I ever say, "Don't smoke, Leroy!" No, I did not say it. I would watch him, chain-smoking those Camel cigarettes, stuffing himself with gravy, cakes, and pie, and I would think, My, my, Leroy, that's going to kill you one day. But I never said it. I even urged him on. I said, "HAVE some more pie, Leroy. HAVE another piece of cake." And now look. Billy in jail and Lily sick, and me raped, Alice crying, the children all gone bad or dead, Darkytown burning to the ground, and no way out whatsoever anywhere, and my own mama standing over me all huge and angry saying, *See what you've done?*

Thus the bitter days went by. And at last the day arrived to go to Court.

Reader, we all three had to go, me and Saralizabeth and Mother Sweet, and I do believe it was not a true Trial—despite the title of this Installment—but something called a Hearing, which is like a little trial with only a judge, and the Judge was Collie Meggs. Now the point of this Hearing was to discover if the Prosecution had a case. If it didn't, why Judge Collie Meggs would throw everybody out of court! He'd have to. Like in Perry Mason. And oh this was my fervent hope and prayer.

For how could they possibly convict Billy Black without his Confession or my Charge. Oh, I am not naive. I knew they wanted Billy Black to hang, and wanted it bad. I also knew, with Granpa Beesly, "When the Fox is judge, the Chicken is found guilty." But on the other side was that great white glare of Publicity. Yes, those reporters from everywhere, those TV cameras. Why, Cachattow County itself was on trial as well as Billy Black, in a manner of speaking, and Governor Colship was reported to have sent a Private Memorandum to Sheriff Peabody and District Attorney Bragg, saying "Do it legal, boys. Hang him fair and square," or words to that effect. Even Leroy wanted them to be correct and proper. And why? To show they *could,* for one thing. And for another, to Read the Scripture from the pulpit: Coddling produceth crime, like we always told you.

Well, Sheriff Peabody came for us in the Sheriff's car and two police cars came along for escort. Me and Saralizabeth and Mother Sweet climbed into the back seat of the Sheriff's car like the Three Graces or the Three Weird Sisters or whatnot, and the photographers took photos of our hind ends climbing in. And off we set. When we got to the Courthouse I saw the reason we had three cars, because a mob was there, a true mob, folks milling around the doors and trying to get in, for all the world like a Western movie. They wanted to see "justice" done, no doubt, and Reader, my veins froze. For it was truly blood they wanted. *Hang him fast or we'll do it for you.* I simply scrunched down in the seat and put my fingers over my eyes and my thumbs into my ears. And we went round back, and whisk, they hauled us out of the car and got us inside mighty fast, al-most too fast for the photographers, but not quite.

Mother Sweet gave a bit of trouble, dragging her feet and squawking her old head off how she had to go back home and change. Somebody gave her the wrong shoe, she hollered. And sure enough, she was wearing one black shoe and one brown, and naturally it was all *my* fault, or else Saralizabeth's fault, depending on which one of us was closer to hand. (Never her *own* fault, Lord no, never all her life long anything her own fault. Well, you have to envy her, I swear! I do, I envy her, for I surely would like to be that way.) Anyways, nobody paid her the least mind on this occasion, mismatched shoes or no. And in we went, into the courtroom, and down we sat in three places saved especially for us, up front. Everybody looked at us.

Saralizabeth had washed her hair, which gleamed like the sun, and she was truly radiant and ravishing in spar-kling all-white piqué and a white headband. I wore a fitted dark-blue linen suit (uncrushable) over which a white lace collar peeped. Mother Sweet wore black, which was no doubt correct, but I avoided black, not wishing to empha-size my bereavement, and Saralizabeth avoided it in the belief that it turned her complexion sallow.

Well, I sat there not daring at first to raise my eyes from my lap, and I heard the sounds of the spectators behind me, jamming the courtroom, and I smelled them too, those hot bodies, and my heart shriveled and dried up like an old gnarled root, but still with some sap in it, still capable of hurt. And when I did glance up, Reader, who did I see across the room but Lily. Oh Lord.

Lily Black in her black dress and wearing my old hat with the pansies. And Reader, she had lost weight (as I had), and she looked tired and sick. But at least, I thought, at least her stroke wasn't serious, for she is up and about now, out of the hospital, able to come to court. Well, I tried to catch her eye, I just wanted to catch her eye and wave and smile, let her know no hard feelings. But she didn't look at me, not once. I swear she was real careful not to look. She just sat there heavy in her chair and stared into the air in front of her, not crying or twitching or showing any signs. My heart went out to her, for I knew her shame and misery. And I took strength from her dignity. Reader, she was dignity itself, and the only time she moved (and just her eyes) was when they came in with her son.

Yes, there arose this ugly murmur in the courtroom, and the marshals with their guns brought in bad Billy Black and two other boys (one of them the same that helped out in our house), and Billy Black had his face somewhat bruised, and also this big ugly scab on the side of his head behind the ear, which he kept lifting his hand to. I wondered, Did I do that? Did I scar him up like that? Or was it—something else? Reader, he looked at Lily and he met her eye, and he smiled at her, just a shadow of a grim smile. And I have to say, when he did that, I remembered other days and other smiles, when he was still the watermelon boy.

Oh I remembered. Like the time I gave him the golden windup locomotive. Him and Johnny playing on the kitchen floor at Christmas time, cute as they could be, one pink and yellow and the other black and brown, and both of them cutting silver paper to make Christmas chains. Cutting paper into strips and gluing them in little sloppy circles, gold and silver chains for the Christmas tree—to keep them busy, out of mischief. And Johnny said, Scrunch up like this. And Billy scrunched up, and Johnny wrapped him round with chains and said, You my slave. And Billy broke open the chains and said, I ain't no slave. And Johnny said, Look what you done, nigger, you broke my chains! and come at him with the scissors and stabbed him right in the cheek and red blood came out. And where was Lily? Out back hanging up the laundry. Well, I rushed over and I swatted that Johnny so hard that his teeth just rattled, and I picked that hurt child up and carried him to the bathroom and I washed the blood and put mercurochrome and a Band Aid on, and he stopped crying and he said I smelt so good. Well I was dressed up to go out and was all powder and perfume, and I gave him one of Johnny's toys, this golden windup locomotive. And his eyes were so big and he smiled his watermelon smile, and he held it in his hand. And I sent him on home and told him he was brave because he hardly cried at all. Well, Johnny screamed and howled for an hour, yes, all because I swatted him, and he told Leroy too, hoping I'd catch it, but Leroy was thinking about something else and said, Run on, son, I'm busy. And it was broken, don't you know. Yes. The golden windup locomotive. Johnny told me afterward, Ha ha it was broken anyway, he said. Ha ha.

Well, time will not stand still, and look at us now. Both him and Johnny gone to the bad, and that's the truth. They grow up, and they go wrong. So cute, they were, the brown one and the pink one. He wore Johnny's castaways. And those piping little voices, break your heart. Oh Lord, if only they stayed little! I wager Lily feels the same.

Bad though he was, I was pleased to see that Billy Black had a lawyer, that smart-looking young white man, too young maybe, in a neat gray suit. I reckon he was paid for by some Nigra group. In fact, maybe MY MONEY helped to pay for him, who knows! Reader, I declare, the ironies all round were thicker than pea soup.

Pretty soon everybody stood up, and Judge Collie Meggs came in. Yes, Collie Meggs the same that talked at Leroy's funeral. And he banged the gavel and declared court in session. Well, I had this knocking and this buzzing in my head, and I said, it isn't real, please Lord, it isn't real. But Lord pleased that it was real. It was Leroy's own Dirty Reality, and no escape, no escape for Prettybelle. No closet to hide in, no clothes hamper, no shotgun, no hospital bed. Well, just automatically I said, Make me a good girl, show me the way, and Alice replied as usual, *Do, Lawd!* My dried up, shriveled, and arthritic heart went pat pat pat, and I could feel my cheeks and neck break out in red blotches, the way they did when I was adolescent and nervous over something, like going to a dance or playing the Virgin Mary in the Christmas Pageant, or else an Angel. They always made me Her or else an Angel, and once I had to kneel and pose so long in my wings and halo that I simply fainted and had to be carried out. And the doctor held smelling salts under my nose and said, "Did you hear about the poor little kid in Darkytown born with four legs?" and I said, "Oh, no, oh no!" And he said, "But its mammy was a nanny goat so THAT's all right!" And ha ha ha.

"Your Honor, the only complication in this case," said District Attorney Bragg strutting up and down like a little barrel-shaped Napoleon "—aside from the nationwide ballyhoo that it's been getting, and the hordes and droves of UNINVITED GUESTS that we are entertaining and showing our Southern Hospitality to and of course we are glad to do it, despite the inconvenience to ourselves and the ingratitude our efforts have provoked—" (and he glared over at the Press) "—the only complication aside from that, Your Honor, is that the Victims of this abominable and revolting crime have been so damaged and so shocked, the outrage to their nervous systems has been so overpowering, that they have thus far been PHYSICALLY UNABLE to give testimony or deposition. I refer, of course, to Mrs. Leroy Sweet, widow of our late beloved Sheriff, and Mrs. Rawlings Sweet, his mother."

A reverential hush fell over the room at the very mention of our names, Reader, but I was not deceived. I knew full well everybody in that courtroom was looking at me and thinking, "By golly, she's been had by a nigger." I tell you, they were thinking of it in Living Color and full detail on CINERAMA, each one embroidering the scene according to his tastes. Well, I nearly died. I could feel seventeen more blotches bursting forth, and I must have looked in the last stages of pityriasis or roseola or bubonic plague, sweaty and hideous, and also my clothes simply hung on me as I had not eaten for a week. And when I finally lifted up my eyes——

God save the mark, my cup of gall ran over, for I saw *Clarence Wimbly* looking at me. Sitting amongst the spectators, calm and suave as you please, with his kindly crinkles and a couple of shaving nicks or whatever down one cheek, and Reader, I wanted to retch. I did, I simply wanted to retch. It was too much. The shame of it. My cup of gall was surely running over.

Well, this Mr. District Attorney Bragg continued his speech, saying how I had been unable to testify and name my assailants. "But we all know who they are," he said, "and they are sitting right HERE!" And he said he had every hope that this afternoon Mrs. Leroy Sweet would be in shape to testify.

So you THINK, I thought to myself.

"In fact," he said, "I believe I can ASSURE Your Honor, that she WILL TESTIFY!" And he bows in my direction and smiles, and makes a sweeping gesture. "In one way or another!" he adds, with heavy significance in his voice.

Well, she will NOT, I said hotly to myself, but my heart went *Scrunch!* What can he be planning? I thought. What trap has he set for me?

And then he sat down, having made his big effect and left everybody buzzing. The Defense Attorney now rose up, and he said with some passion that his clients were innocent, wholly innocent, and were the victims of Cachattow County's hysteria and sick moral climate. He said there was NO SCRAP OF REAL EVIDENCE TO LINK THEM WITH THE CRIME.

I breathed somewhat easier at that, and looked over at Mr. Bragg, but he seemed not the least dismayed, only smugger and rounder and more secure than ever.

And so it began. The courtroom was full to overflowing, as I said, and some folks I recognized and others I didn't. And a veritable wolf pack of reporters. You could tell them by their notebooks and pencils and secret tape recorders. Many of them were Yankees, you could tell that too. One of them particularly caught my eye and he was a corpulent man with a dark face and it doesn't mean I am prejudiced if I say he was plainly a Jew, I am the LAST person to be prejudiced, anyway this fat one kept looking around the courtroom and making notes on everything. And then he'd mop his forehead and make a note of THAT. And it was indeed stifling in there, Lord knows, no air conditioning and they even had to close the windows because of the noise and shouting made by the crowd outside. Well, I followed his eye, and he looked at the walls and the ceiling, and noted down the dirt and the peeling paint and the cracks, and I saw him also take in the Fly Paper, yes, three long rolls of it hanging from the ceiling, and you may be sure he made a fine long note on that, so the Yankees could feel good and superior. And then he followed the antics of a couple of flies and wrote about them, as a comment that even the Fly Paper didn't work, no doubt, and he scrutinized Judge Collie Meggs for the longest time, with his head on one side and then on the other, for all the world as if he were a talent scout and Judge Collie were Marilyn Monroe reborn. Well, he wrote reams about Collie, chuckling to himself, and then he turned to Billy Black, and his eyes grew stern and his fat face fell into round pouting bags of flesh, and he described Billy Black with great slashing notes, whether pro or con I cannot say, and then alas, it was MY turn, and so I can tell you no more about him, being forced to drop my eyes in modesty and acute embarrassment. I reckon he wrote, "The Victim appeared to be suffering from Scrofula." However, I composed myself as best I could and crossed my ankles, and broke out in more blotches, and forced myself to hold my hands still on my lap, and thanked the Lord I had remembered to wear my best white gloves, which neatly concealed the sweaty clammy hands inside. Lily had white gloves too, and Reader, she was just as much of a lady as I was, and likely more!

Ludie Lindley was the first witness, as I recall, and she told about the night of the Rape, and how I looked, and my cut lip, bruised face, and torn and bloody clothes, and the Defense waived cross-examination. Then came on one of the two State Troopers from that night, and his name was Stone, and he told what a mess my house was when he went inside, and everything he found there. A chair knocked over and the couch pillows on the floor, and three spots of wet blood upon the floor and couch.

"Was that blood examined?" says Mr. Bragg.

"Yes sir, it was," says Trooper Stone.

"Was it human blood?"

"It was, type B."

"Now Trooper Stone, do you happen to know the blood type of the Defendants here?"

"I do, sir."

"Was it the same?"

"It was the same as that of the Defendant William Black, sir."

Murmur amongst the spectators.

Well, Billy's lawyer cross-examined, and asked was blood type B a rare type? And the Trooper said, No. And he said, "What is Mrs. Sweet's blood type? Her daughter's blood type?" And the Trooper said he didn't know off-hand. "Then it could have been hers, or her daughter's?" And the Trooper says he reckoned it could for all he knew.

"About how many people have that type of blood, Trooper Stone?" says Billy's lawyer.

"I have no idea, sir. Several million, I reckon."

"No further questions."

Well, I figured this was a mighty victory for Billy's side, but no one seemed to react to it in any special way.

I think there were a couple more witnesses in there, but the next one I remember is old Doc Cunningham, and I do surely remember *him*, for reasons you will shortly understand.

Doc Cunningham takes the witness seat and he swears on the Bible to tell the truth, and you can see the whole business makes him wretchedly unhappy and miserable.

Under questioning, he tells Mr. Bragg how he found me on That Night. Contusions, cut lip, shock and hysterics, plainly the victim of a Criminal Assault. How he gave me a sedative and ordered me to bed, as we all know.

Well, this time Billy's lawyer gets up to ask a few questions himself, and cross-examine, and he is truly a sharp young man, but with this depressingly high schoolboyish voice, in sad contrast to Mr. Bragg's rich baritone which deeply rolls and echoes.

"Dr. Cunningham," says this youngster. "Did you examine Mrs. Sweet?"

"Of course I did, young man," says Old Doc. "What do you think I've been talking about?"

"I mean, did you examine her internally?"

Well, there was a lengthy pause.

"I—uh—examined Mrs. Sweet—to my own full satisfaction," says Doc Cunningham, at last.

"Did you examine her internally?" asks the lawyer once more, in his high voice.

"Well, she was upset."

"Then you did *not* examine her internally?"

"I didn't have to. It wasn't necessary."

"Why was it not necessary?"

"Because, damn it, I knew what I'd find."

"How did you know?"

"Why, she told me," says Doc Cunningham.

"She told you . . . then you are not personally sure whether the attack succeeded or did not succeed. That is, you have no *evidence* except her word."

"Now listen here! I've known Miss Belle for twenty years!" protested Old Doc, getting mad.

"I understand!" said the lawyer, and he took off in another direction. "Dr. Cunningham," he said, "is it not true that Mrs. Leroy Sweet spent four months and three weeks last year as a patient in Pummicami Mental Sanitarium?"

Now honestly! I thought. THAT's a dirty trick.

"Objection!" hollered Mr. Bragg. "Irrelevant and immaterial!"

Well, Judge Collie overruled him. Can you believe it? I vow, the D.A. looked at him all astonished and reproachful. But Collie did it, against his conscience I feel sure, out of downright curiosity. He wanted to know the answer. And so did everybody else, for they bated their breath.

"Well, I—believe she did," growled Dr. Cunningham. "Yes, she did."

"Is it not true that Mrs. Sweet is a *known alcoholic?*"

Gasps from all, including ME, I can tell you. I declare, I did not like that young man one bit, and I was glad and happy when Old Doc simply leaped to his feet and shouted,

"It is NOT true! It is a dastardly lie!"

"Well, what was it, then?" asks the lawyer. "You're her doctor. What sent her to the Sanitarium?"

"Why, it was nerves."

"Nerves," repeats the young man dryly.

"That's right."

"That is your diagnosis?"

"It is, young man, that's what it is."

"Have you ever read Freud, Dr. Cunningham?"

"No sir, I have not and proud of it," says Old Doc.

"Are you aware that a diagnosis of *nerves,* in this day and age, borders on the ridiculous?"

"OBJECTION!" snaps Mr. Bragg.

"Sustained," says Collie.

So Billy's lawyer went on:

"You say, then, that Mrs. Sweet is not and was not an alcoholic."

"That is correct."

"Did she drink to excess?"

"No, SIR! She did not."

(I heard Saralizabeth snort quietly beside me.)

"Well, sir, *did she drink?*"

Doc Cunningham puffed and sighed. "Young man," he said, "what this fine and charming lady did in the privacy of her own home in the company of her husband upon rare occasions of celebration or sorrow is her own affair and none of mine, and I know nothing whatever about it."

"And if you DID know—would you say?" says Billy's lawyer sarcastically.

"OBJECTION, Your Honor!"

"Sustained." And Collie thumped his gavel, and scolded Billy's lawyer, who apologized, and went on:

"Now Dr. Cunningham, on the day after the alleged assault, Mrs. Sweet was taken to Merihew General Hospital where she remained four days. Could you please describe what was wrong with her?"

"It was, uh, a presumed stroke."

"Presumed? A *presumed* stroke?"

"Well, yes, damn it, presumed! I called in two other doctors and they'll tell you the same."

"What do you mean by presumed stroke?"

"I mean, uh, the symptoms were there."

"The symptoms were there. But the tests—?"

"The, uh, tests were mixed."

"I see. The tests were not conclusive?"

"That's right."

"Mm. Mrs. Sweet was left with some aftereffects, is that correct?"

"Yes she was."

"Would you describe them?"

"Well, she has a paralyzed right forearm, a *torticollis* and a light paralysis of the . . ." (he cleared his throat) "the vocal cords."

"The vocal cords!"

"That's what I said."

"You mean, she can't talk?"

"Young fellow, you're mighty sharp in there!" says old Doc Cunningham.

Laughter.

"Now, are these conditions serious? That is, are they permanent?"

"Well, I don't know, sir."

"Is it possible they are *hysterical?*"

Old Doc squirmed and twisted.

"It's possible, I reckon," he said at last with a big sigh. "But what you don't know, young man, is that hysterical symptoms are very damn real to those that have 'em!"

"Well, yes sir, I do know that. But could these symptoms be faked? Could a clever person fake them?"

"OBJECTION!" shouts Mr. D.A., indignant as can be.

"Sustained," drones Collie.

"Let me put it another way. Could a shock bring on these conditions?"

"It's possible."

"Could another shock remove them?"

"It's possible."

"Or could they just disappear one morning?"

"It's possible."

Well, Billy's lawyer looked fairly triumphant at that, and as for me, I felt as if I had been stripped NUDE and exposed for all to see and to examine as they pleased. And my face simply FLAMED. I thought, Oh Lord, if I could only faint like when I was an angel, but no use, no use, for they would only fetch me back soon as I recovered and begin again. The mills of the gods were grinding, and Prettybelle Sweet was on her way to getting ground exceeding small. Nothing on earth could stop it.

Next witness called was Lily Black herself, poor heavy-hearted creature, so good, so weary.

She gave her name in this sweet soft humble voice of hers, and when asked what relative she was to William Black, she said, so gently, with that lilt they have,

"I is his mother."

Oh Reader, I felt so sorry for her, I felt so grieved.

"Now Lily," says Mr. Bragg, "I understand your son William has been up North? In Chicago?"

"Yes, sir."

"Been going to school up there, going to college, is that right?"

"Yes, sir."

"Came back home in early July."

"Yes, sir."

"Now what did he come back for?"

"To see his family, sir."

"And what else?" snaps Mr. Bragg.

"I doesn't know what ELSE," says Lily gently. "That's ALL, far as I knows."

"You're under oath," says Mr. Bragg coldly.

"Yes, sir, I knows that," says Lily.

"He came down here for the Nigra Voting Drive! Now isn't that true?"

And bless her heart, she's a religious woman, and she had sworn on the Book, but she lied for her son. She did.

"I doesn't know nothin' bout that," says Lily.

"He never told *you* to register?"

"No, sir."

"What about these papers found in your own house?" And Mr. Bragg shows some kind of fliers, and I reckon they were urging out the vote.

"In my house?" says Lily, surprised. "Oh, I doesn't think they belonged to HIM. Somebody sho' must have left them in my house, but not him."

Well, he intimidated her and yelled, trying to get her to admit it, but she just repeated her answers gentle as could be, until at last he turned to a new tack.

"On the night of the crime, after you went home from work, when did you next see your son?"

"Why, I saw him that same evening, long bout ten, leven o'clock."

"Did you ask him how his face got all scratched up?"

"OBJECTION!" shouts Billy's lawyer. "She never *said* his face was scratched! Your Honor——"

"Overruled," says Collie Meggs.

Lily sat there patient and placid, motionless.

"Well?" says Mr. D.A. "Did you ask him how his face got all cut up?"

"Oh no, sir," says Lily. "His face warn't all cut up. His face was fine."

"Look at him!" shouted Mr. Bragg. "We have in our files sworn testimony of ten witnesses that your son suffered those wounds BEFORE his capture. From the struggle with his victims. Are you telling this court that those ten witnesses have LIED?"

"Objection!" says Billy's lawyer. "Intimidation!"

"Overruled," says Collie Meggs. "But modulate your tone some, Mr. Bragg."

"Yes, Your Honor," says Mr. Bragg. "Are you saying those men lied?" he asked. "Those *policemen?*"

"Oh no, sir," says Lily. "I only says his face was fine, last I saw him, until now."

Well, he tried some more, but couldn't catch her. Then he pursed his lips, and thought, and asked,

"Lily, you got a key to the back door of the Sweet house, that right?"

"Yes, sir."

"Now Lily. After the crime, when the policemen came to talk to you, they asked you to produce that key. That right?"

"Yes, sir, they did."

"And you could not produce it."

"I knowed it was there, right in my purse," said Lily. "I knowed I *had* it, but I just couldn't lay my *hands* on it."

Mr. D.A. glances triumphantly at Collie Meggs, and also at the spectators. He kind of nods and sneers and looks sly and knowing.

"Oh," he says. "You just couldn't lay your hands on it."

"Yes, sir, that's right."

"But next day, you just happened to FIND it."

"Yes sir, I did. It was right there in my purse. It jus scrunched back inside the lining where it tore. Want me to show you? It slipped right inside the seam."

Oh Reader, the temptation to rush out to her and help her! To say, "I let him in! He rang, I let him in! He didn't use her key!" The temptation almost overcame me, but I drew back in time. For that was not the way to help. Oh, pitfalls and quicksand on every side!

"It wasn't that YOUR SON PUT THAT KEY BACK AFTER USING IT?" says Mr. Bragg sarcastically.

"Oh, no sir," says Lily in her soft voice. "That boy, he wouldn't ever hurt Miss Belle. He doos wrong things, but he wouldn't ever hurt Miss Belle. I knows my boy," she says. "I knows his way. That," she says, "am *not his way*."

Well, I wanted to cry. I choked up and my nose began to run, and I wanted to cry with all my heart, but Reader, they let Lily go, and they turned to *me*.

"Next witness, Mrs. Leroy Sweet."

Small sensation in the courtroom. I clutch my bosom, and shrink back, I gesture at my throat, but no use, I have to stand up. I have to walk across the floor, I have to step inside the witness booth.

Well, this is IT, Prettybelle Sweet, I told myself. You will now find out what he has in mind. ("I can ASSURE Your Honor, Mrs. Sweet WILL TESTIFY.")

Reader, I felt as if my whole future life just hung in the balance. I was petrified. I'd sooner have faced the Ghost of Leroy one million times. I tried to look at Lily Black for courage, I just implored her with my eyes, but she didn't look. She only sat there, gazing blankly at her folded hands. You're all alone now, Prettybelle, said a voice within. You can't climb up on any laps. Not now!

Well, they asked me to take the oath, and I gestured that I could not talk, nor could I place my hand upon the Book.

"Just move your lips, Miz Sweet," says Mr. Bragg with a big smile. "Just move your lips and that'll do nicely."

So they propped up my hand upon the Bible, and sick at heart, I moved my lips in the Oath.

You got to be grown-up now, said the Voice Within. No tears! No laps! But a second inner voice cried out, I can't! I'm just too weak. I'm just too stupid and helpless. I never learned this kind of thing. I never went to college. I'm just too small and ignorant. Please, said this second voice, please, come on, let's faint or hide or something! And the first voice answered, Don't bother me, child, run on, I'm busy. But Reader, I confess it was a bit wobbly when it said it. And oh, as I moved my lips to take the Oath, I felt my eyes simply SINK into their sockets until I looked out gaunt and terrible like some poor starving victim. Every eye was upon me and I could hardly grasp my situation.

I moved my lips in the Oath, and Billy's lawyer said, "Objection!"

"Overruled," says Judge Collie Meggs.

And so I found myself sworn in. Tricks and traps, I thought. Beware of tricks and traps, pitfalls and illusions.

"Now, Miz Sweet," says the D.A. briskly. "I know you are not well, and I am going to make this brief. Brief as I can! I am just going to ask one or two questions."

Well, I gesture feebly with my left hand toward my throat.

"I KNOW you are having trouble with your voice, Miz Sweet," he says sympathetically, swelling out his little barrel chest like a banty rooster. "But I do think you can just OVERCOME IT IF YOU TRY. JUST TRY REAL HARD, Miz Sweet. Consider, Miz Sweet! Consider us trying so hard to protect your good name, punish these criminals. Consider, Miz Sweet! The whole life of the community is disturbed and upset. Miz Sweet," he said, "fires are raging in the Nigra quarter, did you know that? Feeling is very high, Miz Sweet, no telling what might happen to innocent people! Did you know that Violence stalks our streets by night? Blood is running in our streets, Miz Sweet, because of this terrible crime, and JUSTICE MUST BE DONE!"

"Objection!" cries Billy's lawyer.

"Overruled," drones Collie.

"Your Honor——!" protests the lawyer.

"Overruled," says Collie, scratching his left cheekbone.

"Blood in the streets," says Mr. Bragg to me, fixing me with his eye. "INNOCENT BLOOD." Oh Lordy, I thought, he is aiming to give me the Leroy treatment. He is trying to hypnotize me and afflict me. He knows my weakness, he sees my weakest spot. But I will not give in. No, I will not give in. That blood is no affair of mine. I will not even think about that blood.

Well, he went on and on, and I tried not to listen, and above all not to look into his large green eye, which was surely trying to hypnotize me. I would not succumb, no I would not.

"All you have to do, Miz Sweet, to heal our community, to heal its wounds and staunch its blood," he concludes, "is *name your assailants. We are listening!*"

Well, I thought, you won't catch me that way. And I just open and close my mouth like a helpless fish. He waits a good long spell to let the pressure build.

"Your voice still giving you trouble?" he says, finally. "Then let me change my question. Are your assailants in this room? Are they here? Are they here in this courtroom? Just nod your head, Miz Sweet!"

"OBJECTION!"

"Overruled."

I didn't move. I held my breath.

"Objection, objection!" insisted Mr. Young Lawyer.

"Just nod, *or shake*, your head," amended Mr. Bragg, courteously gesturing at his opponent.

I did nothing.

"Are they in this room, Miz Sweet?"

Well, Reader, I felt my *torticollis* coming on. It was coming on strong. I tried to fight it, but my shoulder rose up and my head tipped back and pulled over and then **it** flipped onto my shoulder and there it froze.

And if he didn't take that for a gesture!

"They are!" crows Mr. Bragg. "Yes, they are! Miz Sweet nodded that they are! Miz Sweet *nodded her head.*"

It was on the tip of my tongue to holler, "I DID NOT!" Reader, do you spot the trap? He said I had nodded, when in truth I hadn't. And the temptation and the trap was to get me to protest! Thus exposing the fact that I could talk if I wanted to!

"She nodded!" he proclaimed to Judge Collie. "Miz Sweet has indicated that her assailants are indeed in this room."

Oh, it almost caught me again. I almost spoke. I almost said, "I did NOT nod, I did not!" But I held fast.

Well, do you know, Billy's lawyer did not object, and Mr. D.A. just kept on repeating that I had nodded, and I got more and more upset in my painful and unnatural position, and I wanted to cry out, and I was breathing like a locomotive, and I thought, Is it possible I DID nod? No, I did not nod! Maybe I twitched and they THOUGHT I nodded? Oh Lordy, you can't convict a man on a twitch, can you?

At last Billy's lawyer comes forward, asks permission, and says:

"Your Honor, Mrs. Sweet appears to be in the grips of one of her afflictions. Her *torticollis,* I believe. In my opinion, my learned opponent Mr. Bragg cannot reasonably say she nodded. In fact, in her present position, head to the side, one could more accurately say she is answering his question *in the negative!*"

And they argued THAT one, back and forth, uphill and

down, with me in spasm and torment, until at last Judge Collie banged his gavel hard.

"Get on with it, Mr. Bragg," he said.

"Objection, Your Honor," said Billy's lawyer. "The witness is clearly in no condition——"

"Overruled," said Collie Meggs, and blew his nose with that selfsame terrifying honk that so mortified Saralizabeth at her father's funeral.

Mr. Bragg turns back to me. "Now Miz Sweet," he says. "Your assailants are indeed in this courtroom. You just POINT THEM OUT for Judge Collie."

I didn't budge.

"We know you're sick, Miss Belle," says the D.A., with an edge on his voice. "And we know your right arm don't work so good. But Miss Belle, your doctor has plainly told us there's not a thing in this world wrong with your LEFT arm. SO POINT THEM OUT."

Well, he just YELLED at me. And I didn't budge. Logic or no logic. Left arm, right arm, I held fast and quaked.

He was exasperated. And Billy Black looked up at me perplexed and curious. And Billy's lawyer's eyes just pierced me through and through, and I did not have the heart to look at Lily, no I didn't.

"Objection, Your Honor!" says Billy's lawyer. "It's a disgrace. This witness is not in adequate physical condition!"

"Miss Belle," says Judge Collie, "you all right?"

Well, paralyzed, speechless, spastic, I implored him with my desperate eyes.

"SHE'S all right!" says Collie coldly. "Proceed."

Mr. D.A. leaned on the railing, all sweet again and full of the milk of human kindness. "You can't move your arms, I see, and you cannot nod your head, but——"

And Reader, his eyes were now glittering although his mouth was smiling and I knew the jaws of his real true Major Trap were about to spring shut upon me.

"This is my last question, Miz Sweet," he crooned. "Then you can go back to your seat. Bend your body forward from the hips for YES. Or twist it to one side for NO."

He trots over to his table, and he fetches back an envelope. He waves this envelope before the judge.

"Your Honor, I have here some very crucial evidence, and it will wrap up this case, and it was just found in the basement of the Sweet home, concealed by a rug. I would like to ask the court to admit this SEALED ENVELOPE as State Exhibit No. 12."

Judge Collie agrees to that, and Mr. Bragg comes back to me just smiling, and waving that envelope under my nose. Well, I dimly recognized it.

"Now Miz Sweet," says Mr. Bragg. "Do you observe this envelope?"

Reader, I observed it all right, and my scalp tingled, for it was the selfsame envelope Leroy had dictated to me, and which I had completely forgotten the existence of until now.

"You observe the handwriting on this envelope?" pursues Mr. Bragg. "It is YOUR OWN handwriting is it not?"

I held still.

"Your Honor," says Mr. D.A. smugly to Judge Collie, "it is real easy to establish that this is indeed Miss Belle's own handwriting, whether she acknowledges it or not." He clears his throat. "I will tell you what it says on this envelope. It says, LIST OF NAMES OF THE BOYS THAT RAPED ME."

Sensation in the courtroom, and Reader, I now understood what he meant when he said I would testify one way or another!

"Bend forward at the hips for YES, Miz Sweet," he said. "Is that your writing?"

I gazed at that envelope as a snake gazes at the snake charmer, and I swayed forward at the hips, without knowing what I did. Can you believe I had only the vaguest memory of ever writing out that list?

"Will you read it for us, Miz Sweet?"

I opened and closed my mouth like a stricken trout.

"Very well," he says. "I'll read it. I would like to point out, Your Honor, that this envelope is sealed. With your permission I will open it."

He opens the envelope and he fetches out the paper inside, and he pulls his spectacles out of his pocket so he can read it and before putting them on his nose he shakes out the paper for me to look at, and says "Miz Sweet, this your handwriting?"

Well, I swayed forward from the hips for YES, and my heart gave a big plop, because Lord have mercy, what I had written there in my distress and dismay while the Ghost of Leroy was standing over me dictating (and who would ever believe *that* story) was—just guess—was simply SCRIBBLES. Yes! I had not written down those names at all, I had simply scribbled!

Well, Mr. Banty Rooster affixes his glasses now and reads that paper over quickly to himself, and in a veritable rage, he crumples up the paper, and I vow he almost threw it on the floor and stamped his feet.

"Your Honor," he says, "I apologize for taking the time of the court. The paper is unintelligible. No further questions." And barely able to restrain his curses, he stomped back to his seat. Oh Lordy, I did chuckle within, and I thanked my own Demented Mind for having scribbled like that instead of taking down obediently all that Leroy told me to. O Prettybelle Sweet! You may be mute but you're not so dumb!

They excused me from the stand at last and although my poor neck was still contorted, my heart just sang with triumph, for I had foiled them. I had saved the day! I went back to my seat, and I felt good about myself, delicious inside and comfy-cozy, for I truly figured I had saved Billy and his friends from the hangman's noose. How could Judge Collie hold those boys now? I mean, in front of the world press and all? He would throw us out of court!

So I sang with triumph, but alas not very long. Oh no. For what happened? I was not the final witness, as I had assumed. Mr. Bragg calls one more person to the stand, and who is it? Reader, hold tight, who is it?

Clarence Wimbly!

I sat up with indignation. What could HE know about it? Nothing whatsoever!

He takes the oath all modest and trustworthy and kindly-crinkly-eyed, and answers Mr. Bragg's questions in such a low soothing voice that Judge Collie Meggs had to cup his hand behind his ear and tell him to speak louder.

After establishing what a stalwart citizen Mr. Wimbly was, how he taught history and citizenship as well as Sunday school, Mr. Bragg asked,

"Now where were you, Mr. Wimbly, at about eight o'clock of the night in question, July fourth?"

"I was walking down Liveoak Street, Mr. Bragg."

"Liveoak Street," says Mr. Bragg. "That is the street of the Sweet residence, is it not?"

"Yes sir, it is," says Mr. Wimbly.

"Did you walk near the Sweet residence?"

"Why yes, sir, I passed right by it, on the opposite side of the street."

"Now Mr. Wimbly, did you see or hear anything suspicious as you passed by?"

"Oh yes SIR. I surely did."

Murmur in the courtroom. Reader, I looked at that man, and I listened to his kindly soothing voice, and I vow I hated him worse than ever before, if that is possible.

"Would you tell the court what you heard?"

"I heard a scream," says Mr. Wimbly. "TWO screams. Kind of muffled. I stopped walking, but I thought, oh it's just the television, and I was about to go on. But then— the front door busted open, and a Nigra boy came running out, running to beat . . . all get-out, running just pell-mell, and his clothes were all disheveled, and he ran down the street fast as his legs would carry him, leaving the door wide open. And two others followed after."

"Did you get a good look at them, Mr. Wimbly?"

"Well, yes sir, I did, at one of them. It wasn't fully dark yet, enough light to see pretty good, yes sir."

"And did you recognize him?"

"Well, sir," says Wimbly, "tell you the truth, I did not. Not at that very moment. All I said to myself was, that boy looks familiar to me, I said, I know him from somewheres, but I can't just place him. Now who is he? I said to myself, for I surely know him."

"And would you recognize his face again if you saw it?"

"Oh yes sir, I surely would, I would indeed."

"Is he in this courtroom?"

"Yes sir, he is."

"Would you point him out?"

"Why, that's him right there. The defendant William Black."

Well, I felt sick. I just felt sick. My *torticollis* had eased off, but I felt sicker than ever. The excited buzz mounted up in that courtroom, and Judge Collie Meggs had to hit the desk with his gavel. My heart sank like a stone in the river, for I thought, Lord, Lord, they are going to convict him even *without* my testimony! Oh Lily, I thought. Oh Lily, Lily.

"And could you tell us, howcome you thought you recognized this boy but couldn't immediately place him?"

"Yes sir. You see, he's a local boy, this William Black. Been up North to school, and well sir, I took a . . . certain interest in his return. Because he's one of them in charge of the Nigra Registration Drive. I knew him three ways. One, he's the son of the Sweet family maid and I've seen him at their house, since I was always a good friend of the late Sheriff Sweet. Then, second, I also saw his photo in some . . . well, some photos circulated concerning the Nigra Registration Drive. And you know what else, for third?"

"Please, carry on," says Mr. Bragg.

"At Sheriff Leroy Sweet's funeral," says Mr. Wimbly, "a string of firecrackers were thrown over the wall and landed not forty feet from the grave, disrupting everything, scaring folks half to death, showing disrespect of the dead and defiance of social custom. Well, I know who did it."

"Who did it?"

"Him. William Black! Yes sir. I snuck outside and saw him running off. I saw his face, when he looked back over his shoulder, and I noted his peculiar run, Mr. Bragg. Yes sir, a most peculiar run, with his right foot flung out to one side. Same run as later, when I noted it a second time."

Well, I cast a look at Lily, and she sat cut in stone or ebony. And Billy Black was scowling and breathing hard. The D.A. strutted over to his table and sat down, saying, "Cross-examine."

Poor Billy's lawyer—not much he *could* say after that. But he did his best.

"Mr. Wimbly, is it or is it not true that you are a member of the White Knights, local Klan organization?"

"OBJECTION! OBJECTION!" cried Mr. Bragg.

"Sustained," said Collie Meggs.

And that took care of THAT. So he tried again.

"Mr. Wimbly, do you reside near Liveoak Street?"

"Why, no sir, I live other side of town on Morgan Street."

"What were you doing on Liveoak Street at eight o'clock that night?"

(Well, I was wondering that myself.)

"I was on my way to visit friends on Greentree Street," said Mr. Wimbly.

"Do you always walk, Mr. Wimbly? Did you walk all the way from home?"

"Why, no sir, I took my car."

"Then how did you happen to be *walking* down Liveoak Street? No place to park on Greentree Street?"

"Why, no sir, plenty of space to park on Greentree Street."

"Then how did it happen you were walking?"

"Why, I like to walk now and then, helps keep the old paunch down." (Laughter) "It's my regular practice to park my car a block or two away, wherever I'm going, and walk for exercise."

"I see. Now Mr. Wimbly, if you saw a man come running out of the Sweet house with his clothes in disarray, and leaving the door wide open, would you not naturally have been suspicious?"

"Yes, sir, I would. I *was*."

"Then why didn't you stop him? Why didn't you chase him?"

"Why, I *did*," says Mr. Wimbly. "Didn't I say that? Lord, I took out after him, and chased him two blocks before I lost him, he's a deal younger'n I am, and after two blocks I was used up, I admit it, so I lost him."

Billy's lawyer is just blocked on all sides, and he studies a minute, and says:

"How does it happen you didn't tell anybody about this?"

"Why, what do you mean?"

"I mean, the press, the police."

"Well, sir, I did tell the police. What do you think I'm doing here?" (Laughter) "I didn't tell the press, no sir, none of their business. Besides, I wanted no violence, no sir, no mob violence in Cachattow County."

"When did you tell the police?"

"Why . . . right away. I don't know. Next day."

"Why didn't you tell them that night?"

Mr. Wimbly, very suave, said, "Well . . . tell you the truth, son, they were too busy to listen, and I was too beat up from running the four-minute mile, I couldn't keep on standing round to tell 'em. I went home to bed, it'll keep, I thought, it won't go away."

"You did not go visit your friends?"

"No sir, I did not."

"What did you do?"

"Well, I headed back to the Sweet house, but saw all this commotion going on at the Lindleys, and I knocked on the door, and asked what was going on and somebody told me, Lord, Miz Sweet's been raped."

"Who was that you talked to?"

"I don't rightly remember."

"So it can't be confirmed."

"I don't rightly know if it can or can't."

"Mr. Wimbly, you look as if you've been in a fight yourself. How'd you get those marks?"

"What marks?"

"Why, those festering scratches down your cheek. Looks like fingernails might have done that."

And I thought: What IS he driving at? What CAN he mean? How DID he get those scratches?

"I OBJECT!" cried Mr. Bragg. "Irrelevant, immaterial!"

"Sustained."

"Your Honor," says Mr. Wimbly, smooth as silk, "Lord, I don't mind telling where I got these! I got them struggling with that RAPIST THERE!"—pointing at Billy Black. "I was with the posse that brought him IN! That's how I got them! Ask any of the boys if that ain't so!"

And in the audience some four five heads just started nodding, and muttering that's surely true.

Mr. Defense Lawyer just had to give up, and let Mr. Wimbly go down from the stand, and his evidence was a devastating blow. They were going to hang those boys despite me. They were just bypassing me. Oh Reader, I knew I had to ACT.

Mr. Bragg said he was finished presenting his side of things, and he sneered that Mr. Defense Lawyer could take his turn now, fat lot of good it would do him.

So the Defense called witnesses, but they were just a pitiful parade of black folks all testifying how those three boys were someplace else on the evening of July 4th and not at the Sweet residence at all. But who was listening to them? Nobody. Mother Sweet began snoring and whistling softly, and even old Judge Collie Meggs began to nod his head with slumber and had to prop his chin up with his hand.

Oh Reader, can you taste the sharpness of my torment? I knew I had to ACT. But how? Oh what to do?

If I got up and told the TRUTH, why indeed I would save those two other Nigra boys (and Lord, that was only right, for they TRULY didn't rape me, and were most unjustly and falsely accused, and they had mamas too, named Opal or Lucinda or Pearl crying their eyes out somewhere) —I would save *them*, but Billy Black would hang. Billy would hang, and I could never draw a pure or happy breath again my whole life through, or look another Lily in the eye.

Well, I could LIE. But Reader, that could make things even worse. I could get up and say, "NONE of them did it!" And what would happen? Right away two things would happen. First, they would question and question me, and I (being repossessed of speech) would have to answer all their tricky questions. Sure as Fate, they would trap me, and I would reveal the truth, and Billy would hang anyway. Or, second, if they believed me, oh Lord, Lord, they would let THESE boys go, and FETCH IN A HUNDRED OTHERS. They would fetch in every boy in Darkytown and try to make them confess. They'd burn and shoot and lynch—all in the name of Justice.

Reader, *they had to have their victim!* They could not rest content. They had to have revenge.

Oh, Lord, what a spot to be in. Blood and misery and torment every place I looked. What to do. Oh, Prettybelle, I wailed to myself, is there no solution? There must be something! Think of it, Prettybelle, THINK!

And whilst I was racking my brain and roasting on the spit, the Defense Lawyer, looking uneasy and uncertain, made a quick decision and called *William Black up to the witness stand*.

Well, everybody woke up fast at that, and sat on the edge of their seat. Billy Black himself would testify! I too pricked up my ears, but Lord, I did not dare to hope that somehow he could clear himself.

Well, Mr. Defense Lawyer whispered to him urgently, and Billy Black rose to his feet. Yes, he got up lazy, and he sauntered to the witness stand with his head held high like some kind of black African king or other, and his eyelids were all heavy-laden and suavely sophisticated, even bored, and I mean, oh Reader, you almost would have had to laugh, if your heart was not breaking, and yet it was surely courageous in its way. It was courageous, for how could he help but be scared half to death inside himself, with that mob outside, and all those hostile white faces looking at him, hungry for his blood. Well, he would give them no satisfaction. He would rather die than show that he was scared! They wanted him to squirm and tremble, beg and plead, but he would not. In fact, he was going to put on such an act of majesty and composure that he would leave them purely in a rage. It was Fly Now Pay Later, and go down in glory, I reckon. Only Reader, he was nineteen years old, and thus his act was somewhat overdrawn. And such is my miserable imagination—which is my curse and simply victimizes me—that I truly entered into the mind and body of Lily Black and I WAS Lily Black and I suffered agonies with every defiant word that boy uttered and every bored gesture that he made.

Then for a minute my eyes blurred over and I thought it was Johnny sitting there accused and I thought, Oh my son, my son! And the pain from my *torticollis* moved downward and the pain from my slipped disk moved inward and they both lodged within my very womb. Oh Lily, I thought, the bad bad boys. How we do suffer! How we suffer when they go bad, our sons!—and our husbands too, they also go bad, and we suffer. Now why do they go bad? *We* don't go bad. Why do they all go bad when we women are good and always suffering? *They* don't suffer. They don't suffer over *us*. If a wife or daughter were to slip, go bad, they wouldn't suffer. They would simply toss her out-of-doors and never give it a second thought. Whereas we women are forever loyal and true-blue and suffering. Endlessly endlessly.

Well, Mr. Defense Lawyer questioned Billy about his background and schooling and how he won a Prize for the Best Essay in junior year of high school and was Valedictorian of the Senior Class, and how he went on North to college in Chicago.

"Did you have a scholarship to that college?" asks Mr. Lawyer.

"No I didn't," says Billy Black.

"Well now, tell me, how did you manage to *pay* for that school? How did you support yourself?"

(Uh-oh, I thought.)

"I had financial help," says Billy Black.

"And did you know where that financial help came from?"

"Not at first," says Billy Black.

"Not at first. But later on, you found out?"

"Yeah I found out from my mother."

Well, Mr. Bragg sings out "I object! It's irrelevant!" and

for once he gets overruled. I reckon Collie was curious again, for he was all wide-awake now and hanging on every word.

"Your mother told you the name of your benefactor?"

"Yeah," said Billy Black, very bored, very nineteen years old.

"And who WAS your benefactor."

"It was Mrs. Sweet," mumbled Billy.

"Say it out loud."

"IT WAS MRS. LEROY SWEET," says Billy Black.

Well, sensation. Mr. District Attorney really jumped and growled at that one. He hadn't expected that, and it rocked him. And right away, he started calculating how to counteract it.

"You found out," says Mr. Young Lawyer, "that it was MRS. SWEET HERSELF who financed your trip up North and your schooling there."

"That's right."

Well, I tell you, everybody in the courtroom looked over at me, buzzing and talking, and my cheeks were flaming, it was just horribly embarrassing to hear it said right out in the open, and Saralizabeth looked at me as if she truly could not believe her ears or the full extent of my depravity. Reader, I thought: it's only when MY BLOOD is shed that this Young Lawyer scores a point for Billy Black. I swear, it seemed to be my blood or Billy Black's.

"Now, how did Mrs. Sweet go about giving you the money?" pursues Mr. Young Lawyer.

"She gave it to my mother and my mother sent it to me."

"You didn't question how your mother got all that money?"

"Yeah I did. I kept on asking her. And at last, she told me."

"And it was Mrs. Sweet."

"Yeah."

Oh come *on*, I thought, he's *said* it fifty times now, isn't that enough? My cheeks were still aflame.

"Now," says this young lawyer, "after working at the Sweet house in the afternoon of July fourth, did you, at any time that evening, *did you return to the Sweet house?*"

Well, they all expected him to deny it, and instead he said,

"Yes I did."

Another big buzz in the courtroom.

"You did return. And what was the reason for your return?"

"It was business."

"You returned on business? What was the nature of that business? Was it not to EXPRESS YOUR GRATITUDE TO MRS. SWEET FOR THE FINANCIAL HELP SHE HAD BEEN GIVING YOU?"

Billy hesitated, torn beneath truth and caution, I reckon. Anyway, he said,

"I came to pay back some of the money."

Mr. Lawyer followed up. "GRATEFUL FOR THE HELP SHE HAD GIVEN YOU," he said, "you were EAGER TO COMMENCE REPAYING HER."

Billy Black pondered, and said,

"I wanted to pay her back the money, that's right."

"And did you actually *give Mrs. Sweet any money* on that night of July fourth?"

"Yeah, I did."

Buzz.

"How much did you give her?"

"Thirty dollars."

"And did you tell her you intended to pay back the entire amount as soon as you could?"

"That's what I told her."

"Your Honor," sings out Mr. Young Lawyer. "I recall to your mind that among the items Trooper Stone said he found in the Sweet residence on the night of July fourth was cash in the amount of thirty dollars on the dining-room table!"

Collie Meggs grudgingly nodded his head that he remembered.

Mr. Lawyer turned back to Billy.

"And after transacting this business with Mrs. Sweet, what did you do?"

"I left."

"You left the house."

"Yeah."

"You said good night, and you left."

"I didn't exactly say good night."

"You didn't?"

"No."

"Why not?"

"Well, Mrs. Sweet was——"

"Go ahead, speak up. Out LOUD."

"Well, Mrs. Sweet was——" and he mumbled.

"Nobody can hear you," says Mr. Lawyer.

"SHE WAS DRUNK," says Billy Black.

Well, you know, we won't mention my feelings, but the courtroom surely stirred again. Another gush of blood from Prettybelle Sweet. But at the same time, those people truly did not like to hear such words from a black man. They felt he overstepped the bounds. And Mr. Lawyer sensed this right away, and he hadn't expected it, and he quick tried to cover up.

"She was—under the weather, you said?"

"That's right," says Billy Black.

"Tired out and under the weather? Had fallen asleep?"

"That's right, she fell sound asleep."

"Sound asleep. Now where was that?"

"On the sofa in the living room."

"You mean," says this young lawyer, "you were standing talking to her and she just went to sleep?"

"Yeah, she did," said Billy Black. "Sleep or something."

"So you went home."

"Yeah."

"What time was that?"

"About quarter to eight."

"Can you prove that?"

"No. But it was."

"You left the Sweet house at quarter to eight. And Mrs. Sweet ran over to the Lindley house at quarter AFTER eight. Thus leaving plenty of time for SOMEONE ELSE to come into the Sweet house after you left."

"That's right," says Billy Black.

"Did you leave the door open when you left?"

"I might have, don't recall," says Billy Black.

"Now tell the court how you felt about Mrs. Sweet. You were GRATEFUL to her, weren't you?"

Mumble, mumble, said Billy.

"What did you say? Speak louder."

"I said, I was . . . mmm . . . grateful . . . in a manner of speaking."

Imagine, that boy. "In a manner of speaking." I ask you! Mr. Lawyer winced a bit himself and was perspiring freely.

"You would *never* have treated her with violence," says Mr. Lawyer.

"No," says Billy Black.

"That is," proclaims Mr. Lawyer loudly, "you did not, and would not have raped her, or even thought of raping her—she was your benefactress!"

And hastily—not giving Billy a chance to make one of his grudging answers, Mr. Lawyer turns his back and says, "Your witness," to Mr. Bragg. He then sits down in a weary, soggy slump. He had accomplished much, but feared what was to come.

Now it was Mr. Bragg's turn, and he gets up and prowls around the witness-box, and teeters on his toes, and begins questioning Billy. Before long, he gets him to admit that he is indeed a member of some certain Black Nationalist group in Chicago.

"Now isn't it true," says Mr. District Attorney, very aggressively, "that the avowed and only purpose of that group is to RAPE WHITE WOMEN, KILL WHITE MEN AND DRINK THEIR BLOOD?"

Painful murmur in the courtroom.

Billy Black just kind of snorts.

"Answer the question!" says Mr. Bragg.

"OBJECTION!" says Billy's lawyer, jumping up. "Your Honor, that's ridiculous superstition!"

"Yeah, yeah, that's just what we do," says Billy, snorting and shaking his head. He is being sarcastic, but surely at the wrong moment.

"AH, YOU ADMIT IT IS THE TRUTH!" pounces Mr. Bragg.

"I do not," says Billy.

"Your Honor!" protests Billy's lawyer. "My client was being *sarcastic*."

"Let the witness speak for himself!" howls Mr. Bragg, and the two of them just go to it. Collie Meggs warns them, and then Mr. Bragg pursues it with Billy:

"Is it not the truth that the chief purpose—or let me say ONE AVOWED PURPOSE—of this group is to rape white women?"

"It is NOT," says Billy.

"Rape white women and kill white men, in order to drink their blood," says Mr. Bragg.

"That's a lie," says Billy Black. "That's stupid."

"Drink their blood," continued Mr. Bragg, "in the MISTAKEN AND SAVAGE AFRICAN SUPERSTITIOUS BELIEF THAT SUCH ACTIVITIES WOULD TURN BLACK SKIN WHITE! Is that not the truth?"

Billy Black shook his head in amazement. "Man, you're *flying!*" he said.

Well, there's a fair-sized uproar and Collie Meggs goes rap rap rap with the gavel and says, "The witness will show respect."

So Mr. District Attorney gets Billy Black to admit he came home to Cachattow County not only to see his mama but also to work on the Nigra Registration Drive. And the courtroom murmurs at that, but Mr. Bragg doesn't make as much of it as you might expect him to. Instead he digs right down into the Day of the Crime.

"You worked that afternoon at the Sweet residence, assisting your mother at the funeral reception, is that right?"

"That's right."

"Say SIR when you address me, boy."

Silence.

"Did you hear me?"

"I heard you."

A mutter in the courtroom.

"Your insolence is not the best recommendation for clemency," snaps Mr. Bragg. "You worked there in the afternoon, you left, and then you returned, is that correct?"

"That is correct."

"And when you returned, you had in your possession the key to the back door which you had found in your mother's purse, and you let yourself into the house. Correct?"

"No," said Billy Black, shaking his head. "NOT correct. I didn't have any key, and I didn't let myself in. I rang the doorbell."

"The doorbell," says Mr. Bragg thoughtfully. "Does the back door of the Sweet house have a *doorbell?*"

Billy Black looked him in the eye.

"It was the front door," he said.

Well, at those words, *front door,* a mutter started in the courtroom like big angry raindrops on dry leaves. I declare, they might almost have lynched him for that alone. Folks in Cachattow County are that sensitive about their front doors. Oh, William Black was surely not making a sympathetic impression. And now you could see why Mr. Bragg didn't make so much of the Voting Drive—it was because he had the Front Door up his sleeve.

"You knew, did you not, that you were not supposed to be anywheres near a white neighborhood after sundown?"

"I have heard," drawls Billy Black, "of that local custom."

"You knew it, and yet you came out anyway."

"Yes I did."

"You came where you had no business to be, with rape and violence on your mind."

"No, I did not."

"You did not come where you had no business to be?"

"I had business."

"You had business," sneers Mr. Attorney. "Oh, you had

business. So you came in Miz Sweet's *front door* to talk business."

"Yes I did."

"And then after you gained entry you changed your mind and decided to rape her instead!"

"No I did not."

"Oh you did not! You were there. And she was raped. But it wasn't you that did it!"

"I did not rape her."

"You were there at the time of the rape. She was raped. But it was *somebody else* snuck in the house and did it!"

Laughter.

"I don't know who did it, I don't know anything about no rape," says Billy Black, and he would have gone on, but they shut him up.

"You expect us to believe that!" laughs Mr. Attorney.

"I don't expect you to believe anything a black man says!" shouts Billy, but the tail end of his remark is mostly drowned out by rising voices and Collie Meggs going BAM! BAM! BAM!

"I didn't rape anybody!" cries Billy Black, above the racket.

Collie Meggs is banging away with the gavel.

"But I wish to hell I had!" cries Billy Black.

Well, Mr. Bragg hears that one, and he picks it up, and turns on Billy like a barrel-chested wolf.

"What was that?" he yells. "What did you just say?"

Collie restores enough quiet so you can hear Billy Black's reply.

"I said I did not rape her!" says Billy Black. "But the more I think about it——"

"Go on," invites Mr. Bragg. "Go on!" In the background, Billy's lawyer is dancing with anxiety.

"I mean," says Billy Black, "like, rape would have been the thing. Like don't you see, man, it's a nice expression."

Yes, Reader, that's how he put it, he said a *nice expression*.

"Go on," encourages Mr. Bragg. "Tell us how you raped her."

"I never raped her," says Billy Black. "But I'm going to hang for it anyway—I might as well have had the kick!"

Well, that did it. They got up on their feet and shouted. The whole courtroom just rose up in roaring protest. Billy's lawyer threw up his hands and gave up. Mr. Bragg smiled a secret tiny smile.

"Hang him, hang him!" shouted a man behind me.

And someone else said, "He's hung himself."

Judge Collie banged away with his gavel. I glanced at Lily, and she didn't move a muscle, not even her eyes, but her face had sagged into this mask of hopelessness and pain. Two boys, she was thinking. Two of them and both gone. My own flesh.

As for Billy, he kind of glanced around, and his cool (as they say) seemed to break up just a bit. He kind of stroked his upper lip with his thumbnail and then touched his forehead as if to secretly blot up some sweat, but otherwise he just sat tight, defiant as you please, and calmer than he had any right to be. The two other boys also sat quiet, one looking straight ahead with a blank face, and the other had just the hint of a grim sideways smile.

Yes, Billy Black had surely tied it. And why, why? Who did he do it for, that act of defiance? Did he do it for them, for his friends? But they'd hang with him. Did he do it for us, us white folks? Lord, he must have known how it would boomerang. We didn't see pride or courage, all we saw was one uppity bad nigger got to be punished good and quick.

Worst kind of nigger, got to be stamped out. Did he do it for his mama? To impress her? Oh Lord, my blood hurt me. For his mama, to show her he was a man? When all she wanted and prayed for was that he would NOT be a man, no not a man, just a boy, please Lawd, a good boy, nice boy, be nice, don't be courageous, don't be no man, just be a good boy. Well, Lawd didn't hear that prayer, and far as I can tell, Lawd never hears anything, he's deaf as some damfool post or just too old to care, and we're all a bunch of silly children still clustering round whining for our nickel.

And Lily was thinking, Where did I go wrong, I should have licked him, I should have learned him pain. Why did I protect him? I should have made him suffer, so he'd know. Then his courage would have died inside him, and he would never have tried to be a man, he would have stayed a nice good boy like he should have, like he used to be.

Reader, I looked over at Lily, and she was *crying.* . . . Not making a sound, only crying. Big wet tears just flowing down her cheeks, and her body shaking with it. She was just sitting there silently shaking and crying. I couldn't stand it. You know? It was Alice all over again.

So I rose up.

I knew I had to act. And I rose up.

Midst all that hullabaloo I stood up, and I walked over to the judge's bench, and I beat upon the front of that bench to get his attention, and at last I caught his eye and he kept banging away with his gavel for quiet. And when he saw me, and everybody saw me, things got quiet.

"Miss Belle!" said Judge Collie, leaning forward. "What is it, what is it, Miss Belle?"

I put my hand up to my throat, and showed that I was struggling to speak. Every eye was on me, Reader, and as I struggled there, I saw my whole life in a flash. I did. And my life was a strange journey. The journey of an animal *inside the jaws* of a retriever dog. Yes, I saw it, and I felt it. I felt the hot breath of that running dog. I felt the teeth, which held me firmly. Velvet teeth thus far, Reader, hot breath and velvet teeth. In the very jaws of death I had been riding all my life, and yet, miraculously *safe*. But now? Where was he taking me, this fearful dog? To whom? And for what end? How could I *dare* to turn and bite him? Those jaws could crush my very life at any time, and shake me by the neck till I was dead. And yet I must.

I stood there and I coughed, and choked, and gagged and husked, trying to speak. Everybody stared at me, wondering what would happen next. Judge Collie Meggs looked at me in puzzlement, and glanced at Mr. Bragg, and Mr. Bragg came up to me, all solicitude, to lend me a hand, or lead me back to my seat—but I pushed free of him. I croaked and I burst into sobs, and let them come out free and clear, and in between my sobbing, I called out,

"I can talk now! I can talk!"

Judge Collie banged his gavel and got the room quiet. "I can talk now!" I said. "Judge Collie, I can talk! Your Honor, I have to testify! I HAVE to testify so I can TELL THE COURT THE TRUTH!"

Well, what a melodrama.

Here everybody thought the case was finished and done with, and instead, more thrills. The reporters' eyes just glittered and their noses twitched, and they fished their folded notebooks from their pockets, and poised once more their ballpoint pens.

The judge and the lawyers fussed and conferred, and agreed to let me testify. They sat me in the chair and swore me to tell the truth and I did swear (out loud this time)—

midst the most racking sobs, for it was well-nigh the blackest hour of my life, trapped and caged, and no matter where I turned, all I could see was blood and torment, blood and torment, on my head alone.

I had no idea what I was going to say. I only knew I had to say something. I opened my mouth——

And Reader, a miracle happened. It did. A miracle just happened!

I mean, out of nowhere, the solution burst upon me like a blinding light. I was left breathless by the force of it. Caught up and rigid! I felt as if some laser beam had simply transfixed me. I felt like Joan of Arc listening to the Voices! I stood at the center of a cone of mystical light and rapture.

Oh Reader, I had found a *way out*, and I knew in my bones that it would work. I knew exactly what I had to do, and it would be the BIGGEST LIE and the NOBLEST ACT that I had ever committed in all the days of my life.

My sobs dried up and my hands stopped trembling. I held on to the railing, and my moment had come, and I sang out loud and clear:

"Your Honor," I said, "and Mr. Lawyers, I have to tell this court a terrible and bitter truth. I have to tell it without fear or thought of Self, though it will defame my memory forevermore, I have to tell it in the interests of JUSTICE! For JUSTICE," I said, "is bigger than all of us! Nothing can stop me now." I said. "I am going to tell the truth, the whole truth and nothing but the truth,—which is—THERE WAS NO RAPE!"

Reader, they simply gaped. They did not respond at all. They only goggled at me.

"There was no rape!" I cried. "No rape at all! I made it up. I lied! It never happened! I invented it!"

Well, by now, they began to react. And everybody turned to his neighbor and buzzed, and Mr. Bragg came at me, and Sheriff Peabody appeared just from nowhere, with his bullhorn in his hand, and poor man he was distraught.

"There was SO a rape!" he cried out. "Miss Belle, there was TOO!"

I shook my head. "Uh-uh," I said. "Made it all up, every bit of it."

Well, Collie was banging for ORDER again, and he addressed me from the bench.

"Miss Belle," he said. "This is beyond—beyond—it's not possible. The testimony——"

"Don't believe her," shouted Peabody. "She's out of her head!"

And Mr. Bragg said, "But your wounds, Miss Belle! The blood!"

"Oh, Mr. Bragg. I fell downstairs," I said, inspired. "I just fell right down the stairs, and hit myself on the banisters. And then I walked into the living room, and I laid down on the couch, and I was bleeding, and then I sat down on the floor, and then I swear I don't know what came over me! I just ran over to Ludie Lindley's house, and I told her I'd been raped. It was a lie. A terrible lie. Your Honor, I have no excuse! I reckon I just purely wanted some excitement, that's all."

"But—but—but—" said old Collie Meggs. "What about OLD Miz Sweet? She was raped too!"

"Oh come on now, boys," I snickered. "She's a pretty old lady. She was just crowding in on the publicity!"

Well, you could tell, they didn't believe me . They couldn't bring themselves to believe me. And suddenly, up jumps Mother Sweet, having waked up and heard her name spoken. She lifts her head, like a hound to the horn, and she jumps up and she totters forward, and stands there all alone in the middle of the open floor, chomping fiercely on her false teeth.

And I sang out, real sharp, "Mother Sweet? Who's to blame for all of this? Tell 'em. You tell 'em, WHO DID IT?"

Mother Sweet swung her head around and chewed her cud, working herself up to speech, and then she stuck her skinny finger right in my face, and screeched,

"YOU DID IT!" She turned to Collie Meggs, and hollered, "She takes my things! She reads my mail! She stole my silver thimble! The things she's done," says Mother Sweet, "would fill a book. She tortures and molests me! She thinks she'll drive me crazy so they'll carry me away. But I won't go crazy, I won't go away. SHE'S the crazy one. They took her before, and they'll take her again."

Oh she was in fine form. "Put her in jail!" cries Mother Sweet. "Whatever it is, she's guilty!" Then, swinging her head around, she catches sight of Saralizabeth. "There's another!" hollers Mother Sweet. "Two of them! A pair of vipers in the nest!" And she began jumping up and down, yelling, "Vipers! Vipers!"

Well, those poor stupefied law officers finally got the message and they closed in on her, and held her by the arms.

"Where's my son Leroy?" said Mother Sweet loudly. "LEROY? You come here and help your mammy!" Well, she began to struggle and shout, and she kneed one of them right in the groin, and bit the other on the finger, and Lord, it was a scene! They had to simply drag and carry the poor old struggling creature right out of the courtroom!

"VIPERS!" she was shouting as they carried her out.

"She stole my brassiere!" and the whole routine. And you could still hear her thumping and struggling and screeching like a banshee, calling for Leroy, even after the door closed behind her.

Everybody sat in a heap. I felt obliged to break the spell.

"Your Honor," I said, "on the evening of the fourth of July, that boy William Black came to see me by MY INVITATION," I said. "I wanted to—" (and this was sheerest inspiration) "—I wanted to GIVE HIM SOME MONEY FOR THE NIGRA REGISTRATION DRIVE!"

(*It is a far, far, better thing that I do now, than I have ever done.*)

Well, there is such confusion as you can't imagine and poor old Peabody is practically in tears and his beau ideal is shattered into bits.

"Miss Belle, you KNOW you was raped! You was TOO raped! Why you saying all this, Miss Belle?"

But I stood transfixed in blinding radiance.

"*Why* are you SAYING IT, Miss Belle?" and he commences outright tears and crying. "It's not true," he told Collie Meggs. "It's a LIE. She's lying! She was TOO raped!"

I vow, they all started in to echo him. *She was too raped*, everybody whispered. *She's just lying now, she was too raped*. They couldn't take it in, Reader, they couldn't let go, they could not shift their gears.

"I surely had TOO MUCH TO DRINK THAT NIGHT," I sang out, shaking my head. "I SURELY WAS DRUNK!"

"Don't listen to her!" begged Peabody. "She's cracking under the strain! HUSH UP, Miss Belle."

Don't listen to her, whispered everybody. *She's cracking up!*

Well, Reader, I began to get alarmed. Would my sacrifice be for naught? And I bet you cannot guess who came forward to my rescue, who carried the ball right over the goal line? I bet you surely cannot guess, for it was Saralizabeth. That child! Yes!

She just shoved her way forward and jumped up beside me on the witness seat with her eyes blazing and her arms waving and her cheeks on fire. "I WANT TO TESTIFY!" she hollered, and she stamped those size ten feet, BAM! BAM!

Old Collie Meggs shook his head to clear his mind, and banged the gavel as in a dream, and banged it some more until he quieted everybody down and got them in their chairs again. And for lack of any better ideas, they swore in Saralizabeth, and I vow, I could not imagine what SHE might have to say. And poor old Peabody just stood there with his bullhorn in his hand and the tears a-dripping down his face.

"You tell'em, Miss Sara," he blubbered. "YOU know there was a rape! You tell'em!"

Well, Saralizabeth gathers herself up and scowls and takes a deep breath.

"Your Honor, it's TRUE what she says!" proclaims Saralizabeth. "There WAS NO RAPE! I knew it all the time!"

Everybody goes Oh!

"I knew it!" cries Saralizabeth. "But I didn't speak. Because she's my MOTHER. I was ASHAMED."

Everybody goes Ah!

"She made it all up, and you know WHY? To get attention, that's why! To SHAME my daddy's name, and kick up a big fuss! I was there! I came in, I was there in the house. I passed by the living room! I'd have HEARD IT, wouldn't I? There was NO RAPE AT ALL, and I CAN PROVE IT!"

Everybody exchanges glances and I hear them all repeating, *She can prove it, prove it, prove it.*

"And the proof is this!" cries Saralizabeth. "The proof is this: Would ANYBODY rape my mother who is thirty-eight, and rape my grandma who is eighty-one—AND NOT RAPE ME?!"

Well, Reader, at that, the case was finished and concluded. Over and done with. Yes! Maybe Saralizabeth's proof wasn't strictly legal, but Lord, it surely won the Hearts and Minds of the People. The whole courtroom simply sighed and moaned and gave up the struggle.

I spread my arms out wide. "Y'all can hang me if you want," I said. "Y'all can crucify me. I don't blame you one bit."

My voice trembled, Reader, but oh, I knew, I knew that I was trailing clouds of glory the whole time. All the mighty sufferers of history stood by me shoulder to shoulder, and like Job, my glory was fresh in me, and my bow renewed in my hand. I had delivered the poor that cried, and the fatherless, and him that had none to help him. I had put on righteousness and it clothed me, my judgment was as a robe and a diadem. And I brake the jaws of the wicked and plucked the spoil out of his teeth.

Well, I scarcely remember much more save confusion, but the whole trial broke up, I know, and I remember poor old Peabody with his bullhorn, just heartbroken, saying, "Oh Miss Belle, even if it's true, what did you have to SAY it for? Don't you know your life is going to be plain hell? Everyone will cut you dead, Miss Belle! Oh, Miss Belle!"

And off he went, sniffling and snuffling, to try and pacify the mob outside. And I remember old Collie Meggs, his very last words from the bench, for that same afternoon he had his heart attack. He leaned over and pointed at me, and he said in a shaken terrible voice,

"Miss Belle, you are a WOUND IN THE SIDE OF THE SOUTH."

And I hung my head and cast down my eyes, for it hurt me, but not much, and I said, "I reckon I am, Your Honor."

END TWELFTH INSTALLMENT

The Phoenix

Oh glory, what a moment! Reader, what an afternoon! Finest of *my* life, I can tell you. Never to be forgotten. I only hope my mama was there somewhere, listening, for she would surely have been proud.

Well, today I sit here in the fenced-in park behind our hall at Pummicami, and eight months have passed away since then. Two hundred forty days . . . of glory and of wrath. Yes. Alas, more wrath than glory, I fear, for Cachattow County was seething and raging after that trial like a lion with its tail caught in a meat grinder. As you can well imagine. And naturally it sought to ease its pain and avenge its humiliation by attacking and if possible destroying the very source and symbol of its shame, namely me. Oh Reader, I knew I had a price to pay. I did not expect glory to come free. I was prepared to step into the flame, to burn white-hot and incandescent, and then step out, purged of all dross, purged of all sin and ugliness. I was prepared to burn and be consumed, and rise from the ashes of my life a phoenix of purest gleaming gold.

Yes I was prepared to suffer at certain hands. But what I did *not* expect, Reader, (how could I?) was the absolute *perfidy* of Dr. Dimmer, of all people, and the resultant unbearable crisis in which I now find myself at Pummicami Mental Sanitarium. He was the one man I trusted, and wait till you hear what he did to me.

I mean, the behavior of my family, friends, and neighbors was perfectly normal and predictable. I expected them to treat me like a pariah dog—and sure enough! Saralizabeth packed up and left that very night, departed bag and baggage for a girl friend's house where she ignored my telephone calls. Next day she swept in, gathered up Mother Sweet and simply dumped her in the Old Folks Home. And so I was alone, for the dogs ran off and Lily never did come back to work. If I ventured out of doors, children yelled and pelted me with gravel, neighbors slammed their doors and windows. But that was normal, wasn't it? To be expected. My mortgage was canceled, my life insurance was canceled, my car insurance was canceled, my driver's license was revoked, and my credit was cut off. But Reader, all that was understandable and no surprise. My garbage was not collected, my milk was not delivered, my television broke and no one would fix it, the postman threw my letters in the mud. Salesmen avoided my door. Small boys in Cub Scout uniform collected junk and dog-do and they tossed it over the hedge into my front yard. I vow, the stench was overpowering, and the flies—! Well, I got anonymous phone calls saying *Leave Town!* and I got filthy letters making threats and lewd insinuations. My front porch was bombed, my back stoop chopped with an ax, and the county condemned my property to run a highway through it. Yes.

And Lord, the publicity! Maybe you remember it. Prettybelle Sweet was a dirty joke from coast to coast. A household yak. Standup comics had only to breathe my name

and their contracts were renewed in Las Vegas. David
Brinkley made snide remarks and giggled outright before
saying Goodnight Chet. Walter Cronkite pointed out that
only Luck and Close Scrutiny had prevented tragedy and
bloodshed—but he wound up snickering too. Oh yes. Oh,
ho ho ho. Reader, even the vice-president of the United
States laughed at me, that what's-his-name. In a speech before the Lions Club of Louisville, he declared our nation's
troubles lay 9/10ths inside the mind, and if we could but
"straighten out the kinks" in our emotions, race problems
would vanish in thin air—"just as they did—ha ha—the
other day in Cachattow County Courthouse!" Ha ha ha.
Furthermore, my whole life history was exposed and
picked to pieces in the public press. I was psychoanalyzed
in all the Sunday Supplements and four intellectual quar-
terlies, and I read each and every one of them thanks to my
clipping service. Reader, the number of things wrong with
me would make a strong man blanch.

But wasn't that all normal and to-be-expected? Didn't I
have my purity throughout, my inner self-respect and glowing pride? Oh, I admit it shook me some not having a single
soul to talk to. For we are social animals, like the baboon
and the bee, and ostracism kills. The only company I had
in that forsaken house was Leroy's ghost, and even HE
wouldn't talk. No. He only glimmered feebly into view in
some dark corner or clothes closet, fading in and out like
the Cheshire Cat. Batteries low, I reckon.

Yes I admit that shook me some. It got so I just looked
forward to a dirty phone call. Yes. Or I'd call up the
Weather or the Time, or any old number, just to hear them
say Hello. I even talked out loud, from loneliness; carried
on long conversations with myself. Old songs and commer-
cials kept beating in my head, and I sang them right out.

One was a Christmas Carol. (Didn't I love Christmas, once upon a time!)

> Clad in rags the Christ Child wanders
> Begging at the rich man's door. . . .

Mama gave me presents, oh so many. Books and toys and a bicycle. I suppose my daddy did too, long ago, before he departed this life. Mama always said he spoiled me.

> Clad in rags the Christ Child wanders
> Begging at the rich man's door. . . .

Oh Prettybelle Sweet and the Christ Child wandered a good deal in those days. Hand in hand, poor little souls, begging in the snow.

> Give me but a crumb from your table swept!
> But they gave him none at all.

No, not one crumb of understanding, not one word of true affection. A landscape bare and bleak and freezing cold. Little torn shoes tied on with string.

But Reader, *even so* I had my purity. I had my secret radiance. Even when they cut my phone off, and the lights went out somehow, and the water main got broke, even then—well, I suppose I got a *bit* upset, but not like they claim. No sir.

They claim that I ran howling through the streets in my nightgown—which is ridiculous! They claim I ran to Old Doc Cunningham's office in my nightgown and all the patients in the waiting room hissed and turned their backs on me, and I yelled and lamented and wrung my hands and told about the ghost of Leroy until they had to sedate me and cart me off to Pummicami! Well, it was more dignified than that, I can tell you. I was perfectly willing to come, and Saralizabeth had been arranging for it all along (imagine!). I do remember singing rather loud en route,

> The buzzards and the flies
> Are a-pecking out my eyes,
> Poor little lamb a-crying
> Ma-ma-my!

But that's a perfectly fine childhood song.

Anyway, that's how I came to Pummicami this second time. Yes. And I began my therapy with a certain Dr. Julian Dimmer, who is a pudgy young fellow (I can tell you now) not handsome *at all*, large in size but somewhat soft and weak-looking, yes, with round spectacles that give him a look of constant surprise. He is the main doctor in our wing (Dr. Gamely being in the other wing), and I trusted him gladly from the start, and cooperated, and told him *everything*. Well, I thought he liked me too. I thought we struck it off. We used to laugh together. I showed him all my clippings from the Sunday Supplements where they psychoanalyzed me, and Lord, we had to laugh. All those big words! And I was inspired to write the following poem especially for him, to make him chuckle.

> Keep your distance, friends and neighbors,
> I am someone to avoid—
> Being manic-ly depressive,
> Psychopathic, paranoid,
> Quite precociously demented,

Oh, in very doubtful shape,
Also given to delusions
Of imaginary rape!

Symbiotic isolation
Came upon me very young,
Weaning led to masturbation,
Traumas followed one by one.
Now I'm semicatatonic
With a psychogenic tic,
Schizophrenically chronic
Pathogenically sick.

In my dreams the psychosomas
Chase the somagenics home,
Twenty years of private tippling
Caused Acute-Wet-Brain-Syndrome!
Why, I plainly am perverted,
Masochistical as well—
Anorexia nervosa
Will pursue me down to hell.

> *Well, hoop-a-de doo*
> *And whoops-a-de day!*
> *Come on, fellows,*
> *Just carry me away!*

And etcetera. (There's a lot more along the same line.) But
I never showed it to him, fearing he might actually believe
me! You can't predict psychiatrists. Well, *now* I don't care
if he gets the joke or not, for Dr. Dimmer and I are definitely finished and washed up. Yes. For he insulted and accused me in a scurrilous way, and provoked (along with
Saralizabeth) this dreadful crisis wherein I find myself.

Let me tell you what happened, a bolt from the blue.

And I trusted that man, Reader, and hung on every word he said (few enough, in all truth).

I trotted into his office as usual for our 2 P.M. on Thursday chat, eager and hopeful. And there he was sitting behind his desk, looking pudgy and benign and surprised, as always, and he said:

"Good afternoon, Miz Sweet! Here is some mail for you."

Well, I had three letters.

"Go ahead," he said. "Go ahead, read them."

So I read them, Reader, and the first was from my sister Deedy, whom I hadn't heard hide nor hair of for eighteen years, not since she married that eccentric dentist who carried her off to Brazil. "Dear Prettybelle," she writes. "What on earth have I been reading in the magazines? Did you get raped or didn't you?" Reader, can you believe it? The news of my rape had even reached BRAZIL!

The second letter was from none other than Billy Black. And as he handed that letter over to me, Dr. Dimmer scrunched his eyes up observing my reactions. He had read it first. (They always read your mail, it is one of their lesser torture devices, and they know every word in every letter and can give it to you, or hold it back, or censor it, just as they please.) Well, I was not wholly surprised to receive a letter from Billy Black, for I figured my sacrifice must be weighing heavy on his heart. I suspected all along that one day he would thank me in his way. So I read that letter, and a strange letter it was. First place, he was fresh out of Cachattow County Jail! Yes! I reckon Judge Collie and Sheriff Peabody just couldn't bear to let him go scot-free. Well, he said he'd been in jail six months and had survived it. And now he didn't care if he was Leroy's bastard son or not, he didn't care about my "peculiar" interest in

him or my "peculiar" behavior generally. Reader, honestly!
He said he took back his promise to repay the money, because he figured we were "even." He said he now knew
exactly who he was and what he had to do. And he said—
well, he "kissed me off" or some such expression.

Well, my jaw dropped down and my hand shook briefly,
but I still forgave him, yes, for it was plain he had suffered
a great deal and found the gift I had bestowed on him a
debt too heavy to bear. Well, that didn't bother ME. I
didn't want gratitude, Reader, Lord no. My reward came
from within.

So I finished reading the letter and I looked over at Dr.
Dimmer, and I said calmly, "Well, poor fellow!" And I put
that letter back inside its envelope.

"And here is the third," said Dr. Dimmer, watching me
very close.

Now Reader, that third letter was in a hand I did not
recognize—an ugly blotchy hand. I opened it up and read
it, somewhat reluctantly and with difficulty, not only because it was well-nigh illegible, but also because—after
months of buoyant health—I was seized anew with that
once familiar slipped-disk pain in my lower back.

If that wasn't a lewd and incomprehensible letter! I vow,
I can't remember the wording, but the gist of it was, *I owed
somebody a gigantic sum of money!* Yes! It made no sense
at all. They said I had lost some Million Dollar Wager, but
never mind, they would cancel the debt. And it was signed
by illegible initials.

"Well!" I said to Dr. Dimmer, shaking my head. "This
surely is a doozy. Can YOU make it out?" I said, "for I
cannot."

"Hmmm," said Dr. Dimmer. "Don't those initials mean
anything to you?"

"Why I can't make them out," I said, peering at the letter. "Is it G.M.? What is it?"

Dr. Dimmer had a truly odd and enigmatic expression on his face. He did, and I noted it, but thought nothing special at the time.

"May I look?" he says, reaching for the letter. I let him have it, and he studies the initials. "I make it C.W.," he says.

"C.W.," I repeated.

"Do you know someone with those initials?" asks Dr. Dimmer.

I think and I think (as best I can with that sudden excruciating pain in my slipped disk) and I rack my brain, and I run down the list of my one-time friends and acquaintances, and I come up blank.

"Nobody," I say. "I simply do not know a single soul with those initials. I reckon it is just some nut," I say. "Possibly an inmate of this institution."

"Unlikely," says Dr. Dimmer. And he leans back in his chair, and puts his fingertips together. "Think HARD, Miz Sweet," he says.

So I thought hard, and the silence just stretched out, and nothing came to me, and he stared at his hands.

"Miz Sweet," he said at last, clearing his throat. "Miz Sweet, you've been doing mighty well, lately. You've been making first-rate progress."

"Why I surely am glad to hear that, Dr. Dimmer," I said. "I do try hard, and I cooperate as best I can."

"I know that, Miz Sweet," he said. "I have watched you cooperate, and I have watched you growing stronger day by day, and working hard on that Story of yours. In my opinion, Miz Sweet," he said, "you are now plenty strong enough to face yourself!"

So I laughed, and I said, "Now Dr. Dimmer, aren't you asking a good deal?"

"Yes, I am," he said. "I am asking a good deal. I am asking you to put the right ending on your Story."

"Well!" I said. "And what do you mean, right ending? You mean a happy ending, I trust!" And I laughed, but he did not laugh at all. No, his eyes were glinting behind those round spectacles.

"All I can do is tell the truth, Dr. Dimmer," I said.

"That's exactly what I had in mind, Miz Sweet," he said. And there was something about him made me downright uneasy and alarmed. But I surely was not prepared for his next remark! Lord, no.

"You've been in treatment for some time, Miz Sweet," he said. "And I feel confident that you are strong enough to face YOUR OWN LEFT BREAST!"

Well, I recoiled and I jumped. I couldn't believe my ears.

"Excuse me?" I said. "I didn't quite catch that. Would you repeat that, please?"

And he REPEATED it!

Reader, I ask you! I recoiled and got up from my chair, and I backed away. I was truly shocked. I vow, it flashed across my mind, who's loony now! to coin a phrase. After I had confided so many inmost secrets, trusting his discretion and his sympathy!

"Miz Sweet," he said in icy tones, "your physical examination shows a distinct and fairly recent trauma to your left breast."

"Why no such thing!" I said hotly. "I have a perfectly fine and normal pair of breasts!"

I was indignant. I was hot with shock and indignation.

"Come on, Miz Sweet," he says. "I have confidence in you! You can own up to that, now can't you?"

"Own up to WHAT?" I said. "I have no idea what you are talking about. And I do not CARE for this kind of conversation."

"Miz Sweet," he says, sighing. "Would you remove your blouse and bra? I'll call the nurse."

And he stepped to the door and called, "Miss Curlew, please."

Can you believe it?

Well, I tell you, I clutched at my blouse, and I stepped to the far side of the desk.

"I will do no such thing!" I cried. "You are a HEAD doctor and nothing more!"

"Miz Sweet," he said. "That wound on your left breast. That was a nasty wound," he said. "Must have been mighty painful," he said. "Why, your LEFT NIPPLE WAS HALF BIT IN TWO!"

Reader, I declare, the blood drained from my head, the room went dark, my knees wobbled, I nearly dropped in my tracks. I couldn't believe it. For do you see the mean and twisted thing he was implying? It fairly took my breath away.

Well, when I could speak, I addressed myself to that young nurse, who was advancing on me, and I clutched my blouse, and gasped, "Miss Curlew, I am not about to disrobe for you or anybody, and certainly not for this *doctor* here who in my opinion should have his credentials examined!"

And summoning what dignity I could, I fled out of that office, ignoring his pleas or apologies or whatever, and I ran to my room trembling. I sat on my bed trembling, and I thought, I cannot stay in this place another minute!

I pulled out my suitcase and I threw my few poor clothes inside. I put my hat on my head and I marched out of my

room and down the hall. And at the desk, I told the Head
Nurse, "Kindly call a cab, for I am leaving."

"Why, Miz Sweet, you can't do that," she said with that
big languid smile.

"Why not?" I said. "I haven't been *committed* here."

And do you know, she wouldn't let me go? Wouldn't un-
lock the door?

"You committed yourself, Miz Sweet," she said. "You
signed the papers and you have to stay awhile. Come on
now, take your pill and talk it over with the doctor."

Well, I argued and fussed, but truth to tell, Reader, I
was beginning to remember the Outside World, and where
had I to go? I had no friend, no husband, no home! What
could I do? I slunk back to my room, took off my hat, and
wept.

For I had been HAPPY at Pummicami until now. Oh,
deeply happy. I had planned to remain the rest of my life
and never go Outside again. It cost plenty, but I could afford it. (Reader, do you know that Leroy Sweet had made
himself a wealthy man? He had, and I was about to inherit
half of it. Lord, when I think how I budgeted and saved,
and all the while he was tucking away those tobacco stocks,
and cola stocks and auto stocks right in the safety-deposit
box!) Yes, I could afford it, and I was sleek and happy, and
I planned to stay. Why not? Oh I suffered, naturally, but
it was bearable. In fact, it was *just right*. I mean, if Alice
was still crying, somebody else had made her and not me. I
was a phoenix, Reader, I had risen up. My life was back
in balance once again, and even Pummicami Mental Sanitarium was paradise enow.

And that Dimmer man was trying to wreck everything! I
swear, I could have killed him!

Well, I went to complain to Dr. Gamely, and told him the whole story, but I feared it would be no use, and I was right. He was as bad as the other one. Yes. They were in league together. So I marched out of his office too, and Reader, for two whole weeks I stewed in gloom and black depression. My slipped disk came back and my *torticollis* came back, I had constant stomach distress, and they didn't care one bit—only kept the knives and scissors out of reach the way they do. Then, as if my torment were not complete, one fine morning in the mail I get this big fat Registered Letter from some lawyer, and can you bear it? Saralizabeth is petitioning the court to declare me *incompetent and insane!* My own daughter! Yes. Not content with half her daddy's money, that greedy child, she wanted ALL of it. She'd have me legally insane in the State Hospital! and *her* my *guardian*, no doubt!

Reader, I tell you, the well of my suffering had no bottom. I took that letter, and I rushed into Dr. Gamely's office with no appointment at all, and do you know, he was expecting me? He is a smallish dusty man of maybe forty-five or fifty, with a sandy-colored dried-up beard, but there is an aura of authority about him, I must admit.

"Come in," he said dryly. "I can see you've read your letter."

"I have indeed," I gasped. "And I am speechless. Can she get away with it?"

He observed me in silence, puffing on a pipe.

"Well?" I said.

"Well what?" he said.

"Why Dr. Gamely," I panted. "I have my quirks and crotchets, but I am surely not insane! You doctors will back me up, won't you?"

He puffed away placidly, and said, "Well . . . that depends."

"Depends!" I cried. "Depends on what, I'd like to know!"

Well, he kept on slowly puffing. And my heart began to quail, and beat in frightened little flutters, because I had an awful inkling of what it might depend on.

"Oh NO, Dr. Gamely," I said.

"Sit down, Miz Sweet," he said.

"Oh Dr. Gamely," I said sinking down and shaking my head sorrowfully. "I can hardly stand it. What IS this, a conspiracy?"

"Do you think so?" he asked mildly.

"I mean, Dr. Gamely! What have you got to GAIN by forcing me this way . . . to tell . . . to tell some kind of lie?"

"What kind of lie?" he said. "What kind of lie are we forcing you to tell, Mrs. Sweet?"

"You know perfectly well," I said hotly, the blood just rushing to my face. "You want to FORCE me to lie and say . . . and say . . ."

"Go ahead, Mrs. Sweet," he encouraged me.

"Just try it out for size."

"You're trying to kill me," I cried. "You and that Dimmer man. Haven't I been through enough? You don't understand one thing about me."

"Come on," he said. "You've had two weeks to think it over. You can do it."

"Well of course I could do it!" I screamed at him. "Anybody can tell a LIE if they have to!"

"That's the spirit, Mrs. Sweet," he said in cool professional tones. (I tell you, Reader, I hated him with all my heart. I hate all psychiatrists, I do. They lead you to the very brink of hell, and then they stifle a yawn. It isn't fair!) "Come on," he coaxed, as if I were a little child. "Try and say it."

Well, I rocked back and forth and my mouth opened and this loud keening sound emerged.

"It's *not* the end of the world," he said.

"It is for me!" I wailed. "You're trying to put out my eyes!"

"Now, now."

Reader, I wanted to strike him with my hands and fists, I wanted to trample him with my feet. I vow I almost tried it, but oh I remembered Saralizabeth and insanity, and I only hit the desk. I beat a regular tattoo of rage and despair.

"There you sit smiling," I choked. "But what about ME? What about—my—my——" I was crying too hard to speak the words.

"Your purity?" he dryly said. "Your virginity? Oh Mrs. Sweet, you'll get along without it."

"I will NOT!" I screamed. "What do you know about me?"

"We-ell," he said slyly. "You'll find other ways to expiate. That inheritance of yours . . . that could support a lot of *fine good causes.* . . ."

"Money!" I spat. "Money isn't HALF enough! How could I face LILY?"

"Hm," mused Dr. Gamely, puffing on his pipe. "I imagine she'd be glad of a pension after twenty years."

"Money again!" I cried. "All you psychiatrists can think about is money! Where could I live? Where could I go?"

"There must be someplace," Dr. Gamely mildly said.

"Everyone despises me. I'm notorious!" I wailed.

"You'll be forgotten."

"Well, I won't be," I wept. "They know about me in BRAZIL."

"Brazil," he said thoughtfully. "I could recommend a fine psychiatrist in Brazil."

"Dr. Gamely, what are you *talking* about?" I sobbed.

"Brazil," he said.

"You want me to go to BRAZIL?" I cried.

"Doesn't your sister live in Rio?"

"She hates me," I wailed.

"A good man," mused Dr. Gamely. "A classmate of mine, Dr. Fairfax. He's a Nigra. Teaches at the University."

"I hate him," I wept.

Oh Reader, here I sit in the pretty park behind our hall at Pummicami—hollow and numb where once I was so happy. All around outside the fence, baying and yelping, Leroy's own dirty reality is waiting for me. Here I sit, and my crisis is upon me, my crossroad. Oh Lord, so hard. So hard to be good in this life. They *want* you to be mean and dirty. They worship ugliness, these men.

"You can say it, Mrs. Sweet."

"Well, I can NOT."

Here I sit in dappled sunlight on my favorite bench. All winter long they let me save my daily bread and feed it to the furry squirrels and rabbits here, and all the perky little birds. And now today, with heavy heart, I smell the Spring about to burst. Yes, it is hovering just like a butterfly that flutters down to light on something. A nettle maybe. Or a rose. Like Love.

"You could remarry, Mrs. Sweet."

Reader, help me. Somebody help me. Can I stomach that big black lie? Run away to South America and see a big black psychiatrist? (Imagine!) Why, it's laughable. Leave Saralizabeth behind, and Mother Sweet forever, and what of Johnny? Leave Pummicami and its magic fence, go back outside where mirrors and black windows are, where lions and tigers lie in wait to eat you up? It's ludicrous, it makes no sense. No. Here I will sit on my favorite bench and bite my nail. I don't care. Here I will sit, and dream under the vines, smelling the Springtime, watching the new little frogs jump into the pond. My squirrel friends will come and nuzzle in my lap.

I will lie down on the bench and close my eyes and drift off to sleep. I will dream that far and far away some tight little bud is loosening to bloom, some shy little bird I've never heard before is singing in a thicket. "Miz Sweet," it chirps. "May I present myself?" And do you know, a happy-go-lucky smile begins to stretch and spread just radiant in some dark and enigmatic face, how bright he is, I think, a doctor, yes, a credit to his race. Unmarried, possibly. And there is Alice, singing in the kitchen, yes! or is it Lily? And Mama in amethyst silk taffeta, smelling like jasmine far away, rustling like palm fronds in the wind, sits powdering her pearly shoulders at the dressing table and says . . . and sharply says, waking me up, "Run on, Prettybelle. Mama's busy with the phoenix."

So I sit up hastily and rub my eyes. There is no phoenix anywhere in sight, only a little green frog, looking at me in the strangest way. Am I reborn? Some verses fly into my head and I say to myself, I have finished writing. However (I say to myself), I will just jot down these final farewell lines for Dr. Dimmer. That is, Gamely. Well, for somebody, somewhere.

PROBLEMS OF METAMORPHOSIS

There was a Lady turned into a Frog
(*Hey chug-a-rum bo*)
The Lady turned into a froggy-o
Whether she wanted to or no
(*With a groaken croaken chug-a-rum bo*)
Green and ugly and soft as an udder
She tried to holler for someone to love her
She tried to explain there had been a mistake
She tried to convey that her heart would break
She tried to protest it was hard to adapt
She tried to clamber in somebody's lap—
But all she could say was Chug-a-rum.
Great pop-eyes and a gash for a mouth,
What could she do but swim
And splash
What could she hope but hobble
And hop
What could she catch but lies
And flies
How could she dream except
In green
Who could she love but Somebody
Somewhere
What could she say but Chug-a-rum?
(*With a groaken croaken chug-a-rum bo*)

THE END